MOON SHADOW

WILL OVERBY

BLACK CAT BOOKS

DAWSON SPRINGS, KENTUCKY

2014

Prologue
December 2014

I T WAS THE TIME OF YEAR that filled Tony Sheldon with dread. The late autumn when the trees had lost the very last rag-tag leaves and the wind was sharp with the first whispers of winter. Those days just after Thanksgiving when the streets of the city were festooned with lights and decorations, and the streets were crowded with happy shoppers and expectant kids.

Christmas was coming. And for the past few years he had dulled the apprehension with alcohol, sometimes a little weed when the feeling became too intense, when one more round of "Jingle Bells" threatened to turn him into a raving lunatic. Lori had learned to deal with his craziness, even though she had never understood the cause of it all. When their son had come along fifteen years ago, Tony had made some concessions, including a decorated tree and Santa, and he tried to hide his mounting fear for his family's sake. After all, he didn't want his son to grow up hating the holidays as he did. Tony had tried hard to instill some sort of normalcy in his home, and being terrified of Christmas was not normal. Unless your past was as convoluted and fucked up as his.

When the first death had come in December of 1994, it had seemed a fluke, a mere coincidence. But then came the second death on Christmas Eve 2004, and Tony began to worry. Two deaths. At ten and twenty years after the incident.

And now he was the only one left. And this was the thirtieth year.

So when he pulled into the drive after a long day at the tool shop and saw the object sitting on the front stoop of his small house on Mulholland Avenue, he was not surprised. Not really.

He climbed out of his rattle-trap F-150 truck and stood on the brown, dead grass of the front lawn and stared at it. The breeze was biting, even through his leather jacket, but the cold he felt had nothing to do with the wind. His guts turned to jelly, and he stuffed his hands into his pockets, pacing back and forth, keeping his eyes on the thing as if any moment it might fly off the stoop and attack him.

It was a mood ring – a small, plain band no larger than three-quarters of an inch in diameter. It lay square in the center of the concrete stoop. He thought at first he might be hallucinating it. After all, he had imagined all sorts of things over the years, especially this close to Christmas when his nerves were raw. He closed his eyes and counted to ten, hoping that when he opened them the ring would have miraculously disappeared. But it was still there.

He knew where it had come from, of course. From the shores of Harper's Lake back home, the last place he had seen it. Where the whole episode had happened.

He pulled out his phone and dialed Lori's number. He wasn't supposed to call her when she was in the middle of her shift at the hospital, but this was an emergency. He had to warn her.

He had to tell her the truth.

Part One:

December 1984

THE HARPER'S LAKE THREE

1

I T WAS GOING TO BE A WHITE CHRISTMAS in the sleepy resort town of Harper's Lake. The first in almost twenty years.

Everywhere around the eight-hundred-acre lake, among the shops, pubs and empty boat docks, decorations hung gaily, blowing gently in the snowy winds. Up from the shore in the town square, the bells in the stone tower of St. Paul's pealed out Christmas carols at the top of each hour, the music eerie and haunting as it floated out across the water.

This was off-season. The town was dormant except for the three thousand or so year-rounders that called Harper's Lake home. Business was all but non-existent at the three rambling hotels that graced the shore. Vacation homes lay empty, waiting for warm summer sunshine and people to return with their hot, golden days. And boats were stored away until next year when they would sail over the crystalline waters. But now the lake was as gray and lifeless as the thick clouds hanging low in the sky overhead. No one ventured out on the water in the winter except for a few die-hard fishermen intent on drinking a few beers and getting away from their wives for a bit.

Up on the hill at the high school the last bell of the day rang, signaling the start of Christmas break.

Tony Sheldon hurried out of English class, weaving through the crowd of other students to his locker. Joyous laughter and conversation filled his ears as he deposited his books, grabbed his coat, and maneuvered his way through the hall to where Lori was just pulling on her school band jacket.

"Hey," he said. He gave her a quick kiss, fully aware that it was against school rules, but not caring.

"Hey," she said, and kissed him back.

They had been going together since the middle of the summer, when Tony finally got the courage to call and ask her out to see a movie downtown. To his amazement, she had accepted. The movie was some stupid monster flick, but he'd seen hardly any of it. Mostly he had watched her, admiring the way she filled her jeans and how her breasts pushed up against her pink oxford. Finally, he had put his arm around her, drawing her close and experiencing the scent of her hair, the feel of the burgundy sweater draped over her shoulders, the warmth of her fingers on his thigh. And after the movie, as they sat outside on the curb talking and laughing like old friends, he had given her his initial ring and asked her to go steady. She had said yes. As a joke, she had taken the mood ring off her finger and slipped it onto his pinkie. They had laughed then, but he was still wearing it. It was a plain, color-changing band, and sometimes it left green streaks on his finger, but he still thought it looked pretty cool.

Their arms encircling each other's waists, he

walked her out across the snow-covered lawn in front of the high school to the parking lot across the street. The morning's snowfall had only skimmed the town, covering the ground but just dusting the roadways. Not enough to cancel school and give them an extra day of vacation.

"Sorry I missed you at lunch," she said. "Mrs. Carlton wanted to have a quick meeting with the yearbook staff, and by the time I got down to the lunchroom you were gone."

"Yeah," he said. "Craig and Gabe wanted to shoot some hoops in the gym, and I wasn't sure how long you'd be." In truth, he had been more than willing to wait for her at the lunch table, but Craig and Gabe were seniors, and when a senior befriended you and wanted you to do something, you did it. Especially if they were jocks. Especially if you were a scrawny sophomore and they had risked their reputation by helping you out when you were getting the shit beat out of you at the flagpole after school because some football player thought you had made a pass at his girlfriend. "What do you want for Christmas?" he asked her. It was a dumb question, because he already had her present – a gold locket embedded with a diamond chip that had cost him a month's allowance.

She shrugged. "Don't know. Call me later and we'll talk about it." She nodded toward a dark blue Chrysler. "There's Mom." She kissed him on the cheek. "'Bye."

He watched her walk toward the car, a vision in Calvin Klein jeans and Frye boots.

Her mother rolled down her window. "Hi, Tony." Her eyes were invisible behind round, black sunglasses.

"Hey, Mrs. Wilson." Nice parents, too. Her mother

often invited him to stay for dinner when he was there, and when he accepted he was never disappointed. Mrs. Wilson was about the best cook around, even better than his own mom. Lori's dad was cool, too. Right before Halloween he had gone fishing with Tony and his dad. They hadn't caught much but they had a lot of fun. They had even let Tony have a beer. That had been right before cold weather set in, and now he supposed they would have to wait until spring to do it again.

A car horn sounded behind him. Craig was getting impatient. Tony ran for the red Camaro and hopped in the back. "'Bout time," Craig said.

Gabe turned and winked from the front passenger seat. "For a minute I thought we'd have to hire a tow truck to get you away from her."

Craig Marston and Gabe Devons were pretty cool guys. They were two of Tony's best friends, ever since the flagpole incident at the beginning of the year. After they had pulled the other guy off him – some lunk named Corey Preston – they'd invited him back to Craig's basement to listen to Rush and smoke a joint. Not that he'd had a great interest in getting high, but he figured he should at least be sociable. Since then, Craig usually gave him a ride to and from school, and hanging out with them had become a regular thing. Sometimes, like that first day, they got stoned at Craig's house. Mostly they cruised the empty streets of Harper's Lake, drinking beer and blasting tunes. Except for Saturdays; Saturdays he reserved for Lori, and they understood that.

Tony had never really understood how Craig and Gabe had become such good friends. Aside from being on the football team together they were nothing alike.

For one thing, Craig's family had money. A lot of it. They lived in the Rockcastle Shores subdivision, a cluster of sprawling homes with private boat slips and winding drives on the south end of the lake. Going to Craig's house that first time had been an event, like stepping into one of those magazines Tony's mom subscribed to, and one that he never expected to repeat. But even though Craig had all the usual trappings – nice clothes and this Camaro he'd received brand-new on his sixteenth birthday – he was never pretentious. He tried hard to be just a regular guy, something Tony couldn't help but respect him for.

Gabe, on the other hand, was a different story. If there had been railroad tracks through Harper's Lake, Gabe would have come from the wrong side. He lived on the east end of town near the junk yard. And while the house he called home might have been nice once, since his father had been off from work with a disability for a couple of years, there was no money to keep the place up. What broke stayed broke. Gabe's mom waited tables at The Sail restaurant, but what she made wasn't enough, even in the summer when the business and tips were good. But Gabe's family had their pride, and most of their pride was in their son, the linebacker. They were at every game, cheering him on. Gabe's dad, a bear of a man and always in a worn green army jacket and camouflage cap, could always be heard above the crowd yelling "Go, Gabe!" Football had been Gabe's life, and now that his senior season was over, he had deflated somehow. Although he had been a good player, he was not a standout, and there would be no football scholarships in his future. Not that Gabe was college material anyway, but Tony thought it would have been nice for him to have some ticket out of his shitty life in Harper's Lake. But Gabe seemed resigned to the fact that he'd never leave here after graduation. He already had a part-time job with Anderson's Garage pumping gas, a position he'd been assured he could have full-time next summer. Gabe would be all right. He was a survivor.

Gabe turned to Craig now. "We going riding around tonight?"

Craig glanced at him. "You're not working?"

"Nope. I'm off until the night after Christmas. Mr. Anderson told me to eat, drink, and be merry."

Craig laughed. "Well, I'm all for the drinking part. I'll pick you up around six-thirty. I've got some shit to do first. Maybe we'll go down to the fishing hole and build us a little bonfire." Craig and Gabe had a clearing in the woods down an old dirt path at the water's edge, a secluded spot where the lake formed a small inlet and the shore was sandy and smooth. In the summer they would sometimes camp overnight, fishing and drinking and talking bullshit. Craig caught Tony's eye in the rear-view mirror. "You coming, Tony?"

"Sure," Tony said, though he really didn't want to. What he would rather do was lie on the couch and talk to Lori on the phone, playing old scratchy Christmas albums and watching the lights on the tree. It was the holidays for crying out loud. Time to be nostalgic and be with the family. Time for traditions.

But not even tradition would make him give up free beer.

* * *

Tony's house was on Lakeview Drive, not to be confused with Lake *Shore* Drive which was three blocks south and circled around the water. Lakeview Drive was misnamed, at least as far as Tony was concerned. The only way he could even get a glimpse of the water was by craning his neck out his bedroom window and looking way down to the left.

He climbed out of the Camaro and headed up the drive toward the English Tudor-style house. The pine wreath on the front door had accumulated a good dusting of snow, and the candles in the windows glowed warmly in the winter gloom. The bell tower downtown was chiming "O Come All Ye Faithful." Tony felt a rush of warmth go through him. Christmas was here, and everything felt just perfect.

He stepped through the front door and pulled off his boots in the foyer. "I'm home!"

"I'm back here," his mother called from the kitchen above the din of the dishwasher and the television. "How was school?"

"Fine." He hung his coat on the rack by the door and headed toward the back of the house.

Kathy Sheldon dried her hands on a dishtowel and pulled a strand of graying brown hair from her eyes. "Made some cookies," she said, nodding toward a platter on the counter. "Help yourself."

Tony grabbed a frosted sugar cookie – shaped like snowman wearing a stocking cap – and headed up the stairs to his room. "What's for dinner?"

"There's a plate of leftovers from last night in the fridge for you," she called up to him. "Your father and I are going to Dr. Ross' party tonight, remember?"

Oh, yeah, he had forgotten. The Annual Shindig. Dr. Ross invited them every year to a get-together at his place, which wasn't too far from where Craig lived. Tony was always invited, too, but he'd never gone.

The thought of watching grown-ups, especially his parents, mill around and booze it up bored him to tears.

The cookie was still warm, and after the first bite he wished he'd thought to get a glass of milk to go with it. He pulled off his jacket and tossed it on the bed, biting off the rest of the snowman's head. He looked at the record still on his turntable, the one he'd been playing last night, and decided he wouldn't mind hearing it again. Strings and horns and choirs were just what he wanted with Christmas only a few days away. The new Springsteen album, an early gift from Lori and still wrapped in plastic, lay on his desk, but it would have to wait until the holidays were over. Priorities.

He started the record and some crooner came on warbling about chestnuts and Jack Frost. He couldn't remember who it was – Perry Como? Bing Crosby? It didn't matter. All that he cared was Christmas was here and he was home for two weeks and the cookie was warm and sweet in his mouth and tonight would be a blast hanging out with Craig and Gabe.

His phone rang, and he crammed the rest of the cookie into his mouth as he picked it up. "H'lo?"

"Hey," Lori said. She laughed. "Are you eating something?"

He swallowed, really wishing now he'd brought up that glass of milk. "Cookie. Mom made 'em."

"Sounds good," she said. "Hey, you want to come over tonight? My parents are going to Dr. Ross' party."

"So are mine." He smiled. "Are you saying it would be a good opportunity for some alone time?"

She giggled. "Not really," she said. "I'll be babysitting Danny."

In the background, Lori's little brother called out, "I'm not a baby!"

Lori sighed. "Relax, short stuff, it's just a figure of speech," she told him.

"Stop calling me that!" A door slammed and Lori sighed.

"Sounds like it would be a wonderfully romantic evening," Tony said. "Besides, you know our parents would freak out about us being alone together, even if the munchkin was there."

"Yeah, you're right. But sometimes I get tired of being one of the good girls."

"I know," he said. "And I get tired of being one of the good boys."

In fact, Tony desperately wanted to be bad, and he wanted to be bad with Lori. The most they had done ever was while locked in a basement closet at Kelly Sharp's birthday party in October, and even then he had barely brushed her breast through her bra with his shaking fingertips. They had been so caught up in kissing and tasting each other that they'd come out blinking and disoriented in the light like moles when their Seven Minutes in Heaven were up. But it was over, and he had Wimped Out. He wondered often what else might have happened if they'd had just a few more minutes in that closet, or what they could do if they were ever alone again. But it was not likely to happen soon. Maybe in the spring, when he finally had his driver's license and his promised car, he'd take her up to the cliffs overlooking the lake and they would be alone finally, and they could make out in the back seat and this time he would show her. This time he wouldn't Wimp Out.

"Tony, you there?"

"Yeah," he said, realizing he was probably coming off as a dork with his silence. "Just thinking."

"'Bout what?"

"Nothing really." *About kissing you and holding you close and feeling our naked bodies together and. . .* and after that he wasn't sure. He knew of course *what* was supposed to go *where*, but he had no idea exactly how to do it. Or what a girl felt like down there. He'd heard Craig and Gabe and other guys talk about girls "getting wet" and "fingering" and all kinds of other things he didn't really understand but always pretended that he did. Sex was an abstract idea that both terrified him and drove him insane with want. He wondered if Lori felt the same way, and if she ever fantasized about him the way he did about her. He tried to imagine her hot and sweaty in her bed, pleasuring herself furiously the way he did often, and he couldn't do it. He wondered what she looked like down there, but all he could picture was a vague, shadowy mound covered in silky hair, just like he'd seen in magazines. If only they could have had another seven minutes. Just seven more minutes. If only he hadn't Wimped Out.

"Well, it sounds like you're preoccupied with your cookies," she said. "I've got to get off here anyway. Mom wants me to help her with her hair for the party tonight. You cruising around with Craig and Gabe later?"

"Yep. Most likely wind up at the fishing hole."

"You be careful," Lori said. "I don't trust those guys."

"I'll be fine." The idea that Lori didn't trust Craig and Gabe shot a thrill through him and made him feel as if he were doing something dangerous.

"Please don't drink too much."

"I'll be all right," he said, feeling slightly irritated. "I promise I'll be home by midnight so I don't turn into a pumpkin. How's that?"

"Call me when you get in," she said. "I won't go to sleep 'til I hear from you."

"Sure." He loved Lori having her own private line; it gave them the freedom to talk at all hours of the night.

"Listen, babe, I've got to go," she said, "Mom's calling me. Love you."

"Me, too."

He hung up the phone and stared at it. The remains of the cookie was pasty in his mouth. He would have to break down and head to the kitchen for some milk.

2

CRAIG PULLED THE CAMARO INTO THE DRIVE and sat for a moment, listening to the last few chords of "Photograph" on the Def Leppard cassette and drumming his fingers on the steering wheel. He loved this song, even though it was old and they hadn't put out a new album since. It was hard to beat Leppard.

He grabbed his jacket and stepped out into the frigid air. Fuck, it was cold. Maybe he could persuade Gabe and Tony to just come over tonight and watch a movie. They could still have a good time. His parents would be gone to that stupid party at Dr. Ross' tonight and they'd have the whole house to themselves. They could even watch the big TV in the den instead of the dinky one down in the basement. Yeah, that's what they could do. Then they wouldn't freeze their asses off down by the lake. He wasn't looking forward to that wind whipping off the water, even if they did have a good fire going.

Inside the front door, he tossed his jacket across a chair and headed toward the kitchen. He needed something to eat, and he hoped his mom had picked up some Doritos like he'd asked her to. "Mom, you here?"

"In the den." He followed her voice into the darkened room and switched on a lamp. Celia lay on the sofa with a washcloth across her forehead. She was in a rumpled housecoat and her dark brown hair was splayed across the sofa pillow.

"You okay?"

She nodded. "Migraine. Started coming on a couple of hours ago."

"You take one of your pills?"

"Yes, but it hasn't helped." She pulled the cloth from her head and gave him a faint smile. "So. . . out for Christmas break, huh?"

"Yep." He looked about the room, at the unlit Christmas tree and the blank television. Through the windows that stretched from floor to ceiling, he could see the deck, its furniture covered with black tarps for the winter, and the gray lake beyond. "Dad still at work?"

"Board meeting today," she said, and gave him a knowing look. Jeffrey Marston was president of the Harper's Lake Bank and Trust, and over the years Craig and his mother had both learned that board meeting day usually turned out to be a Bad Day. He would be home late, and most likely in a foul disposition. Craig had learned to avoid him on these days, which usually wasn't hard because his dad would veg out in front of the TV with a whiskey and Coke.

"Well," Craig said, "at least you've got your party tonight."

His mother draped the cloth back over her forehead. "Yeah, I don't think we'll go."

Great. There went his plans for the evening.

She closed her eyes. "My head's about to split open and there's no telling what kind of mood your father will be in. I just don't think I can deal with all that tonight. I may take another pill and go to bed early." She opened one eye. "You can find something to eat for dinner, can't you?"

"Sure." He started to turn toward the kitchen but stopped himself. "You need anything?"

She smiled. "That's sweet, but no. You can turn the light out, though."

He switched off the lamp and made his way to the kitchen. The Doritos were on the counter. He grabbed them and a Coke from the fridge and headed up the stairs.

His room was at one end of the house, where both sides of the roof sloped upward to form an "A." As a little kid, he'd loved this room because he could pretend it was an Indian teepee, and later it was an adventurer's tent on the African plains or the throne room in some giant castle. But now that he was older and close to six feet tall, the place was stifling and cramped, and he bumped his head against the ceiling at least once a week. He had plastered the walls with posters, but now he wondered if that had been a mistake, if that contributed to the claustrophobic atmosphere of the room.

He set the Coke and the chips on his desk and stepped into his tiny bathroom. It was just big enough to accommodate a shower, a toilet and a miniscule sink. He took a quick leak and washed his hands, drying them on the fresh towel Celia had brought up today. He leaned over the sink and grabbed both sides of the medicine cabinet, pulling it straight out from the wall, unleashing a flurry of sheetrock dust in a puff of frigid air. In the alcove, nestled between a two-by-four and a sheet of insulation, was his stash: a Ziploc bag of grass and some rolling papers. He pulled it out and held it in his teeth as he set the cabinet back into place. This was the shit he'd told Gabe and Tony he had to do. He needed some time to be alone. To not have to think.

He flipped on MTV and cranked the volume. They were playing Quiet Riot, which was a good band on its own, but not in the same league as AC/DC or The Scorpions. He brushed a pile of cassettes and papers to one side of the desk and carefully rolled a joint, then lit it and sucked down the first sweet smoke. He grabbed the Doritos and the Coke, then flopped back into the tangled sheets on his bed and sat propped up against the headboard, staring at the *Playboy* centerfold he'd tacked to his wall back in the spring. He'd first put it up as a sort of joke, wondering how long it would take his mother to notice it. But if she had, she'd never said anything about it, just like she never said anything about the occasional stains on his sheets or, like now, the aroma of marijuana that was surely drifting from his room. He'd come to the conclusion that either she was completely clueless about such things or she didn't want to confront him. And his dad would never bring up any of it because he was too busy worrying over his precious bank and whether he would still have a job after being raked over the coals by the Board. No doubt Celia and Jeffrey would get into it once Jeffrey got home and found out she was having another of her "spells" and the evening's festivities were off the table.

He wondered what would happen to them once he left for college next year, whether they would even stay together. They barely spoke as it was. Most evenings they spent in the den, staring at the television like emotionless robots, not even smiling at the sitcoms they were constantly blaring. Jeffrey spent most Saturdays down at the bank (doing what, Craig couldn't imagine), and Sundays found the three of them dutifully parked on a pew in the First Baptist Church. But his parents weren't fooling anyone, especially him. They didn't even sleep in the same room anymore; his dad had moved to the guestroom two years ago because of his "snoring." It was just a matter of time before they split, and Craig would bet money it would happen within the next year.

He took a long drag off the joint and held it, then let the smoke taper out through his nostrils. He couldn't wait to get out of here and get to college. Joey Patterson, who bought Craig his beer when he came in from State on weekends and who sometimes supplied him with grass, told him college life was the best thing ever. Parties and girls and freedom, and all of it happening seven days a week. Sure, there were still classes and homework, but the smart guys knew how to balance studying and partying, and Joey promised to show him the ropes if Craig went there next fall. Hell, Joey had fun and still managed to keep a 3.0. The secret was moderation, Joey said, and if you weren't careful, you'd burn out before the first semester was over. He'd seen it happen, seen guys with full-ride scholarships go down in flames. Craig was determined not to let that happen; he'd had a good meeting back in November with an assistant coach from Florida State, and the coach had told him he was a front-runner for a football scholarship. He damn sure didn't want to lose his ride and have to come back here. Not ever. What would he do? Pump gas like Gabe? Pick up some classes at the community college in Springfield like a second-class loser who couldn't hack it at a real university? And worse, would he have to move back here to the house of joy and harmony? Hell, no. Not if he could help it.

He had two weeks here in this hell-hole with all of them pretending to be full of good cheer, but at least his dad would stay down at the bank for the most part. Somehow they would get through Christmas Day, and he hoped his parents could at least be civil to each other for twenty-four hours. If it got to be too much, maybe he could talk Gabe into heading over to Cedar Hill to catch a movie. He was sure Gabe would welcome any opportunity to escape his shitty existence for a while. Tony wouldn't go, because he'd either be having Christmas dinner with his fairytale family or be so far up Lori's ass he couldn't see straight.

There were times when Craig thought having a girl-friend would be a nice distraction, but usually those times were at night when he was horny and alone. Jessica Alvarez had filled the bill for a while, and she'd had some special talents with her mouth. But as time went on, she became whiny and jealous, and when her family moved to Kansas at the end of his junior year, it had been a relief. Being single had allowed him to con-centrate on football, to work overtime on basic fundamentals like throwing, and the extra effort had paid off when he caught the eye of the coach from Flor-ida.

Besides, a girlfriend would keep him from Gabe, and Gabe needed him. Gabe needed a lot of things, es-pecially a place to hide when things got too rough. Craig wondered what would happen next fall when he was gone and Gabe was still living at home. He hoped Gabe would move out when he turned eighteen, that his job working for Mr. Anderson would pay him enough to get his own place. Even if it was some crappy trailer on the north end of town. Even if he had to scrimp and go on food stamps to survive. Anything would be better than where he was. Anything.

He stubbed out the roach and tore open the Doritos. The grass had made him hungry and drowsy. He popped a chip into his mouth and popped the tab on his Coke. Quiet Riot had given way to Twisted Sister on MTV, which was a faggot group if he'd ever seen one, if their videos were any indication.

He took a sip of Coke and let it trickle down his throat. He had plenty of time to take a nap before he picked up Gabe and Tony, and maybe he could sleep through whatever might erupt when his dad came home. And who knew? Maybe the board meeting was going well. Maybe Jeffrey would come home in a good mood. Maybe he wouldn't care that Celia was laid up with another fucking migraine and their plans for the evening were shot.

Right. And then maybe monkeys would fly out of his ass.

3

GABE SAT CROSS-LEGGED ON HIS BED in the darkness, holding the cat in his lap and feeling it purr against him. If he sat very still, maybe his father wouldn't know he was home. Maybe he would settle down in front of the TV with his bottle of Kessler and be passed out before Craig came by at 6:30. Maybe he would get caught up in Phil Donahue or Hour Magazine and forget he hadn't seen Gabe since he stumbled through the door.

Gabe could hear him in the kitchen now, slamming cabinet doors and cursing about, of all things, some editorial he'd read in the paper about unfortunate people like himself – army veterans no less – who were forced to draw disability and other benefits and how they were sucking the system dry. It was the sort of rant he went on when something pissed him off and Gabe's mother had moved the bottle. And she moved it often. Gabe could only guess that she was reasoning that if he couldn't find it, he couldn't get drunk. And if he couldn't get drunk he wouldn't pass out. But she was safely waiting tables at The Sail, and she didn't have to deal with her husband when he was pissed off and sober. She had no idea how ugly things got if Curtis Devons couldn't get his drunk on. Or maybe she did and that's why she worked double shifts.

The cat darted from Gabe's grasp and sat in front of the closed door. It reached out and pawed at the door, softly at first, barely audible, and Gabe thought surely his father wouldn't hear it over his raging. But the cat's pawing became more insistent until it sounded more like knocking. Gabe let out a breath, knowing there was no way his father wouldn't hear that.

The door opened and a sliver of light spilled into the room. Curtis' eyes narrowed behind his wire-frame spectacles and he frowned beneath his bushy gray beard. "What the hell you doing in there in the dark?" The cat flew out between his feet and he chuckled. "Playing with your pussy?"

Gabe hauled himself off the bed. "I wasn't doing nothing." He followed his father into the kitchen. "I was tired. Taking a nap."

Curtis grunted and resumed pulling open cabinet doors. "What the hell's your mother done with my goddamned whiskey?" He peered into the narrow space above the refrigerator.

Gabe shook his head. His mind was still groggy from his short nap. "I don't know."

"You didn't take it, did you?" He whirled and glared at him. "You take my whiskey, boy?"

"No, Daddy," Gabe said. He sighed and rubbed his eyes. "You check on top of the hutch in the dining room? She puts it up there sometimes."

Curtis lumbered through the doorway into the darkened room and felt along the top of the hutch. "Bingo," he said. He pulled it down and blew off the dust. He looked at Gabe over the top of his spectacles. "What's for dinner?"

Gabe shrugged. "How 'bout mac and cheese?" Now that his mother was spending less time at home, it frequently fell on Gabe to cook their meals and clean up the kitchen, a fact he resented but had resigned himself to.

Curtis nodded. "Call me when it's ready." He moved toward the flickering television in the living room, colliding with a dining chair and muttering a curse. "Don't burn it."

"I won't."

Gabe pulled a pot from the cabinet and filled it with water, then set it on the stove and turned on the flame. His father hadn't always been like this. Once, years ago, he'd been active and happy. They had gone places, done things together as a family. But a debilitating back injury in the coal mine three years ago had put him out of work, and the constant pain had driven him to Darvocet and whiskey. And he had changed, almost overnight. He was easily irritated, and quick with a smack to the side of the head if you got in his way. And Gabe and his mother did everything they could to stay out of his way. She had taken the waitressing job at The Sail, and Gabe began spending more time with friends, especially Craig.

Not that Curtis Devons was completely heartless. He had attended every home football game and cheered Gabe on during every play. Gabe had often heard him over the rest of the crowd, shouting his name. Sometimes his mom would come, if she wasn't working, and she would stand and cheer. And afterwards, sometimes Curtis would meet him outside the locker room and tell him he'd played a good game and slap him on the back; or if things hadn't gone so well, Curtis would tell him he needed to brush up on his fundamentals, and Gabe would smile and nod and pretend he didn't smell the whiskey on his dad's breath. Those were the times when Gabe had almost believed everything was normal. That he was just another guy on the football team with two normal parents and he could go home to a normal house and live a normal life. That the next day Curtis wouldn't smack him upside the head for forgetting to take out the trash or scoop the cat shit out of the litter box. Or that he wouldn't see his mother daubing makeup over a fresh bruise on her cheek as she got ready for work.

The water on the stove began to boil, and Gabe stirred in the uncooked noodles, then turned the heat down on the burner. He realized he hadn't checked to make sure the milk in the fridge was still good, and a jolt of panic seized him. He pulled out the gallon jug – still half-full – and sniffed it. It had soured. He screwed the cap back on and looked at it. For a moment he considered using it anyway, wondering if his dad would even notice. But if he did, things would get ugly. The macaroni was at a rolling boil now, and Gabe would have ten minutes to get to the store and back before it was done. Ten minutes. That wasn't near enough time. The macaroni would boil dry. He sat and watched the noodles boil for the full ten minutes, then turned off the flame and topped the pan with a lid.

In the living room, Curtis was stretched out in the recliner watching Dan Rather. One hand held the bottle of Kessler and the other idly stroked the purring cat in his lap. He looked around at Gabe. "Goddamned Reagan's gonna ruin this country."

"I need to run to the store for some milk," Gabe said. "I won't be long."

Curtis turned back to the television. "You know where the keys are."

Gabe grabbed his coat off the hook by the front door and the keys to Curtis' Chevy truck off the top of the small bookshelf. Outside, night had descended, thick and cold. The McMillens' dogs next door were barking at something on their side of the fence, but then they were always barking at something. Gabe slid onto the cracked vinyl seat of the pickup and cranked the engine. It roared to life and the radio came on blasting Barbara Mandrell crooning "I'll Be Home for Christmas." He snapped it off, and backed out of the drive, holding his breath as the tires slid on the packed snow. All he needed was to run over a phone pole or the fire hydrant at the edge of the street.

C's Market was still open, he saw with relief, and inside Mrs. Claskey greeted him as he entered. "Just barely made it," she said.

He gave her a smile and grabbed a gallon of milk from the case. "Out of milk," he said, and set the jug on the counter. "Can you put this on our tab?"

Mrs. Claskey eyed him over the top of her spectacles. "I can," she said. She rang up the sale and sighed. "Tell your father he needs to start paying on his bill. It's darn near two hundred dollars now."

Gabe nodded, but didn't look at her. "I'll tell him." He grabbed the milk and headed for the door.

"Merry Christmas," Mrs. Claskey called.

Back at the house, Curtis still sat in the same position in the recliner. He didn't stir when Gabe came in, and Gabe wondered if he was asleep. It was too early for him to be passed out.

In the kitchen, Gabe drained the noodles and stirred in the milk and the cheese packet. The macaroni had cooled while he'd been gone, and the cheese clumped on the spoon. He turned the burner back on, and heated the contents of the pan, stirring it and watching the powder dissolve. Too late he realized he had scorched the sauce slightly, and he jerked it off the flame. Hopefully his dad wouldn't notice.

Curtis still sat motionless in front of the television. Gabe touched his shoulder. "It's ready."

His dad stirred and looked around, his gaze drowsy and confused. He set the bottle on the table beside him and knocked the cat from his lap, then followed Gabe into the kitchen. "Boy, you're gonna make somebody a good wife one day." He grabbed a plate from the cabinet and heaped it full. He sniffed it. "You goddamn burned it."

Gabe blew out a breath. "Sorry. I didn't mean to."

Curtis shook his head. He pulled a fork from the drawer and settled at the table. "There any tea?"

Gabe checked the refrigerator. "Yeah, looks like Mom made a pitcher before she went to work."

"Pour me glass."

Gabe poured the tea – no ice, no sugar – and set the glass on the table. "Mrs. Claskey said we need to start paying on the grocery bill."

Curtis shoveled a forkful of macaroni and cheese into his mouth. "She'll get paid when she gets paid." He let his fork fall to the plate with a clatter. "This tastes like shit. You can't fucking do anything right."

Gabe scraped the last of the noodles from the pan onto his own plate. "Sorry, Daddy."

Behind him, Curtis snorted. "Ain't no man gonna marry you if can't cook any better than that."

Gabe bit his lip, feeling the rage burning in his gut. God, he hated him sometimes. He wished now he had told Mr. Anderson he would work all through Christmas. He would gladly sit on his ass down at that drafty garage all night and watch the passing traffic to get away from this bullshit. Maybe he should give him a call tomorrow, offer to fill in for anyone who might want some extra days off.

He might even volunteer for double shifts.

4

TONY HEARD THE CAMARO HONK in the driveway and made his way through the upstairs hall to the door of his parents' room. He knocked. "Craig's here," he said. "I'm going out."

The door opened, and his dad stood staring at him. Greg Sheldon was a big guy, six-two and stocky, and he kept his sandy blond hair and reddish mustache trimmed with the same military precision from his army days. He was a formidable presence that easily intimidated his clients in the law office, and when dressed in a dark suit and tie, he had been known to elicit confessions from the most hardened criminals during their first meetings. But right now he was wearing only white briefs and black dress socks, and Tony hid a smile behind his hand. Greg tilted his head. "Where're you guys going?"

"Just riding around, like usual," Tony said.

Greg's green eyes narrowed. "Drinking?"

"No, sir," Tony lied. "Probably go down to the fishing hole and build a fire."

"Awful cold. Why don't you guys stay here and watch TV or something. You'll have the whole house to yourselves."

"Dad. . . "

Greg held up a hand. "I know. Not near as much fun." He gave him a wink. "You guys be careful."

"We will."

"Girls?"

"Nope. Just the three of us. Lori's babysitting tonight."

Greg grunted and started to ease the door close. He stopped. "Tony? No booze."

Tony nodded, but he couldn't meet his father's eyes. "Yes, sir."

"I mean it. Especially if you're driving around."

The Camaro's horn sounded again. "I gotta go. Enjoy the party."

Downstairs, he grabbed his jacket on his way out the door and was still pulling the sleeves over his arms when he opened the Camaro's door. "Sorry." He chucked a thumb over his shoulder. "My dad."

Craig grinned at him from behind the wheel. His eyes were red-rimmed and the car reeked of pot. "No problem."

"Where's Gabe?"

"Left him down at the hole. Supposed to be getting a fire going."

Tony slid into the seat and pulled on his seatbelt. He caught Craig's gaze. "What?"

Craig shook his head. "Nothing." He put the car into gear and sped off down the street. Van Halen was pumping through the speakers, and Craig reached over and turned it down. "Gabe's in a bad mood," he said.

"What's wrong?"

Craig shook his head. "Evidently his dad was giving him a bunch of shit right before I picked him up."

"As usual," Tony said. "What about this time?"

"Who knows. Gabe didn't want to talk about it."

"He never does."

Craig slowed at the stop sign and pulled out onto Lake Shore Drive. "Whatever it was, it's got Gabe pretty upset." He glanced at Tony. "I think he's been crying."

Tony blew out a breath. "Jesus."

"That's why I left him at the hole. I think he wanted some time to himself." He reached over and turned the heat down a notch. "So if you don't mind, we'll cruise around a bit before we head back there."

"Sure."

They drove the circle for a while, then turned down toward Rockcastle Shores. Tony watched the passing houses with their façades perfectly outlined in lights and their massive front entrances illuminated like stage settings. He knew one of the partners in his dad's firm lived out here, and once Tony had asked his dad why Rockcastle Shores was full of doctors and bankers and lawyers, but the Sheldons still lived in town. Greg had looked Tony in the eyes and said, "Because a lot of what you see out there isn't necessarily paid for. And living in town keeps me honest." He had remembered that conversation many times, especially during that first visit out here to Craig's, and it never failed to make him wonder about the people who chose to live here. And just like he didn't want to know all of what went on behind the walls of Gabe's house, he found himself glad the private lives of the residents out here remained shrouded in mystery.

Dr. Ross' house came into view, a two-story monstrosity built of white limestone and lit up from cellar to roof like some kind of national monument. Lanterns lined both sides of the winding drive like an airstrip. Even from the street Tony could see a massive Christmas tree twinkling in the parlor windows and people milling about in the rooms beyond. He thought of his parents inside, hobnobbing with the elite, and was glad once again he'd decided not to go.

"Looks like some party, huh?" Craig said.

Tony shrugged. "I guess."

"My dad loves going to that party every year. I wonder if he went on without Mom?"

"Would he do that?"

Craig snorted. "Wouldn't surprise me. My parents get stranger by the day. I don't think I ever want to get married."

"Yeah, I know what you mean," Tony said. Although he really didn't. But if a person had to be married to someone like Gabe's dad, he could understand. That must be pure hell.

Just past Dr. Ross' house was Craig's, and Craig slowed down to take a look at the dimly-lit windows. "Can't tell if they're both home or not," he said. He sped up and headed toward the intersection with Lake Shore Drive. "Not that it matters, I guess. If they stayed home, Dad will be bitching at Mom. If Dad went, Mom will be bitching at *him*."

Tony looked at him. "What if they both went?"

Craig shrugged. "Then I guess everyone will be happy as pigs in shit."

5

CRAIG PULLED OFF LAKE SHORE onto a gravel strip. Yellow crossbars with a sign proclaiming "NO VEHICLES BEYOND THIS POINT" barricaded the road. From here it was on foot to the hole. Through the trees he could see the orange glow of Gabe's fire. Shit. They'd have every deputy from Lake County out here. He popped the rear hatch and climbed out. "Case of Busch back there," he told Tony. "You want to grab it?"

He grabbed a flashlight from the console and flicked it on, then led the way around the barricade toward the clearing. The air was colder, and the thick pinkish clouds drifting through the black sky looked heavy. Behind him, he was aware of Tony struggling with the beer, his boots crunching on the snow-covered gravel. "You okay back there?"

"I'm all right."

"Don't drop it," he said, and stifled a grin as Tony let out a sigh.

Around the bend the woods opened up. The fire

roared at the water's edge and Gabe sat on a log staring into the flames, poking at the burning logs with a long stick. The snow was melted around the fire, leaving a brown ring of sodden earth. Gabe looked up and saw them and jumped. "Jesus, you scared the shit out of me."

Craig motioned at the massive fire. "What the hell are you trying to do, signal aircraft? I said a small fire, Gabe. *Small* fire."

Gabe shook his head. "Sorry, I guess I just got carried away."

"We'll have the fire department out here."

Gabe glared at him. "We'll just let it die down. It'll be fine." He looked at Tony. "Toss me a beer."

Tony tore into the package and pulled out a can, then handed it over to Gabe. "Hey, man, you okay?"

Gabe's eyes narrowed, and he shot a dark look at Craig. "I'm fine."

Craig grabbed a beer and sat back on the log beside Gabe. He popped the tab and raised the can in a toast. "Merry Christmas, mother fuckers." He took a sip, and it was cold and good over his tongue. "So, Tony, tell us. How's things going with Lori?"

Tony looked over, his hand poised over his can of beer. "Fine," he said, and his face flushed red.

"Sticking it to her every chance you get, right?"

Tony looked away. "You know it."

Craig looked at Gabe and they exchanged a smile. "Hope you're using rubbers."

Tony stared at the beer in his hands. "I'm not stupid, you know." He popped the tab and white foam exploded from the can. "*Shit!*"

Gabe laughed. "Hey, that looks like my last date."

Craig smacked him on the shoulder. "Looks like all

your dates – a little premature."

"Shut the fuck up," Gabe said. He took a gulp of beer. "At least I've had some since you have."

Craig raised an eyebrow. "Oh, really? That's news to me. Who was it?"

Gabe grinned crookedly. "Kelly Harris."

Craig laughed. "You're fucking crazy. You're telling me you did it with Kelly Harris?"

"Who's Kelly Harris?" Tony said.

"Oh, you know her," Craig said. "Blonde hair, largish tits. Usually hangs around with Lisa Meyers and her crew." He looked back at Gabe. "So you and Kelly, huh?"

Gabe took another sip of his beer. "We didn't really *do it*," he said.

Craig snorted. "That's what I thought."

"She came by the garage one night. We messed around in the office and she gave me a blowjob."

Craig stared at him. "So when was this, and why am I just now finding out about it?"

Gabe watched the fire. "Back about a month ago. I just forgot to tell you about it."

Craig laughed. "You're lying. You are fucking lying to me."

"Am not," Gabe said, flashing a grin. "I swear to God."

"There is no way Kelly Harris put your nasty dick in her mouth."

Gabe waved his hand. "Whatever." He hooked a thumb at Tony. "This is the guy who needs to be telling us what it's all about. He's getting it a lot more often than we are."

"Yeah," Craig said, "tell us about it, Tony. I bet you're tearing that thing up."

Tony's face was blood-red. "Yeah," he said. "Every weekend."

"Damn," Gabe said, "I bet she's tight. Is she tight, Tony?"

Tony took a sip of beer. "Yeah," he said, giving them a smile that looked more like a grimace. "Almost too tight for my big cock."

Craig covered his mouth with his hand, stifling a laugh. He would bet a million bucks Tony was still a virgin, that he and Lori had barely made it to second base. If that far. He doubted Tony had ever even *seen* a tit outside of watching HBO.

"Hey boys," a voice called from the edge of the woods.

They all turned.

A thin man wearing a dark jacket over a blue work shirt stood at the edge of the clearing. A Peterbilt cap was perched atop his head, slightly off-center, and his black hair stuck out from beneath it in oily tufts. Craig recognized him at once, and his stomach gave a lurch. Melvin Hart worked over in Cedar Hill at the toy factory, and Craig often wondered how many little cars and trucks came out with crooked parts because Melvin was too soused to glue them on straight. "Hey boys," he said again. His round eyes drooped at the corners, their rims red and watery, and all Craig could think was that Melvin Hart was a most unfortunate looking man. He had heard Melvin made a pass at Gabe's mother years ago, that Curtis had beaten the shit out of him and that they'd danced around each other for years like bantam roosters until they discovered they shared a fondness for booze. Now Melvin spent nearly every weekend draining a few beers with Curtis, shooting the shit and playing a few hands of poker. To hear Gabe tell it, he was about the only person Curtis Devons could stand since he'd taken up with the bottle, and the only one of his friends who still came around.

Gabe stood and shoved his can of beer behind his back. His face was nearly drained of all color. "Hey. Hey, Melvin. What are you doing out here?"

Melvin looked at them, his gaze glassy and unfocused. "Just coming home from work," he said. "Saw the fire. Thought I better stop. Didn't realize it was just you boys." He pointed to the opened case of beer sitting in the snow. "What's that you got there?"

"Just some beer," Gabe said.

Melvin grinned. "Your daddy know you're out here drinking?" He looked at Craig. "What about you? Your daddy know you're here?" He laughed. "No, I bet he's too busy counting other people's money."

Craig could feel his jaw working. "Go home, Melvin." Poor Gabe was already looking like he'd seen a damn ghost, and they didn't need an old drunk like Melvin fucking up their night.

Melvin grinned and stepped closer. "Now that's no way to be." He caught sight of Tony and nodded. "Looks like you got a new recruit." He took a seat beside him on the log and stuck out a hand. "Melvin Hart."

Tony shook the man's hand. "Tony Sheldon."

Melvin stroked his chin. "Sheldon. Sheldon. You related to Greg Sheldon? The lawyer?"

Tony nodded. "My dad."

"Ah." Melvin grinned. "Your dad." He pointed at the case of Busch. "Hand me one of them beers and maybe I'll forget I saw you boys out here."

Tony glanced at Craig, then pulled a can from the box and slipped it to Melvin.

Melvin took it, eyeing Tony as he did so. "You're a little young to be hanging out with these punks, ain't ya?" Tony shrugged, and Melvin laughed, popping open the beer. "What are you, thirteen? Fourteen?"

"Fifteen," Tony said with an edge to his voice.

Melvin took a swig from the can. "Fifteen." He grunted. "I remember fifteen."

Gabe continued to stand. His eyes were watery. "What do you want, Melvin?"

Melvin looked at him. "Now, don't get your panties in a wad, Gabe. I ain't gonna tell your daddy nothing. Sit down here and relax."

Gabe sank back down on the log and stared into the fire, his brow knitted. He brought the can up to his lips and took a sip. "You just surprised us, is all," he said, his voice low. He looked over. "How come you're not over at the house? It's Friday night. Dad's probably looking for you."

"Let him look," Melvin said. "I'm gonna sit here a while with my young friends. A banker's boy, and a lawyer's boy, and. . . " He peered around at Gabe. "Whatever you are."

Craig saw Gabe's cheeks flush, and he quickly said, "Melvin, you got some smokes?"

Melvin felt around in his shirt pocket and pulled out a pack of Winstons with a Bic lighter stuck inside the cellophane. "Help yourself."

Craig shook the pack and pulled out a cigarette with his lips, then lit it and handed the pack back to Melvin. "How's the toy factory?"

"Slow," Melvin said, grabbing a cigarette for himself and twirling it in his fingers. "Cut us back to two shifts. Always like that this time of year. Ramp up production during the summer for the Christmas inventory, then slack off mid-October. I'm lucky I got some years in so's they keep me on during the slow season." He lit his cigarette and blew out a long stream of smoke. "Tell your dad I'll be down to the bank next week to make my truck payment."

"Okay." Craig hated people talking about the bank. Like he gave a shit. Like he even knew any fucking thing about it. Like his dad came home and blabbed all about his customers and their accounts and who was behind in their payments and who was rolling in money. He knew his dad hated getting asked about bank business outside the office, too, especially people calling him at home and bitching about being overdrawn or why they got turned down for a loan for little Susie's braces. He and his mom usually screened the phone calls in the evening and on weekends, which was easier now that they had an unlisted phone number. But there were still the dumbasses that would corner you in public and blab your ear off about their financial woes. Craig had learned, though, it was easier just to nod and promise to give his dad a message. Which he never did. It was pointless; what the hell would his dad do about somebody's account at ten o'clock on a weekend night?

Melvin stretched his legs out toward the fire and sipped his beer. He was looking really comfortable and talking bullshit with Tony. Craig blew out a breath. So much for their Friday night. They'd never get rid of him now.

6

ELVIN WAS TELLING SOME CORNY SEX JOKE to Tony and Craig. Gabe huddled on the end of the log and gazed into the flames and tried to tune out his slurred, booming voice. Maybe if Gabe sat still and didn't make a sound, if he didn't acknowledge Melvin was even here, Melvin would leave him alone. Maybe Melvin would forget about him all the way on the other end of the log. Maybe if he concentrated hard enough, he could even make himself invisible.

He clutched the beer with both hands, dimpling the aluminum with his fingertips and letting the dents pop back out. He had been looking forward to being with Craig and Tony tonight. Just the three of them, sitting out here at the hole and having fun. Not thinking. Not worrying. Not locked in his room wondering whether his father would come pounding on the door bitching about something before the whiskey graciously took over and quieted him down. And certainly not having to listen to this old drunk asshole going on about booze and women. Why didn't he go on over and see Curtis?

Then Curtis could tell him all about how Gabe had ruined dinner but he'd made him pay for it. Gave him a smack upside his worthless faggot head. And then they'd laugh and down a few shots and Melvin would ask, "Where's that woman of yours, anyways?" And Curtis would say, "Slaving her ass off down at the café, where she belongs." And they'd laugh again and Curtis would bring out the cards and say, "I'll deal the first hand."

But instead the prick was here. At the hole. And it made Gabe sick. This was the one place he'd always been able to come and hide from everything. To get away from home and school and the garage and not have to deal with any of it. It was sacred, like a church. And seeing Melvin perched down here was almost profane, like a turd being placed in front of a holy altar.

Gabe ran his fingertips along his cheek where his father's meaty palm had connected. It was tender, and he wondered if there would be a bruise there tomorrow. He figured there would be. But like his mother, he'd become adept at lying about mysterious marks and contusions, often blaming them on football or spirited basketball games during lunch period. Craig, to his credit, had never mentioned the bruises or even the occasional black eye, but Gabe knew he wasn't stupid. One night back in the summer, Craig had even brought up the idea of Gabe moving in to his house for their senior year, and though he'd mentioned it with the idea of partying in mind, they both knew the real reason. Craig was a good friend. He was good at keeping secrets.

Melvin guffawed at something, and Gabe stole a quick glance at him. Skinny and sunken-eyed, with pasty flesh and a nose that jutted out like a hawk's beak. What his mother had ever seen in him, he would never know. What she continued to see in him was even more of a mystery.

He had always known, of course, that Melvin and his mother had been an item when they were in high school. She had never made a secret of it. He had seen the old faded snapshots, the portrait from the 1958 prom, the love notes and letters from Fort Hood where Melvin was stationed during his stint in the army – all of it stuffed in a cardboard box under his parents' bed. And he wondered often what Curtis thought about that box of memories, or if he even knew it was there.

And then there were the rumors – that Gabe's mom and Melvin had been seeing each other for years. That while Curtis was still working at the mine on thirds, Melvin was keeping his wife company during the cold nights. Gabe had heard talk that his father had confronted Melvin, that they had come to an *understanding*. Exactly what that was or why Melvin and Curtis remained friends was anybody's guess. And the more Gabe thought about it, the more he didn't *want* to know. Especially after what he had stumbled onto lately.

The first time Gabe had seen Melvin and his mother together was back one evening in the late winter of junior year. He'd been out on his bike, coming home from watching an early basketball game at the gym, and he'd had decided to stop by the café for a Coke before heading home to deal with his father. Since his mom waited tables at The Sail, she could let him have a fountain Coke for free; the manager didn't mind, and sometimes he would sit and chat with Gabe, asking him about school and whether the team would make it to state this year. Gabe had parked his bike out on the sidewalk, shivering against the sharp breeze in his sweaty t-shirt and pulling his letter jacket up around his neck, and started up the steps to the front door of the restaurant. That's when he saw them through the window, framed by the steam on the glass. Sitting in a corner booth. Sheila Devons, dressed in her white uniform and apparently on break, twirling a strand of her dark hair where it peeked from beneath her cap. Melvin leaning in close, saying something that was making her blush and smile. Gabe froze, one foot on the step and his hand on the door. His stomach felt as if he'd swallowed hot coals. They continued to stare at each other, never noticing him through the window. His mother reached over and took Melvin's hand and squeezed it. That's when Gabe bolted back to his bike and pedaled hell for leather toward home, his heart pounding sickly in his chest all the way. At the house, he debated on whether to tell his father, but decided he'd better leave well enough alone. He would keep it a secret. But he couldn't get the image out of his head of how they had been looking at each other. The way he'd seen guys and girls look at each other in school. The ones who had been dating for a while. The ones everybody knew were having sex on a regular basis.

And then there was the incident in the summer. Gabe had worked a rare day shift at Anderson's, and he was coming home, pedaling along his street and thinking what a loser he was because here he was at seventeen without a fucking car and having to bike everywhere in town, when he rounded the curve and saw Melvin's truck sitting in his driveway. He was used to Melvin showing up on weekends to visit with Curtis, but this was a Wednesday afternoon. And while Curtis' Chevy was nowhere to be seen, his mother's white

Monte Carlo was parked at the curb. Gabe stopped in the street, balanced on one foot, and watched as Melvin came out the front door and climbed into his truck, started it, and coasted toward him down the street. He pulled up beside Gabe and let his arm dangle out the driver window. He gave him a tobacco-stained grin. "You tell anybody about seeing me here today and I'll cut your goddamn balls off." He drove off, leaving Gabe to stare after him, dumbfounded. Inside the house, his mother was sitting on the sofa in her housecoat, smoking a cigarette and watching *Wheel of Fortune*. She smiled at him and said, "You're home early." He looked at her, then wordlessly passed through toward his room. He never told anyone about what he had seen, not even Craig. It wasn't just from the fear of Melvin, but also because he knew all hell would erupt if word got back to his dad. And as much as he hated Curtis, as sickened as he was by Melvin and his mother, he didn't think he could handle that. Nobody should have to handle that.

And now here the bastard was, drinking their beer and taking up their time and generally just being a goddamn nuisance. Gabe's stomach burned hot and sick, and he wondered when Melvin would just shut the fuck up and go home. Why did he want to hang out with a bunch of kids, anyway? Was he some kind of. . . whatever that word was for adults who got turned on by kids? *Pedophile*. That was it. Maybe Melvin was a pedophile. On top of being a mother fucker. Gabe snorted and tried to cover it with a cough. Melvin was literally a mother fucker. It was goddamn funny when you thought about it.

"What're you grinning about down there, Gabe?" Melvin said.

Gabe glanced at him. Melvin's beady eyes bored a hole through him. He sat ankle-over-knee, his cigarette smoldering between two nicotine-stained fingers and his can of beer poised halfway to his mouth. Gabe swallowed. "Nothin', Melvin."

Melvin shook his head and took a sip of beer, then turned back to Craig and started yapping again. The conversation had turned to football, and Melvin was saying what a great quarterback Dan Marino was, and that the Dolphins were sure to make it to the Super Bowl this year, but that they'd never have another perfect season like they had back in 'seventy-two. And Craig was nodding in agreement, although Gabe could see the boredom etched across his face like a flashing neon sign. And you'd have to be stupid or drunk (or a little of both) to miss it.

At the other end of the log, Tony was resting his head in his hand and poking at the fire with a stick. No doubt daydreaming about Lori. Gabe wished he was down there on the other end, sitting with Tony and out of Melvin's line of vision. At least he could be talking to someone and not just listening to Melvin ramble. He could get up and go down there, but that would require passing by Melvin. And he didn't want to draw any more attention from Melvin than he had to. No, it was safer just to sit here and be quiet. And invisible.

Melvin drained his beer and stretched, giving a loud yawn. He crumpled his empty can and tossed it into the fire, then flicked his cigarette butt in after it. "Guess I'll let you boys get back to business," he said. He stood, and Gabe heard his knees crack above the roar of the fire.

He staggered a bit, and Craig reached out to steady him. "Whoa, there, Melvin. You okay to drive?"

Melvin gave him a crooked grin. "I'll get there. Always do."

"Be careful," Craig said, giving him a pat on the back.

Melvin paused in front of Gabe. Gabe kept his eyes on Melvin's shoes. Black scuffed leather work boots. The lace on the left one was loose and dangling and dragging the ground. "Tell your daddy I'll see him tomorrow night."

Gabe nodded, not moving his eyes from the boot lace.

Melvin's hand reached out and grabbed Gabe's chin, tugging his face upward to meet his gaze. Melvin grinned at him. His yellow teeth gleamed in the firelight. "Say hi to your mama for me." He winked, then gave Gabe a playful slap on the cheek.

That was when Gabe exploded.

7

A T FIRST, Tony thought Melvin had stumbled. He saw the man pinwheeling his arms, falling backwards into the flames.

But then he saw Gabe on his feet, his fist in the air, the expression on his face a mixture of rage and hurt.

Melvin landed in the fire with an eruption of sparks and ashes. For a second – a second that seemed like hours – he simply lay there, dazed and surprised.

Then the screaming started.

Craig dove toward him, grabbing for his kicking feet. But Melvin's legs were pumping furiously, and Craig couldn't take hold. He glanced at Tony. "Help me!"

Tony was beside him at once. He caught Melvin's ankle, but the man jerked away, nearly pulling Tony into the fire.

Melvin continued to scream, his voice now high-pitched and piercing. He wallowed in the flames, whether trying to roll out or gain leverage with his arms, Tony couldn't tell.

Melvin's foot connected with Tony's chest, and Tony went sprawling backward, falling on his back into the snow, his breath knocked out of him. For a moment, all he could do was gasp, the cold air burning his suddenly starved lungs.

Melvin's coat was on fire now. His arms flailed wildly, and his screams were turning to sobs.

"Gabe! Help me!" Craig cried.

Gabe stood like a stone, his wide eyes fixed on the sight in front of him.

"Gabe!"

Gabe's paralysis broke, and he lunged toward Melvin's thrashing feet.

"Melvin!" Craig screamed. "Stop kicking!"

Somehow Craig and Gabe grabbed Melvin's feet and pulled him from the fire. His body was engulfed in flames. And his head. . .

Oh, God, his head is on fire.

Melvin's screams had become guttural moans. He writhed on the ground, his arms and legs jerking with spasms. Craig shrugged off his letter jacket threw it over him, trying to smother out the flames as best he could. "The water!" Craig cried. "Get him to the water!"

Gabe and Craig pulled Melvin by the feet toward the shore, leaving behind a swath of blood and. . .

But Tony couldn't look at it. He knew what that was. It was chunks of Melvin's burned flesh fused with the melted nylon of his coat. He turned away and gagged, and then the beer was crawling up his throat and he was vomiting up something sour and hot into the snow. He closed his eyes, squeezing them tight, hoping this was some alcohol-induced dream and that he would wake up in his bed. He could hear Craig and Gabe splashing into the water, and Melvin was moaning.

His head was on fire.

He sank against the log, breathing deeply and trying to keep his stomach from heaving again. The bark was cold and rough against his cheek, and the ground was sodden beneath his jeans. He focused on these two things. Anything. Anything to keep from thinking about that streak of gore leading toward the water.

Melvin moaned.

Tony opened his eyes.

Melvin lay half in the icy water. Gabe and Craig were on either side of him, both up to their thighs. Craig was in his shirt sleeves, shivering, his gaze locked on Melvin. Gabe was gray, and his brown eyes bulged from their sockets. Tony couldn't see Melvin's face. He was glad he couldn't see it. The fire illuminated only a blackened, misshapen, moaning figure lying under a red-and-white jacket in the mud. That was enough.

"We need to get somebody," Craig said finally. "We need to get an ambulance. The police."

"No!" Gabe cried. "He'll tell them I did it! He'll tell them I knocked him into the fire."

"It was an accident," Craig said. "He needs help." He dug into his pocket and pulled out a set of keys. "Tony! Can you drive my car?"

Tony pulled himself to his feet. "I guess so."

Craig tossed the keys toward him. They landed in the blood-smeared mud. "Take my car down to the police station. Tell them we need an ambulance."

Tony grabbed the keys and wiped them on his jeans. "What do I tell them?"

"Tell them Melvin fell into the fire. Tell them what happened."

Tony headed down the trail toward the trees. Behind him, he could hear Gabe crying. "I don't want to go to jail, Craig. I can't go to jail!"

The limbs crowded over the trail, blocking out the light from the fire, and too late Tony remembered Craig's flashlight sitting in the snow by the log. But the snow was bright, even though the moon was shrouded in clouds, and he was able to make his way back toward the yellow crossbars. He saw the chrome glimmer of the Camaro's driver-side door handle. He'd never driven very far before, only run his dad's Oldsmobile to and fro along the driveway. He didn't even know whether he'd be able to back Craig's car out onto the road.

He stopped. Melvin's truck sat crossways of the turn-off behind Craig's car, completely blocking it in. He could see the glow of the fire glinting off the windshield. *Damn it.* He rounded the front and pulled open the driver's door. The stench of whiskey and cigarettes assaulted him and the dome light illuminated a heap of papers and work clothes and fast food wrappers spilling off the seat into the floorboard. No keys in the ignition. He felt around through the stash of receipts trapped above the sun visor. Nothing. He probably had them with him. Most likely in his pocket. Which meant they would have to fish them out.

Tony wound his way back down the path. Craig and Gabe now stood at the water's edge. Melvin's moans had quieted to barely audible grunts. Craig looked up at Tony. "What is it?"

"Melvin's truck has us blocked in. He must have the keys, I couldn't find them."

Craig blew out a breath. "Jesus Christ." He bent over the figure lying at his feet. "Where are the keys, Melvin?"

Melvin let out a breathy, wheezing groan. His torso was still covered with Craig's jacket. The once white letters spelling "MARSTON" across a red field were now smudged with ashes and mud. And what Tony knew was blood.

"Are they in your pocket?" Craig felt through the man's charred clothing. "I think I feel them." He pulled his hand away. "God, they're hot!"

Tony stepped closer. He caught a whiff of smoldering nylon, of singed hair. And something else. Something sweet. Melvin's blackened flesh. He buried his nose in the sleeve of his coat, clenching his gut against the rising sickness.

Craig was trying to dig his fingers into Melvin's pocket. The fabric had fused together in the heat. Melvin let out a guttural cry, and Tony realized the pants had melted onto his skin as well. "Melvin, I've got to get your keys," Craig said, but his voice was barely a whisper. "We've got to get you some help."

Melvin cried out again, and this time Tony caught sight of his charred face, the blackened skin cracked and revealing bloody red flesh beneath. The bill of his cap had melted and jutted out at a drunken angle. Tony looked away, forcing his gaze to the ground beneath his sneakers. A bottle cap lay trapped in the mud. Ski. He hadn't drunk a Ski in ages.

Suddenly, Melvin screamed, his voice loud and shrill like a woman's. It echoed off the lake like the cry of a ghost. His hand shot up and grabbed the leg of Gabe's jeans.

Gabe's eyes bulged. "Let go!" He tried to pull free of Melvin's grasp, but the man's seared fingers held tight.

"Calm down," Craig told Melvin. "Just let me get

your keys. We've got to take your truck."

Melvin screamed.

"Let go of me!" Gabe cried. "Let go!" He kicked at Melvin with his other leg.

"Gabe, stop," Craig said. "You're hurting him."

"Make him let go!"

Melvin screamed again, piercing and long.

Gabe kicked.

Craig held up his hands. "Gabe, stop it!"

How or when Gabe picked up the piece of driftwood, Tony would never be sure. One minute Gabe's hands were empty, the next he was wielding the broken stump like a club. "Let go! *Let go!*"

The wood came down against Melvin's skull with a hollow thunk, then rose and fell again.

Melvin lay quiet and still.

Craig fell back into the mud, his eyes wide with horror. "Gabe! What the *fuck!*"

Gabe stood with the wood held over his head, his face frozen in a mask of terror.

Tony stood like a stone. His feet had gone numb. "Gabe. What. . . ? Why did you do that?"

Gabe's gaze met his, and the hand holding the driftwood sank down to his waist. "He wouldn't let go of me. He wouldn't let go."

Craig looked at Melvin. "He's not breathing." He clambered up on his knees and took the man's hand. The charred skin sloughed off like a glove. "Melvin!" He looked up at Gabe. "My God, Gabe, I think you killed him."

Gabe shook his head, his eyes welling with tears. "He wouldn't let go."

Craig leaped to his feet. "What the fuck's wrong with you? *What's wrong with you!*"

Tony took a step forward, his gaze locked on the blackened torso beneath the jacket. "Are you sure, Craig? Maybe he just passed out."

Craig's eyes were dark and wide. "He's dead, Tony! Gabe clubbed him like a goddamned fish!"

"I didn't mean to," Gabe said, his voice barely audible. "I just. . . he wouldn't let go of me. He wouldn't let go!" Gabe sank to his knees, sobbing.

"You better cry," Craig said. "You have gone and fucking done it now. He's dead and you killed him, you *fucking killed him!*"

"I didn't mean to," Gabe said through hoarse, choking sobs. "I didn't mean to!" He looked up at Craig and Tony. Tears had left white streaks down his smudged face. "Oh, God, I'll go to jail. I'll go to fucking jail!"

Tony's lips were tingling, and his heart threatened to beat right through his ribs. "What're we gonna do? We can't get the police out here now. They'll haul Gabe in for sure."

Craig glared at him. "Hell, Tony, they'll haul *all of us* in. We were all here."

Gabe's eyes were round and panicked. "Don't call the police, Craig. Please, don't call the police."

"Well, what are we supposed to do?" Craig spat. "Just leave him here? Everybody in town knows this is our spot. Hell, even the cops know, they've chased us out of here enough times."

"Can't we just tell the police he fell into the fire?" Tony said. "Like we were going to from the beginning?"

Craig whirled around. "Gabe bashed his fucking head in, Tony. How do we explain that?"

Tony took in a deep breath and slowly let it out. His

stomach trembled with every beat of his heart, and he felt like he was going to vomit again any minute. He stared at Craig's jacket, wishing and praying he would see it rise and fall with Melvin's breath, but it remained still. Stopped. Dead. "So what do we do?"

Craig clasped his hands behind his head and brought his elbows together, covering his face. "I don't know," he said. "Just let me think for a goddamn minute."

8

I N SPITE OF THE COLD BREEZE blowing in off the lake, and regardless of the fact that his jacket now covered the dead man at the water's edge, Craig's body was coated in sweat. He stood facing the dying fire and looked at the scattered logs and glowing embers. What the hell were they going to do? Calling the police would certainly be the end for Gabe. He would go to jail. And not juvie.

This was big-time shit.

Gabe would never survive in prison, not surrounded by hard-core criminals. Craig knew what would happen to him, knew he would be some big guy's bitch within the first week. He had heard enough horror stories to know that. Gabe was fragile. Jail would finish breaking him.

Tony would be fine, no matter what. His dad would find a way to get him out of this. Fair or not, Tony would come out smelling like a rose. All those lawyers knew each other, helped each other out. Someone would pull some strings. Hell, Tony was only fifteen.

And he hadn't even put a finger on Melvin. But would he tell the cops what Gabe did and save his own skin? Maybe. And Craig wouldn't really blame him if he did.

And what of himself? A scandal like this would kill the football scholarship. Even if he ratted Gabe out, even if he was able to prove he had tried to help Melvin. No school wanted that kind of publicity. No coach wanted his team tarnished with gossip and allegations of murder. This could spell the end of Craig's football career, could kill his future.

All their futures.

He knew of course why Gabe had lashed out. That snide remark of Melvin's. *Say hi to your mama for me.* And talk was all over town about Melvin and Sheila Devons. Had been for months. And there Melvin was, playing cards and chumming around with Curtis and all the while banging his wife on the side. Melvin had been a prick. Craig had never said anything to Gabe about what'd he'd heard about his mom and Melvin, and he never would. God only knew what else Melvin had been involved in, or what he'd doled out to poor Gabe. On top of what Curtis gave him on a regular basis.

He looked at Gabe now, hunkered down in the snow, his shoulders quivering as he cried. *Gabe* had killed Melvin. Not Craig. Not Tony. Gabe. But Craig couldn't let Gabe face this alone. He just couldn't. He couldn't let this be the capstone of Gabe's shitty existence. No matter what happened to himself, there was no way he could let Gabe take the complete fall for this. It would kill him. If Gabe was sent to prison, they would find him hanging in his cell within a month.

Goddamn Melvin. This was all his fault. Why couldn't he have just minded his own business? Why did he have to stop here? Why did he want to hang around with a bunch of high school guys? Why hadn't he just gone on to Gabe's house?

Craig sank down onto the log and stared into the fire until his eyes felt dry as stones. He held his hands toward the flames, barely feeling the heat with his frozen fingers. His wet jeans were icy and tight around his legs. His toes squished inside his shoes and he thought fleetingly of frostbite.

Tony sat down beside him, keeping his gaze on the muddy ground in front of the fire. They sat in silence for a few moments, watching the last flames burn down and listening to Gabe cry.

Tony shrugged out of his coat and draped it over Craig's back. Even though it was too small and barely stretched around his shoulders, the sudden warmth seemed to melt something inside him. "Thank you." He suddenly felt completely hollow. No emotions. No sensations. If someone were to prick him with a pin, he would deflate into nothing. And that would be a blessing.

Tony rubbed his hands together and crossed his arms over his chest. He was wearing only a thin sweatshirt, and Craig knew he must be freezing. "So what are we gonna do?"

Craig shook his head. "Not sure." He had an idea, but he needed few minutes to let it gel, to work out the details in his head. He reached into his pocket and pulled out his knife. He unfolded it, and the blade caught the reflection of the firelight and reflected it back into his eyes. "We need to get Melvin's keys."

* * *

It was Craig who cut Melvin's keys out of his pocket. They were still warm. The nylon from Melvin's work pants had melted into a black glob and held the keys together like glue. In the end, he also had to cut the mass loose from Melvin's leg, gagging as he did so, then managed to pry away the Chevy's ignition key and scrape it clean. "Got it," he said, and his mouth was dry as cotton.

He stood and looked down at the body. Tony had pulled Craig's jacket up over Melvin's face, but Melvin's arms were bent upward as if pleading for help. The sleeves were tight around the forearms, looking like black melted candle wax.

"We'll have to carry him to the truck," Tony said.

Craig looked at him. "I know." He shivered. Tony had taken his coat back, and the wind was whipping off the lake like a gale. It would snow tonight for sure. "Let's go. Gabe, grab his feet. Tony and me can take his arms."

Gabe slogged silently into the water and picked up Melvin's legs by the ankles. Craig and Tony grabbed the upper arms. Something gave under Craig's fingers, and it took all his strength to keep from vomiting. For as tall as he was, Melvin was surprisingly light, and Craig imagined that had something to do with Melvin's steady diet of alcohol and cigarettes. They carried him past the smoldering remains of the fire, now nothing more than glowing embers, and up the trail. A sharp limb stabbed his temple and Craig muttered a curse, blinking back sudden tears. He could not bring himself to look at Melvin, even though the face was still covered with the jacket and the ambient light was barely enough to guide them through the woods. The smell was bad enough. He forced his gaze to remain on the trail winding through the skeleton trees, forced his nose to concentrate on the icy wind, forced his fingertips to ignore what they were squeezing into. At one point the world tilted sideways, and he thought he would pass out. But an intake of breath from Tony brought him around.

"Someone's coming," Tony said.

The glow of headlights appeared on the road ahead. A truck by the sound of the engine. The three of them stood frozen, not daring to move. They were still behind the barricade, far enough off the highway that no one could see them. But in a moment of panic, Craig thought of the vehicles parked on the turnout. His and Melvin's. The truck whisked by without slowing. They stood unmoving until the taillights disappeared around the bend.

When they reached Melvin's truck, Craig unfastened the tailgate and they laid the body in the bed. Craig slammed it closed and looked at Tony. "You still got my keys?"

Tony nodded.

"You and Gabe take my car. You drive, Tony. I don't think Gabe can."

Gabe stared at the ground, not meeting Craig's eyes. "I'm so sorry," he whispered. "I'm so sorry I got you all into this mess. But I can drive. I can do it. Tony doesn't even have a license."

Craig reached out and touched him on the shoulder. "You sure?"

Gabe nodded and his eyes filled with fresh tears.

Craig looked at him. "You know where we're going?"

"I think so," Gabe said. "I'll just follow you."

"Don't speed," Craig told him. "Stop at all the

signs. Do everything you're supposed to. We're not going into town, but we don't want to do anything to call attention to ourselves. Got it?"

"I got it."

Craig pulled an old sweatshirt from the Camaro's back seat. He'd left it in the car after the last home football game a month ago, and he'd been meaning to take it home and wash it. It smelled of stale sweat and wasn't much to keep him warm, but it was better than nothing. He wriggled into it, then took a last look at Gabe and Tony and climbed into the cab of Melvin's truck. He slid the key into the ignition and fired up the engine. Some whiny-ass country song came blaring over the radio and he fumbled to turn it off. He certainly didn't need that right now.

He pulled out onto the road and sat idling, watching in the rearview mirror as Gabe backed out from the pull-off and followed him. They headed south, away from town, toward the turnoff onto Route 232. It was a sparsely populated area, and at this time on a Friday night, no one would be out and about. Nobody lived out there but farmers and old folks who went to bed with the chickens. And besides, where they were going there would be no one to see them.

Decades ago this area had been quarried, leaving large hollowed out scars which quickly filled with water once operations had moved away and the sites abandoned. Some had been stocked with fish, bluegill and small-mouthed bass mostly, and these were good places if you didn't like the crowds around the lake and wanted a secluded spot to cast out a line or two. Some, like the one they were headed to, were rumored to be over a hundred feet deep. Craig had heard his father bitching once about a deadbeat customer who was behind on his payments and ran his car off into the quarry and reported it stolen to collect the insurance money to pay the bank off, and how no one would have ever known about it except the fool couldn't keep his mouth shut. God only knew how many other secrets lay at the bottoms of these pits, but there would soon be one more.

He took a slight right onto 232 and watched the Camaro's headlights follow. So far Gabe was doing well – better than Craig expected given the circumstances. He wasn't weaving, and he was keeping a steady speed. Good. If he could just keep it up all the way to the quarry.

Headlights topped the hill ahead and Craig instinctively dimmed his brights. The white car passed, and Craig's blood froze in his veins as he saw it was a state trooper. He watched the taillights vanish in the side mirror, certain the car would spin around and come after them, blue lights blazing and siren blaring, and pull over Gabe in the Camaro. Or worse, Craig.

What's that in the back? Well, sir, you wouldn't believe me if I told you.

But the trooper kept going and the taillights faded out of sight.

Craig took a deep breath and loosened his grip on the wheel. He was suddenly weary, as if all his strength had been sucked away. He had no idea if this would work, or what they would do if it didn't. Or what would happen if they were ever found out. He could only hope no one would ever know, that neither Gabe nor Tony would ever talk. That guilt and fear would never drive any of them to mention anything about this night.

He slowed as the lane appeared out of the darkness,

veering off through a stand of pines and leafless oaks. The snow atop the gravel was undisturbed, and he wondered how his Camaro would make it. But there was no time to think about that. He pulled off the highway and felt the snow crunch beneath the truck's tires. The headlights played across the bare trees as they passed, and Craig felt his heart leap as eyes suddenly rose out of the darkness. But it was only a deer – a buck with at least ten points on his rack, and it sauntered across the road without giving the truck a second glance.

Gabe was following slowly. So far, so good. The snow wasn't deep, but Craig knew the Camaro's tires didn't have the best traction. And Gabe wasn't used to driving it. Had probably never even driven in snow, as a matter of fact. Craig touched the brake pedal and felt the truck slip sideways a little then resume coasting.

He hadn't been out here in a year or two, not since his dad and a friend had brought him out here to fish off the cliff. He remembered the surface of the water a good fifty feet below, and how it shimmered in the summer sun, and his father saying, "This is the spot here where the bastard did it. Stuck a rock on the accelerator and let it drive itself right in. So dark down there those divers the insurance company hired almost didn't find it." And his dad's friend – Jerry Something-or-other, saying, "Never would've found it if the dumbass had kept his mouth shut." And them laughing and cracking open a couple more beers.

The headlights glared on a faded yellow sign sticking up out of the snow at an angle. DANGER – HIGH CLIFF.

Craig pulled the truck to a stop and put it in park, letting the sputtering engine idle. Gabe pulled up behind, and Craig winced as the Camaro's brakes gave a squeal; he'd have to do something about that soon.

He climbed out of the truck and stepped toward the sign, peering over the edge into the blackness below. He couldn't see the water. In fact, he couldn't see anything at all. It was like peering into a great void of nothingness.

Behind him, Gabe said, "What if it's frozen?"

Craig shook his head. "Hasn't been cold enough." But a doubt crossed through his mind. *Had* it been cold enough? He couldn't remember. It had been freezing and snowing the last couple of days, but surely not long enough to solidify the surface of the quarry pit. He imagined the truck careening off the cliff and nosediving into a solid wall of ice below. What the fuck would they do then? He turned to them. They were silhouetted by the headlights and he couldn't see their faces. "Let's get this over with."

With Gabe taking Melvin's feet and Tony and Craig grappling with his arms, they managed to pull him from the bed of the truck. The letter jacket fell to the ground and Craig stared at it. He would have to do something with that. He couldn't very well send it over the cliff with the truck. And he couldn't take it home, not in its current state. But he would deal with that later.

Putting Melvin into the truck was easier in theory. Craig climbed into the cab, keeping a grip beneath the dead man's armpits, and pulled him in after, struggling to raise him high enough to clear the seat. The stench of scorched flesh flooded his nostrils and he clenched his jaw to keep from gagging. "I think he's stuck," Craig said. "Push up on him, Tony."

"I can't," Tony said, his voice cracking.

"Do it, goddammit!" Craig cried. "I'm about to drop him."

Below Melvin's blackened torso, Craig caught sight of Tony's tear-streaked face. His eyes were closed, but his hands were reaching beneath the body and pushing. Pushing upward. Craig pulled, and Melvin suddenly slid forward. Craig fell back against the passenger door of the truck, striking the back of his head against the glass.

Melvin's head was in his lap, his charred face staring up at him, the eyelids half-closed, the mouth open and slack. Craig looked away, fighting the rising sick in his belly. He fumbled for the door handle, his fingers like frozen sausages, his breath caught in his chest and his heart fluttering like a trapped bird. He managed to throw open the door and stumble back out into the darkness, his stomach clenched with horror and nausea. He took gulps of the frigid air, feeling the sharp bite of the cold in his lungs, his eyes wide and staring into nothingness. He slammed the door closed and made his way around to where Gabe and Tony stood like lumps of clay.

"What do we do now?" Gabe said.

Craig took a deep breath. "We send it over the edge." He reached in and felt around the steering wheel for the gear shift and shot a glance back at Gabe. "Hold my belt. Be ready to pull me out as soon as the truck starts moving." He felt the tightening around his waist as Gabe did as he was told. He had seen a small red toolbox on the passenger floorboard, and now he reached in around Melvin's legs – still wet and muddy from the muck of the lake – and grabbed it, pulling it over the transmission hump with a clatter. He shifted the truck into drive, jumped as the truck rolled forward slightly, then set the toolbox on top of the accelerator.

The truck shot forward with a roar, and if he hadn't

had the presence of mind to have Gabe pull him back, Craig was certain it would have taken him with it. He and Gabe landed in the snow just as the taillights disappeared over the edge of the cliff. The side of his head hummed where the fender had grazed him, and his elbow screamed in pain.

Tony was already at the edge, peering over. "It's in!"

Craig and Gabe were with him at once, staring at the lights descending into the murky depths below, and all Craig could think was, *It wasn't iced over.*

The lights dimmed, and then they were gone.

9

Back in the Camaro, Gabe collapsed into the passenger seat. He looked at Craig and was shocked to see a trickle of blood down his temple. "Looks like you hit your head."

Craig looked at himself in the rearview mirror and swiped at the blood, smearing it across his face. "Yeah." He slammed his door and the interior of the car was plunged into darkness.

Tony leaned up from the backseat. "What do we do now?"

Craig shifted the Camaro into drive and turned around. "We need to go back to the hole."

Panic seized Gabe's gut. "Why?"

"I want to make sure we didn't overlook anything."

Gabe shook his head. "I can't go back there, Craig. I can't."

"So stay in the car." Craig was staring straight ahead at the ruts in the snow-covered lane. "Dammit."

"What?"

Craig motioned with his hand. "The snow. The tracks in the fucking snow. The truck left tracks in the snow. Anybody will be able to see something went over the cliff."

Gabe's breath left him. He thought of the state trooper that had passed them on the highway, imagined him coming back this way and following their trail down the gravel road to the quarry. Imagined him shining a flashlight on the tracks that disappeared over the edge. Imagined him radioing in to dispatch, and remembering the vehicles he passed on the road earlier. The red Camaro following the old blue pickup.

"It's supposed to snow again tonight," Tony said. "I saw it on the news."

Craig glanced at him, then back at Gabe. "You two better hope to fuck it does."

They rode in silence the rest of the way to the turnout at the hole. The sickness in Gabe's stomach gnawed at him like a rat. He kept feeling the driftwood in his hand, kept feeling the thud as it connected with Melvin's skull. Kept hearing that horrible scream as Melvin cried out in pain. And Craig's voice: *Gabe clubbed him like a goddamned fish!*

Craig pulled the Camaro to a stop in front of the yellow crossbars and killed the engine. He looked at Gabe. "You coming?"

Gabe nodded. He didn't want to. He never wanted to see the hole again. All he wanted was to go home and forget this night ever happened. To climb into his bed and hide beneath the covers and never come out. To forget that panicked look in Melvin's eyes when he held onto Gabe's jeans. To forget that horrible sound of wood meeting skull.

The embers of the fire still gave a ghostly glow, flowing and ebbing like a living, breathing thing. Tony poked in the stick he'd used earlier, and yellow sparks floated upward like snow from hell.

Craig found his flashlight and shined it on the muddy swath that led to the water's edge. The snow-lined edges were tinged with blood. "We need to do something about that," he said, and his voice was strained.

Gabe reached out his boot-clad foot and scattered the snow, trying not to think about what was looking at. The red stains disappeared and faded into the mud.

"Did Melvin have anything with him?" Tony asked.

"His cigarettes," Craig said. "I gave 'em back to him. I saw him put the pack in his shirt pocket." He was holding his letter jacket by the collar, its sleeves dragging the ground.

Gabe nodded at it. "What're you gonna do with that?"

Craig looked at it. "I don't know. It's ruined. I can't ever wear it again." He swallowed. "Not that I'd want to."

Tony stepped closer. "Should we burn it?"

Craig shook his head. "I'm not starting another fire. Not tonight."

Gabe looked off toward the water, and his gaze lit on the riprap lining the lakeshore. "We could bury it," he said.

Craig looked at him. "What?"

Gabe pointed. "Bury it. Beneath those rocks."

Craig followed Gabe's line of vision, then looked back at him and nodded. "All right." He strode off toward the water's edge, his flashlight leading the way, and climbed up amid the stones. They were large, about the size of basketballs, and covered with moss and leaves. He looked back at Gabe and Tony. "Help me."

The three of them knelt and began dislodging rocks until they had dug a small pit, and Gabe shuddered as he thought, *Just like digging a grave.* Craig folded the jacket and set it into the hole, and then they piled the rocks back on top of it. The light showed no trace of the jacket to be seen among the rocks, and the stones were heavy enough and far enough up from the water's edge that nothing would disturb them.

Wordlessly, Craig led them back down and grabbed the box of remaining beers from behind the log. Gabe and Tony followed him down the trail and climbed back into the Camaro. Craig opened the hatch and set the beer inside, then slid into the driver's seat.

They sat there, listening to each other breathing for a few minutes, no one daring to break the silence. Snow began to fall, and they watched it accumulate on the windshield.

Craig gripped the steering wheel and stared straight ahead. "We don't ever talk about this," he said finally. "Not one word to anybody." He looked into the rear-view mirror. "Tony, you don't say anything to Lori, got it?"

Tony nodded. "Yeah."

"We were here, partying all night. Melvin stopped by, had a beer with us and then he left." His eyes met Gabe's. "He left, do you understand?"

Gabe swallowed. "Yes." He tore his gaze away from Craig and looked toward the outside, toward the faint glow of town through the trees. Tears stung his eyes and he fought to blink them back.

Craig started the car. "We go home. We get up tomorrow and *we don't know a goddamned thing about Melvin.*" He looked at Gabe and Tony again. "Right?"

"Yes," Tony said. He leaned back in his seat.

"Gabe?"

Gabe took a deep trembling breath. "Yes."

Craig swiped the snow from the windshield with his wipers and backed out of the turn-out, then headed toward town. The snow was falling thickly now, heavy and wet, and the flakes reflected in the headlights like passing stars. The wipers thumped back and forth like a heartbeat. Like the old man's in that Edgar Allan Poe story they read in English class right before Halloween. And Gabe wondered if like in the Poe story the sound would drive him insane before they reached town.

They rode the rest of the way in silence. Craig dropped him off at the end of the drive, and Gabe watched the taillights fade into the distance down the street. He stood for a moment, watching the snow float down in the pool of light beneath the streetlamp, listening to the stillness of the neighborhood. The snow had covered the street already, and everything seemed muted and stagnant. And dead.

His mother's car was in the drive, and he wondered if she might have come home expecting to find Melvin and Curtis playing a drunken game of cards at the kitchen table, and whether she had been disappointed when he wasn't here. He decided it didn't matter, and he tromped up the snow-covered steps to the back porch and let himself in the back door.

His dad was in the recliner, watching an old black-and-white movie. *A Christmas Carol.* On the screen, Scrooge was huddled on a snow-covered street, peering up at a black-cloaked figure. A figure with no face. "I am standing in the presence of the Spirit of Christmas Yet to Come?" Scrooge asked, and the figure nodded.

"That you Gabe?" his father called, making him jump.

"Yeah, Dad." He pulled off his wet, muddy boots and set them on the rug.

"'Bout damn time."

He hung his jacket on the hook and yanked off his wet socks. "It's snowing."

"That's what your mama told me." He reached under his sweatshirt and scratched at his stomach. "Guess Melvin decided to stay home tonight. Didn't hear from him all evening."

Gabe felt a jolt at the mention of Melvin's name. "I guess he was busy."

Curtis snorted. "Yeah, busy with a bottle. Or some whore he picked up in Springfield."

Gabe winced, and wondered again just how much his father knew about Melvin and Sheila. He turned away. "I'm gonna take a shower."

"If you see your mama, tell her to bring me in another beer."

Gabe stepped into the dimly-lit kitchen and saw his mother leaning against the counter with a glass of water. She was wearing a light blue housecoat, and he thought it made her look much older, that her skin looked pale and lifeless under the fluorescent light mounted over the sink. Her hair was pulled back into a ponytail, but a strand lay across her forehead. She looked at him with her dark eyes gave him a crooked smile. "I heard him."

Gabe sank into a chair at the table. "I figured he'd be passed out by now."

"Yeah. He's been waiting on Melvin all night." She downed the rest of her water and set the glass in the sink. "I hid his new bottle of whiskey in the hall closet. Why do you keep giving it back to him?"

"Why do you keep telling me where you hide it?" She smiled at that, and he looked at the floor. "He's not as mean when he's drinking. He leaves me alone."

Sheila nodded. "I know." She reached out and touched his cheek, then frowned at him. "How'd you get so dirty? What've you been into?"

He turned his head away. "Nothing."

She sighed and shook her head. "Go get cleaned up. You're nasty."

She tousled his hair and gave him a weak smile, and he felt something melt inside. At that moment he saw her not just as his mother but as a sad, lonely woman, married to a man who didn't know how to love her without showing her with his fists. A woman trying to catch some happiness in any small way she could, even if that meant rekindling a romance with her old high school boyfriend.

And now Gabe had taken even that away.

He stood and kissed her on the cheek, then hurried to the bathroom before the welling tears spilled down his face.

With the door closed and locked, he pulled off his shirt and wriggled out of his wet jeans and stood shivering in his briefs, trying to will the tears to stop. He reached over and turned on the faucet in the tub. The roar of the water would drown out the sound of his crying. He fell to his knees and knelt over the side of the tub. The porcelain was cold, and he pressed his chest against it as the sobs wracked his body and the tears stung his eyes. He sat until the water was hot and the mirror above the sink had fogged over. He had no idea what would happen now. Had no idea how he would get through this.

The wood came down against Melvin's head.

Gabe clubbed him like a goddamned fish!

His arm rose and fell, wood cracking against bone.

Gabe! What the fuck!

A knock made him jump, and then he heard his mother's voice over the sound of the water, muffled through the bathroom door. "Gabe? You okay?"

"I'm fine."

"All right. I thought I heard. . . "

He wiped his eyes. "What?"

"Nevermind."

He pulled the lever on the faucet and water sprang from the showerhead. He stepped out of his briefs and into the hot flow, feeling the pulse against his skin. The sudden heat made him realize how cold he was. His feet and fingers were like ice, and his scrotum had shriveled into a numb lump. He couldn't stop shivering. He had never been so cold.

He wondered if he would ever be warm again.

10

CRAIG CAME AWAKE SLOWLY, reluctantly rousing from a dream where he was making out with Jennifer Jason Leigh. He could still taste her lips, could still feel her breast beneath his fingertips. His hand groped for the stiffness between his legs and he let out a contented sigh because it was Saturday and the first day of Christmas break and –

Gabe bashed his goddamn head in!

And the memory was suddenly in his head, clear and sharp and horrifying. His gut clenched, and he rolled over and stared at the gray light seeping through the window blinds.

Melvin was dead. They had killed him.

He sat up and shivered as the covers fell away, then reached over and grabbed a sweatshirt off the floor and pulled it over his head.

He closed his eyes and his heart thudded dully in his chest as the sight of Melvin's blackened, upturned face swam before him. The feel of his fingers sinking into burned flesh. And the smell. Oh, God, the smell. He would never be able to get that smell out of his nostrils.

Craig swung his legs out of the bed and stepped into

a pair of sweats, then padded to the window and peered around the blinds. Snow was thick across the lawn and driveway, several inches from the look of it, and it continued to fall. Enough snow to cover their tracks from last night at the quarry. Enough to obliterate everything at the fishing hole.

He took a deep breath and felt it rattle in his chest as he trembled. It would be okay. Everything would be okay.

In the bathroom, he pulled his stash from behind the cabinet and sat on the toilet as he rolled a joint on the side of the sink. Something to take the edge off, to dampen that vision of Melvin's charred face. He lit the roach and pulled the smoke into his lungs, holding it and feeling the shakes subside. He sat smoking in the dark silence until the joint was burned down to a nub and his mind was thick and dull and empty.

Downstairs the Christmas tree was dark and silhouetted against the windows, and outside the lake was a gray smear through the swirling snow. He curled up in his father's chair and covered himself up to the neck with an afghan and watched the flakes dance through the air. The snow on the deck was level with the bottom of the sliding doors, and the patio furniture was a set of white lumps. The wind caught a loose tie from one of the tarps and knocked it against the side of the house. *Tap. Tap. Tap.*

Last night he had slipped in the front door and up the stairs before his mother could stir from her pill-induced haze on the sofa and give him the third degree. As he was stripping off his muddy clothes in his room, he noticed the darker stains on his jeans. That wasn't mud, and he was pretty sure it wouldn't come out no matter how hard he scrubbed. His gray sweatshirt was also streaked with gore. He stood naked in the center of the room, looking at the pile of clothes and wondering what to do. He couldn't very well just toss them in the laundry basket for his mother to see. He would have to get rid of them somehow. In the end, he stuffed them under his bed for the time being, deciding he would deal with it later. He stood in the shower with the water as hot as he could stand it, feeling the blood begin to flow through his limbs until he at last felt human once more, then he bundled up in sweats and lay on his bed watching MTV and trying to get his brain to shut off.

There had been no sound from his parents' rooms this morning as he had tiptoed past, and he figured they were sleeping off whatever they had drunk last night after his father had stumbled in from Dr. Ross' party. He had heard them cursing and shouting, even upstairs in his room above the music on his TV. His dad telling his mother she was lazy and antisocial and his mother screaming back that he never appreciated her and never took her feelings into consideration and that all he cared about was his precious bank and schmoozing customers. And then things got quiet, and before long he heard them trudging up the stairs, his father saying something he couldn't quite make out and his mother answering in that high girlish tone she had when she'd been drinking. He heard them go into the master bedroom, and he turned the volume up on the TV so he couldn't hear them messing around. They were disgusting, both of them.

Beneath the unlit tree wrapped packages spilled out across the floor. It looked to be another big year at the Marston house. Yesterday he had been feeling the anticipation of opening gifts on Christmas morning, hoping for a new stereo or a VCR, looking forward to visiting the grandparents over in Springfield and sitting down with aunts and uncles and cousins for a big meal and watching football afterwards. But none of that mattered now. He looked at the pile of presents and felt an urge to take the whole lot of them and dump them in the lake. He felt oddly detached from himself, as if all of this were happening in some stupid made-for-TV movie and he was playing the part of the angst-ridden teen.

"You're up early." He turned and saw his mother standing in the doorway to the kitchen. "I figured you'd be in bed until noon."

"Couldn't sleep."

She knelt beside the Christmas tree and plugged in the lights, then stepped around to the window. "Isn't it beautiful? Wonder how much we've got." She stood smiling, staring out at the snow, her breath fogging the glass. "The weatherman predicted six to eight inches. I think we've got at least that already." She looked at him and frowned. "You feel okay?"

He took a deep breath. "I'm fine."

She bent over him and felt his forehead with the back of her hand. "You don't feel feverish."

"I'm not sick," he said.

"You just don't look good."

He closed his eyes. If only she would just shut up and go away. "I'm all right," he said.

Outside, the snow billowed across the deck and the tie from the tarp knocked again on the siding. *Tap. Tap. Tap.* Like bare-boned fingers rapping on the wood.

* * *

A little after three he called Gabe's house. By then the snow had all but stopped, but the day remained gray and dull. He needed to talk to someone. Sitting in his room with nothing but the TV for company was making his nerves raw. Gabe answered on the first ring and his voice was weak and ragged. "Hey," Craig said. "What'cha doing?"

Gabe sighed. "Nothing. Watching TV."

"Me, too." He glanced at the football game on the screen. "The Citrus Bowl is on. You watching Florida pound Georgia?"

"No. We got a movie on."

"Hm." The silence rose up between them, thick and menacing. "I was hoping we could do something to-night, but I think I'm pretty well snowed in out here."

"Yeah," Gabe said. "I don't think I feel like doing anything anyway."

"I understand."

"I'm so tired," Gabe said. "I was awake almost all night."

"Yeah." Craig closed his eyes, thinking *Don't say it, don't say his name.*

Gabe's voice became a whisper. "It's going to be okay, right? Nobody's gonna find him. Right?"

"It'll be all right," Craig said. "Don't panic."

"Somebody's gonna miss him. They'll go looking for him."

"Who? Your dad? Your mom?" Craig bit his lip, wishing he hadn't said that.

"He had friends at his job, too," Gabe said with an edge to his voice. "Don't you think they'll be con-cerned when he doesn't show up for work?"

"Calm down." Craig told him. "Sure they'll be concerned. I'm sure somebody will call the police. But we can't lose our heads. Remember what I said last night. If anyone asks, Melvin stopped by and had a beer with us, then he left. That's all we know. That's it, Gabe. We don't say anything else."

"But what if they search the quarry? Like those divers that found the car you told us about?"

"If they find him down there, they'll assume he was drunk and drove over the edge."

"But he's *burned*, Craig. They'll know that didn't happen from going over a cliff. What then?"

Craig blew out a breath. "For God's sake, Gabe, I don't know. We don't know *anything about it*. Got it?"

Gabe sighed. "I got it."

"Just don't panic. Everything will be fine. Everything will be all right."

11

S O WHAT DID YOU GUYS DO at the lake?" Lori
asked. "You were kind of vague when you called
me last night."

Tony lay on the floor in the living room, staring up
at the Christmas tree and twisting the phone cord
around his hand. His mom hated him doing that because the cord would inevitably end up in a gnarled
mess. He threaded the cord through his fingers and
looked at his left pinkie where Lori's mood ring had
been. He'd been wearing last night, he was sure of it.
But at some point in all the commotion he must have
lost it. Whether at the hole, in Craig's Camaro, or if it
was now lying at the bottom of the quarry beside Melvin's truck he had no idea.

His parents had retired to their room an hour ago,
leaving him alone to talk to Lori in private. He had put
one of the old records on the stereo – one of those albums his mom had picked up at Grant's or True Value
Hardware or some such place years ago – and was trying to get some kind of holiday feeling inside him.
Something to make it seem like Christmas. Anything to
replace the horrible, sick gnawing in his gut.

"Tony?" Lori said over the phone. "You still there? You didn't fall asleep did you?"

"I'm here." He sat up and pulled one of the brightly-wrapped packages with his name on it from under the tree. It was light and made a soft shuffling noise when he shook it. A shirt. Maybe a sweater. "We just drove around like I told you," he said. "Went down to the hole, had a fire." He closed his eyes and tried to brush away the vision of Melvin wallowing in the flames, the sound of his garbled cries. The smell of scorched nylon and flesh.

"What do you guys do down there, anyway?"

"Oh, you know, sit around and talk." He lowered his voice to a whisper. "Maybe drink a beer or two."

"I figured that," she said. "I just don't get guys and their fascination with beer. It's nasty."

He pulled one of the ornaments off the tree – a china Santa Claus that once belonged to his great-grandmother. The glazing was spiderwebbed with tiny cracks but the hand-painted details were still vivid and sharp. Santa's eyes were bright and merry, but there seemed to be a slightly cruel expression around the mouth. Something he'd never noticed before. Almost as if Santa knew what had happened and was taunting him. *Like you think you're getting anything under the tree from me.*

Lori sighed. "Well, it sounds like you're preoccupied. I'll let you get back to. . . well, whatever it is you were doing before I called."

"I'm sorry," he said. "I'm just really tired. I hardly slept at all last night. I just don't feel good."

"Think you're coming down with something?"

He hung the Santa back on the tree. "I don't know. Maybe."

"I've got some gifts to wrap anyway. Including yours."

He picked up a small box with a bright red bow. Lori's locket. "I've got something for you, too."

"Well, I hope so." She giggled. "Maybe the roads will clear up tomorrow so we can see each other. This is the first Saturday night we've spent apart since the summer."

He lay back on the floor. "Yeah."

Suddenly, he wanted to tell her everything – all about Melvin and what had happened. About the fire and the accident. About sending the truck plummeting to a watery grave at the quarry. About the real reason he had been unable to sleep, and why his belly felt as if it were being eaten away by guilt and fear. But he couldn't tell. He couldn't tell anyone. They couldn't risk anyone else finding out.

But maybe she could help them sort things out. Maybe she would know what to do, would think of something he and Craig and Gabe had not. She could be a voice of reason.

But no. Craig would kill him if he told. And as much as he loved Lori, he wasn't sure he trusted her with such a secret. It wasn't just that he thought she would tell out of spite. He knew such knowledge would be a burden. That the weight of *knowing* might be enough to make her crack. And while he couldn't do that to *her*, he also couldn't do that to *them*.

Lori blew out a breath. "Well, you obviously don't feel good. Why don't you get some sleep."

"Yeah."

"Call me tomorrow?"

"I will."

He hung up the phone and lay on the floor in the

glow of the multi-colored lights. The record had ended and the turntable clicked off, leaving the house in heavy silence. His stocking hung from the fireplace mantle, empty and limp, his name spelled out in glittery script, the same stocking he'd had since he was a baby, and he wondered if his parents had hoped for more kids, for more stockings on the mantle, each one adorned with a different name. What would it have been like to have a brother or a sister? Or both? Would he have confided in them what had happened? And would they have helped him or turned the three of them in?

Outside, a gust of wind howled about the house and Tony shivered. It was the loneliest, coldest sound he had ever heard.

A sudden clattering at the front of the house made him sit straight up, and he thought of that old song, "'Zat You, Santa Claus?" He got to his feet and crept down the dark hallway toward the front door. Even if he were a kid and still believed, he knew Santa wouldn't be creeping around the front stoop. He would be sliding down the chimney into that cold, dark, drafty fireplace.

He peeked through the window out into the darkness and breathed in relief. The snow shovel had been propped against the side of the house. The wind must have caught it and now it lay across the front steps. That's all.

In the multi-colored glow cast by the lights around the front door, the cleared walk wound across the snow-covered lawn toward the street where it ended abruptly in a mound of ice thrown off by the snowplow. Earlier in the afternoon the kids across the street had built a huge snowman, and now it stood sentinel over the neighborhood. Its expression, barely visible in the half-light, was glowering and dark, not at all happy. Two stone eyes were capped by downcast eyebrows made of twigs, and the mouth was dotted by sharp-looking rocks for teeth. It was damn creepy when you thought about it, and the little urchins probably just wanted to shock the neighbors. It was the kind of thing Tony might have done when he was younger, and he blew out a breath wondering if he would ever feel that carefree and innocent again.

He had just started to turn away from the window when he caught sight of something at the corner of the neighbors' house. Something in the shadows. Something that looked like a man. Standing at the edge of the light. A man in a dark jacket and a cap.

Tony's blood froze and his legs suddenly felt rubbery.

He blinked his eyes and the figure was gone. If it had ever been there at all.

12

B Y MONDAY, Christmas Eve night, Gabe had only slept a few hours in almost four days. The nights were spent tossing and turning and being jarred into consciousness every time he felt himself drifting off by the hollow sound of the driftwood hitting Melvin's skull. Early Monday afternoon he was finally able to score a couple hours' sleep from sheer exhaustion, but even that had been restless and plagued with strange dreams of dangling over a pit filled with the moaning living dead, their rotting hands reaching for him and their eyes glazed and vacant. He came awake with a start, his face and chest coated in a thick layer of cold sweat, his heart thudding like a bass drum.

Christmas morning dawned sunny and clear, and by noon the snow had begun melting with a steady dripping off the roof that sounded like rainfall. They exchanged their gifts in front of the small tree in the living room. Gabe received a new pair of Levis and the new Foreigner cassette. He gave Curtis a pocket knife he'd purchased at Kesterson's Hardware Store and Sheila a pair of fake pearl earrings from Rite-Aid. Then they sat down to a dinner of baked ham and sweet potatoes and corn and rolls and a store-bought pecan pie before stretching out in front of the television for the annual Blue-Gray football game. Curtis drank only beer and was asleep before the first half was over.

Wednesday night, Gabe returned to his job at Anderson's, grateful to be out of the house and away from Curtis and into some sense of normalcy. The night shift at the garage was slow, and the office was cold as shit, but Mr. Anderson had a small black-and-white TV under the counter and Gabe knew where Gerald, the assistant mechanic, kept his stash of porn magazines in the men's restroom, so there was plenty to keep him entertained. Craig called and kept him on the phone for a couple of awkward hours; neither of them mentioned the previous Friday night. They kept the conversation on Christmas – what they received and what they gave – and how many days were left until school started back. After they hung up, Gabe went to the restroom and vomited.

He had just come back out to the office and settled in the desk chair to watch the last part of some dreary Christmas miracle movie when movement out the window caught his eye. He squinted to see through his own reflection in the glass, peering out into the darkness at the drugstore across the street. Someone was standing there, bathed in the red glow from the neon sign. Facing the garage. Looking at him. A man in a dark jacket and a cap. Gabe's heart lurched in his chest. *It looks like. . . .* But he wouldn't let himself finish the thought. It was too crazy. And too horrible.

He circled around the desk and went to the window, cupped his hands around his eyes and pressed his face against the glass. Nothing. Just an empty sidewalk mounded with melting ice and snow pushed up by the snowplows.

He blew out a breath and massaged the back of his neck where a dull throb was beginning to make itself known. He was seeing things. That's all. Whether it was guilt or fear or just plain losing his mind, he didn't know. Maybe it was all three. But there was nothing out there. There *hadn't been* anything out there. He flopped back into the chair and forced his gaze to stay focused on the flickering television screen. He couldn't crack up. Not now.

On Thursday Sheila heard Melvin was missing.

She came home that night from The Sail and announced it to Curtis and Gabe, and Gabe noticed a glimmer of hurt in her eyes. Melvin was late with his rent, she told them, and his landlord had come knocking on his door Wednesday evening but got no answer. Then he tried calling him at the toy factory that morning, but Melvin's boss said he hadn't shown up for his shift the past two days. The landlord was afraid Melvin might be in trouble, given his reputation for getting hammered and driving around all over the countryside. No one at the restaurant had seen him in a few days, and had Curtis heard from him? Curtis assured her that he hadn't, but he tried immediately to call him and when he got no answer he speculated that maybe Melvin had run off with one of those women over in Springfield he was always with. Gabe noticed his father didn't use the word "whore" this time, but Sheila closed her eyes and blushed just the same.

Friday morning, a sheriff's deputy stopped by the house. Gabe saw the black Crown Victoria pull up in the driveway and his knees buckled. He sat at the kitchen table as his father answered the door, sweating and shaking and nauseated until he realized the deputy just wanted to ask Curtis a few questions. Had he heard from Melvin? When was the last time he'd seen him? Did he have any idea where he might have gone? Satisfied, the deputy left. When he was gone, Gabe locked himself in his room and cried into his pillow.

So that night, when Gabe looked up from behind the counter in the garage office and saw Craig's Camaro pulling into the lot, he was relieved to finally have some company – someone who understood the uncertainty and dread of the past few days. Tony was with him, and Gabe was shocked to see how gaunt and pale he looked. They entered the office, and Gabe nodded at them.

"Hey," Craig said. He was wearing a new coat, and Gabe immediately thought of the letter jacket buried under the rocks at the lake. "What's up?"

"Not much. Working."

"Cold as a witch's tit out there," Craig said, sinking down onto the cracked vinyl chair next to the big glass window.

Gabe shoved the space heater closer to Craig and Tony with the toe of his boot and felt the cold descend on him like a cloud. "There's coffee if you want some."

Craig shook his head. "Nasty stuff."

"Got any hot chocolate?" Tony said.

"Nope," Gabe told him, surprised at his own disappointment. "Just coffee. But you could add a bunch of creamer and sugar to it."

Tony shrugged. "All right."

Gabe nodded at the pot behind the counter. "Help yourself."

"So how are you?" Craig said.

Gabe took a deep breath. "I don't know. Talk's all

over town about Melvin. People saying he ran off because he owed somebody some money. All kinds of
crap. And my dad's all in a funk. He thinks Melvin
left town without telling him, thinks he ran off with a
woman." Gabe didn't tell Craig, but Curtis was also
drinking more, even for Curtis, and Sheila hadn't bothered trying to hide the bottles the past couple of days.
In fact, Gabe wondered if his mother might have been
drinking as well. She had been somber and moody, and
sometimes her eyes were tinged red, as if she'd been
crying. As if she wished Melvin had run off with *her*.

Craig nodded. "Yeah, I've been hearing that stuff,
too."

"And there's something else. A sheriff's deputy
came by this morning and talked to Dad."

Tony looked up from stirring his coffee. "What did
he want?"

"Just to ask him a few questions. And of course
Dad doesn't know anything, so he didn't have anything
to tell him. He didn't stay long." Gabe felt the fear
rising in his chest again. "But what if he comes back?
I'm scared."

Craig looked at him. "Remember what I told you.
Just keep quiet and don't panic."

Gabe suddenly felt weak. "I'm so tired, Craig. I
can't sleep. And when I do, I keep having these horrible dreams."

Tony sat next to Craig and took a sip of coffee from
the foam cup, then hunched over its warmth. "Me, too.
I keep dreaming about him – about Melvin. And last
night I dreamed I told my parents about it."

Craig's eyes narrowed. "Stop it, both of you. Get
hold of yourselves."

The covering was ripped along the arm of the chair,

and Gabe fingered the flap of green vinyl and the yellow foam underneath. He thought of what he had seen Wednesday night – no, what he *thought* he'd seen – and debated on whether to tell Craig. But one look at Craig's stern expression told him he'd better keep it to himself. "Maybe we should just go to the cops."

Craig shot him a glance. "And tell them what? You *killed* him, Gabe. You killed him and Tony and I helped you hide him. Do you know what that would mean, going to the cops?"

Gabe looked away, feeling his eyes water. "We don't have to tell them everything."

"Well, what parts are you planning on leaving out? Because I can't think of any fucking way that wouldn't land all three of us in jail." Craig leaned closer and his voice was softer. "You can't go to jail, Gabe. They will eat you alive in there."

"But – "

Craig looked at him. "And *I'm* not going to jail. I've got a future. Tony's got a future." He stood and looked out at the parking lot, his back to them. "You've got a future, too, Gabe, but you can't blow it. We've just got to stay quiet."

Gabe took a deep breath. He looked at the calendar on the wall and watched it turn blurry as the tears finally welled up in his eyes and spilled down his cheeks. "I just want this to be over." He wiped his face quickly before Craig or Tony could see.

Craig turned and his face softened. "I know, buddy."

Gabe felt rage well up within him. "Do you really? Because you act like all this is nothing."

"Why? Because I'm not freaking out? Because I haven't turned into a blubbering sack of shit like the two of you?"

"That's not fair," Gabe said, even as he felt more tears slipping out.

Tony looked at Craig. "I think what Gabe means is that you seem like you're not worried at all."

Craig flopped down onto the chair. "Look. You think I'm not worried? I'm as worried as you two are. But you both have to calm down. You start acting all psycho and it's going to raise some eyebrows." He leaned forward, his elbows on his knees. "It'll blow over. Trust me. But we've got to stick together. All of us. Like 'The Harper's Lake Three' or something." He held out his hand. "I'm making a promise, here and now. I'm never going to tell another living soul about this. I'm not ratting anybody out. It's going with me to my grave." He looked at Tony. "Tony?"

Tony stared at Craig's outstretched hand, then placed his own on top of it. "Me, too."

"Swear?"

Tony nodded. "Yeah."

Gabe looked at the hands in front of him. He could feel Craig's eyes on him, and though he tried desperately to hold them back, tears were tickling his eyelashes. He reached out his hand to the other two. "I swear."

13

CRAIG POURED THE POPCORN out of the pan and into a large bowl. He had made too much, but he figured he would eat it anyway. It would probably be his dinner. Jeffrey and Celia had gone after-Christmas shopping over in Springfield and most likely would stop at a restaurant on the way home. They'd invited him to go along, but who wanted to be closed up in a car with them while they bickered and picked at each other? Fuck that. He would just stay home. Even if it was Saturday night. Gabe was working again and Tony was with Lori. Craig had come close to calling Shelley Parker and asking her to go to the movies tonight, but decided he didn't want to fool with her. She was a junior, and he'd heard just before Christmas break that she'd broken up with her boyfriend. He'd always liked Shelley, and she was certainly fine to look at. But girls didn't like it when you asked them out at the last minute. And besides, he wasn't sure he'd be very good company tonight.

The late afternoon was dreary and gray, and the den was dark except for the Christmas tree. He switched on a lamp before flopping onto the sofa and grabbing the

TV remote. But after flipping through the channels he realized there was nothing on. No football, no basketball. Just old black-and-white movies and reruns of *Gunsmoke*. He turned to MTV for a minute, but they were doing a year-end video countdown and he just didn't give a fuck. He turned the TV off and listened to the silence. He'd received several new tapes for Christmas, but nothing he wanted to listen to right now. The quiet was actually peaceful; no yelling or arguing, no banging around in the kitchen, no shrill ringing of the phone. He could almost get used to it.

He lay back on the couch with the bowl on his chest, looking at the Christmas tree and shoving popcorn into his mouth. He hated the way the tree looked after Christmas. All the gifts gone and nothing but the plain red tree skirt beneath it. It was depressing. Like arriving late to a party and finding everyone had already gone home. Even the nutcracker by the fireplace looked dejected. He hated that thing, hated its wide painted eyes and white chomping teeth, and he could never understand why his mother put it on display every year. It had never cracked any nuts that he knew of, and he'd been looking at it every Christmas since he was little. It was just another decoration, one more thing to gather dust and clutter up the place.

Outside the wind had picked up, and the bare branches waved stiffly in the breeze. He could hear them rattling together like bones, and he shivered. It might snow again this week, and he hoped if it did it wouldn't keep them from going back to school Wednesday. It wasn't that he wanted to be back in class, but he needed to be around people again. Someone other than Gabe and Tony. Those two were going to drive him crazy with all their worrying and crying and bullshit. It wasn't helping anything and was just pissing him off.

Yesterday afternoon while his dad was at work and his mom had been preoccupied with cleaning the house he had pulled the bloody clothes from under his bed and stuffed them in a trashbag, then carted them downstairs to his car. He had no idea what he would do with them at first, but found himself on the road heading toward Springfield. A half hour later he was in the parking lot behind the mall, sipping on a Coke from McDonald's and watching people coming and going through the side entrance. Close by was a large dumpster used by several of the stores; he could see it overflowing with boxes and trash. When he was satisfied no one was around, he drove over to it and flung the bag of clothes inside, then pulled away and headed back to Harper's Lake. No one had seen him and no one had stopped him. The clothes were gone and he was pretty sure they couldn't be traced back to him. And if his mother missed them he figured he could tell her he'd left them in the locker room at school. She would forget about them before long. She hadn't even noticed he was no longer wearing his letter jacket.

On his way back he had made a detour out to the quarry, just to look things over. Most of the road in was still a slushy mess, and it didn't look like anyone else had been out here since that night, since the big snow had obliterated the Camaro's tracks. At the top of the cliff, he parked the car and climbed out into the sharp December air. Thick clouds sat on the horizon behind the bare trees on the other side of the pit and the last feeble rays of the dying sun shone on the jagged rock walls, turning them a deep amber. He squinted at the dark water below. His eyes searched for any telltale glint of chrome or glass, but there was nothing below the smooth surface. It was as if it had never happened. Satisfied, he climbed back the Camaro and headed for home, and last night he slept better than he had in days.

Outside, another gust of wind howled and the limbs of the dogwood scratched against the siding with a raking shriek. Craig set the popcorn on the coffee table and moved toward the window. The lake was choppy and dark, and he wondered if the snow might come sooner than expected. The houses across the water were colorless in the gloom, and only a few faint lights glowed coldly. The Harrisons must have already taken down their Christmas tree because he could no longer see it in their living room window.

He pressed his nose to the glass. Someone was standing on the Harrisons' dock. Was that Mr. Harrison? What the hell was he doing standing out there in this wind? He cupped his hands around his eyes, shielding his vision from the light in the room. It was definitely a man. Someone wearing a dark coat and a cap. Staring back across the water at him.

No. It couldn't be.

He remembered the binoculars, the ones his dad kept in the side table. He kept them here to look at the girls on the lake during the summer although he told Celia he was birdwatching. He took one more glance at the figure on the dock, then reached for the drawer. The binoculars were right on top of a jumble of catalogs and papers. He grabbed them and peered into the eyepieces.

The dock was empty. He searched up and down the shore but there was no one there. He put down the binoculars and looked back through the window. Nothing.

But someone had been standing there. He was sure of it.

Someone that looked like Melvin.

14

TONY SAT ON THE CHURCH PEW, staring at the preacher in the pulpit, but hearing nothing. He was wearing the new red sweater he'd received for Christmas, and it was hot as hell. He pulled it away from his neck slightly, allowing just a trickle of cool air inside. Two rows ahead Carrie Kennedy sat between her mom and dad, her honey-blonde hair pulled back into a ponytail and tied with red ribbon, looking perfect as usual. He wondered if her parents knew about all the wild rumors flying through town about Carrie and Joey Miller and what they'd done down at the boat dock a couple of weeks ago; if they did, they'd have her down at the altar before the service was over.

Last night he had met Lori down at the movie theater in town. They were rerunning *Gremlins* for Christmas, and Tony wanted to get another look at Phoebe Cates. The theater had been almost empty, even on a Saturday night, and he and Lori had the whole back row to themselves. She was wearing the locket he'd given her for Christmas, and the diamond chip sparkled as if it were full of electricity. The lights had barely gone down before they were wrapped

around each other, their hands exploring, their fingertips like fire on each other's skin, their lips pressed
together and their tongues exploring, and all Tony
could think was *Please don't let me Wimp Out this
time*. His erection was straining against his jeans. He
pushed Lori's hand closer to the bulge, but she knew
what he was doing and pulled away. "Not here," she
whispered, leaning back in her seat.   Tony's fingers
traveled along her leg, moving up toward her center,
but she caught his hand in hers and held it firmly
against her knees. "Watch the movie," she said, and he
knew he would have to wait. He hadn't Wimped Out,
but she was setting the rules, and somehow that excited
him. He kept his eyes on the screen, but he concentrated on the feel of her fingers interlaced with his.

After the movie he walked her back to her house
along the dark silent streets, and they were holding
hands and talking about the movie and other pointless
stuff when she said, "So what happened to my ring?"

"What ring?"

"The mood ring.   The one you've been wearing
since summer."

He was suddenly aware of his naked finger in the
cold air. "I'm not sure," he said. "I guess I lost it."

"When?"

He thought back to the night at the lake and felt ice
along his spine. "Last week I think."

"If I'd known that I would've gotten you a new ring
instead of that Devin cologne. A *real* ring this time."

"Don't you like the way I smell?"

She grinned. "I love the way you smell, but I just
like the thought of you wearing something that tells
people you're mine. You're hot property, Tony Sheldon. I want all the other girls to know they have to

keep their hands off of you."

Tony snickered. "I don't think you have to worry about that."

"I'm not so sure."

"Well, I am," he said. He nodded toward the house in front of them. "Besides, you're home now."

She eyed the house, then sighed. "So I am." She leaned in and gave him a quick kiss. "I'd invite you in, but it's kinda late."

"Yeah."

"Call me when you get home?"

"I will."

She skipped up the steps, then turned on the porch and blew him a kiss before she disappeared through the front door.

Tony shivered. It seemed colder somehow now that he was alone. He watched the house until the light came on in her upstairs bedroom, then headed back down the street toward home six blocks away. Somewhere a dog was barking, a lonely, mournful sound. He pulled the collar together on his coat and picked up his pace. The wind wasn't blowing, but the night was definitely colder than it had been before the movie. He sniffed the crisp air and caught the faintest hit of wood smoke and wondered if his dad might have a fire going in the fireplace when he got home.

But fires no longer made him feel warm and cozy, and he wondered if they ever would again. That smell would always be linked now to fear and guilt and horror and the sound of a man screaming while he burned alive. It wasn't fair.

And now, sitting in church and doodling with a pencil on the back of the bulletin, he realized Christmas was ruined forever. It was gone, and he would never be able to get it back. A hollow, sick feeling rose inside him, filling him at once with both sadness and rage. Damn Melvin. And damn Gabe and Craig, too. They had taken Christmas from him. He tried to remember how he was feeling just a week ago, how happy and excited and warm, but now everything was still and black and cold.

Like a dead fire.

When the service was over and they were headed across the parking lot toward the car, Tony's dad rested a large hand on his shoulder. "Want to go out with me to see the Hendersons later?"

William and Clara Henderson were an elderly couple that lived out on 232, past the quarry where Melvin now rested under the murky water. Each year they allowed Tony and Greg to take a Christmas tree off their land, and Greg always paid them back by checking on them through the winter. Tony liked the Hendersons, but the thought of spending most of a Sunday afternoon in their museum of a house made his head hurt. Truthfully, all he wanted to do was go home and go back to bed and sleep until spring and forget this Christmas had ever happened. But he found himself nodding and saying, "Sure." Maybe he needed to get out and get his mind off of things.

* * *

An hour later he was seated beside his dad in the Bronco, heading up the hill away from town and passing the hole. He craned his neck to see through the stand of pines, but he could barely see the water, let alone anything on the shore.

His dad caught his gaze. "You and Lori have a

good time last night?"

"Yeah."

"What'd you do?"

"Went down to the Princess and saw *Gremlins*."

"Again?"

Tony shrugged. "It's a Christmas movie."

Greg stared at the road ahead. "Look, I don't want you to think I'm prying, but is everything going okay with you?"

Tony looked at him. "Yeah. Why?"

"Because you haven't seemed yourself the last week or so. You've been. . . distant. Almost sad."

Tony looked away at the passing trees. "I'm all right."

"You'd let me know if something was wrong. Right?"

Tony looked at him. "Of course."

Greg glanced at him and gave him a crooked smile. "Lori's not pregnant, is she?"

Tony felt a jolt. "What? No!"

"Just checking. You know about using protection."

He could feel his cheeks burning. "Jeez, Dad, we already had that conversation."

"I know, but I like to remind you once in a while."

Tony shook his head, wishing his dad would just stop talking. They were coming up on the turnoff onto 232, and Tony's heart had begun to thud in his chest. He could even feel the rhythm in his belly – a nauseating ripple through his gut.

"You and your friends aren't doing any drugs, are you?"

Tony blew out a breath. "No, Dad. We don't do anything like that."

We just kill people.

"Look, Tony, I know you guys drink some. Hell, *I* drank when I was in high school. That doesn't mean it's okay."

"I know."

"Especially if you're out cruising around town."

"I know that. Okay?" He stared out the window, looking for the turnoff to the quarry. If only his dad would shut the hell up.

"You could ruin your life quicker than you can imagine."

Suddenly, he spotted the turn. The snow was almost all gone from the gravel road back into the trees. If there had been any trace of them from the other night, it was gone now. He felt himself relaxing a bit. He took a deep breath and turned to face the highway. Maybe everything was going to be all right.

He wondered if anyone had been out here looking for Melvin, or if anyone would. The word in town now was that Melvin had gone south. A co-worker had told the police Melvin was always talking about packing up and heading down to Mexico. And if that was the case, if the co-worker was credible and there was no evidence to the contrary, maybe the investigation would be dropped. Other than Gabe's dad (and of course his mother), no one really missed him. No one was demanding a more thorough investigation.

Maybe Craig was right. Maybe it would all blow over.

* * *

The Hendersons lived in a ramshackle white clapboard farmhouse that sat comfortably at the crossroad of Route 232 and Pumpkin Center Lane. Tony hadn't been here in years, but it still looked the same. The shady side of the rusty metal roof was still covered in snow, and cozy, black smoke came from the brick chimney.

Greg knocked softly on the door and within seconds, Clara appeared behind the steamed windows of the door. She was a plump, pigeon-like woman with warm bespectacled eyes and cottony hair. "Greg!" she said, and beckoned them into the kitchen. "Didn't hear you drive up."

"Just thought we'd check on you," Greg said, stomping the snow off his boots on the worn mat. The small, pinkish-beige kitchen smelled of beans and bacon and coffee, and Tony's stomach rumbled in spite of the lunch he'd just eaten.

Clara was dressed in an uncomplicated cotton dress, matching the simple, practical and ordered furnishings of the house. Her gaze fell on Tony. "Why, this can't be your boy!"

"Yep," Greg said.

Clara smiled wider and Tony grinned. "Last time I saw you, you weren't big as nothing. How old are you now?"

"Fifteen," Tony said.

"Land's sakes, he's nearly as big as you are, Greg!" She grabbed Tony's shoulder and squeezed it affectionately, then looked back at Greg. "How's Kathy?"

"Fine."

Clara waved them on into the house. "Come on in. We'll find William."

She led them through the kitchen and into a warm, snug den. Like the rest of the house, it was plain and simple, yet homey and practical. The hardwood floors were immaculate and buffed to a shine so bright Tony could almost see his reflection in them.

"William, got company!"

The shriveled man stirred from his sleep in the rocker by the fire and stared up at them. "Well!" he said in a voice fermented by years of cigarettes. "Howdy!"

Clara pointed to Tony. "You know who this is?"

"Course I do," William said. "How are you, Tony?" He winked behind his glasses.

"Good," Tony said.

Clara began moving over some chairs. "You have a seat here by the fire."

"Oh, don't fuss," Greg said. "We won't stay long. Just thought we'd stop by and see if you needed anything." He looked at William. "Got anything I can help you with while we're here?"

"Well," William said, "I hate to ask you, the weather being as cold as it is, but it costs so damn much for the garage in town to come out. . . "

"What'cha need?"

"Truck's stuck down at the old barn. Batt'ry's giving me a little trouble. You mind going down there and giving me a jump?"

"I'd be more than happy too, William," Greg said.

"I'd sure appreciate it." William rose and slipped into an old frayed coat that had been hanging on the back of his chair. "Get stiff if I sit there too long." He looked at Greg. "You wouldn't know anything about that, of course."

Greg smiled. "The hell I don't."

"You take your cap and gloves, William," Clara said. "It's *cold* out there."

William zipped up his coat. "Give me time, woman."

Greg looked at Tony. "Why don't you stay here with Clara while we're gone? No sense in you freezing to death out there." He glanced at Clara. "That all right with you, Clara?"

"That's fine," Clara said, putting an arm around Tony. "He can help me peel some potatoes for supper."

When William and Greg had gone, Tony sat at the kitchen table while Clara worked on her potatoes. She had supplied him with enough milk and gingerbread man cookies to last a year. "I make them for the grandkids," she said, "but I take a little nibble every now and then. Doctor says I ain't supposed to eat cookies. I'm diabetic. But sometimes I just gotta have something sweet." She sliced at a potato skin with her paring knife. "So, did you have a good Christmas?"

Tony swallowed a bite of cookie. "Yeah," he said, wishing he were telling the truth. "Best part was being out of school."

"How's school going?"

"Fine."

"You got a girlfriend?"

"I do."

"What's her name?"

"Lori."

"She pretty?"

Tony felt his face flush. "Yeah. She is."

Clara looked down at the scraps of potato skin on the table and smiled. "I'll never forget my first boyfriend," she said. "Jimmy Potter. Used to walk me home every day from the one-room schoolhouse. He had jet-black hair – the blackest black you ever saw – and a big, strong, muscled body from working hard on his daddy's farm." Her eyes had gone misty and she stared into space. "He used to tease me a lot. We'd be walking home and he'd say something like, 'We're gonna get married one day, ain't we?' And I'd tease back, 'Yeah, I already got my dress picked out.' And then we'd just laugh and laugh. But then he joined the army. I'll never forget him getting on that train in Springfield. He was waving and calling, 'You wait for me now, Clara, you hear?' And I hollered back, 'Yes, I will!' He yelled, 'I love you!' and then he was gone. I never got the chance to tell him the same thing."

Tony pulled a raisin eye off a gingerbread man. "What happened? Did he find somebody else?"

She stabbed a potato. "He died. Killed over in France in the war – World War One." She took a deep breath. "But I guess it all worked out for the best. If I'd married Jimmy I'd never have met William." She looked at Tony suddenly, as if she'd forgotten he was there. "Well! Listen at me, just going on and on. You must be bored to death."

"No," Tony said, meaning it. Listening to her talk was exactly what he needed to keep his mind off Melvin.

"You can go in the front room and watch TV if you want."

"No thanks," Tony said. "I'm not bored. Really."

Clara smiled. "You're sure not like most kids your age. All the ones I know are all rowdy and vulgar. You're just really nice."

Tony gave her a crooked smile. "Thanks." He could have told her that he did occasionally get rowdy and vulgar, that he enjoyed a beer or two now and then and that most of his waking moments were spent wondering what Lori looked like naked. And what would she think of him if she knew about Melvin? He stared into his milk. He didn't deserve her praise. He didn't deserve anything good. Not anymore.

Clara yawned and rubbed her eyes beneath her glasses. "Oh, you'll have to excuse me. I haven't been getting much sleep lately. Been having a lot of dreams. Bad ones."

Tony looked up. "Really? What about?"

Clara turned back to her potatoes. "Well, I have this one where I'm running down our road at night. There's no light but the moon. It's summertime, but everything's real quiet – no crickets or whippoorwills or anything. But the wind's blowing through the trees like ghost people shushing each other. I keep on running until I'm down to the wooden bridge across the creek, way past the barn. I look down at the water rushing over the rocks. And the more I look, the more I think I see Jimmy's dead face staring up at me from the sludge of the creek bed. Then I look up and see these men – soldiers, four or five of them – stumbling along the road towards me, like they've been drinking. But when they get closer, I can see they're really dead, and their eyes are all red and glowing-like. Then one of them reaches out and touches me on the cheek. It's Jimmy. And his hand is cold and wet. But he's not real. Just a trick of the moon – a moon shadow. That's what my mama always called a ghost." She shivered and looked up, her eyes suddenly bright as if she'd just awoken from a trance. "I haven't told anyone else about that dream. Not even William."

Tony broke off the gingerbread man's leg and dipped it in his milk. "I've had a lot of bad dreams lately, too," he said, then wished he hadn't. He put the bit of cookie to his lips and hesitated. "You think. . . ?" Then he shook his head and popped the leg into his mouth. He didn't want to voice what he knew – that the guilt and fear over Melvin was invading his sleep and giving him nightmares. And he sure didn't want to tell it to this sweet old woman.

Clara put down her knife. "What's wrong, Tony? Is something troubling you?"

He shook his head. "No, I'm fine. Just tired." He felt his eyes water, and he blinked back the tears before they could start.

She placed her hand on his. "Look, I don't claim to know the problems of young men – William and I raised two daughters – but I can tell when someone's in trouble." She looked at him. "What is it? Drugs? Something with your girlfriend?"

Tony shook his head, staring at the broken gingerbread man on the table. "It's nothing like that." He wanted to tell her, to tell *someone*, to get it out before it ate him alive. But he knew he couldn't. Just like Craig had said – it was something they would have to take to their graves.

"It's all right. You don't have to tell me anything." She patted his hand. "But I'll pray for you."

The back door banged open and Tony jumped. Clara screamed, shrill and panther-like, dropping her pot and scattering white potatoes across the floor.

But it was only Greg and William. "Sorry," Greg said. "Didn't mean to scare you."

Clara bent to pick up her potatoes. "That's all right," she said, laughing. "I can just wash these off." Tony grabbed a couple and dropped them into the pot, and Clara smiled up at him. "Thanks."

"Sure appreciate your help, Greg," William said.

"No problem," Greg told him. He looked at Tony. "You ready, son?"

Tony nodded and shoved the rest of the last gingerbread man into his mouth. "Thanks for the cookies," he said to Clara.

She patted his shoulder. "Thank *you* for the conversation. Don't get much company out here, least of all anybody that cares about what a couple of old coots have to say."

"You're not old coots," Greg said.

"Oh, you'll know one day," William said. "You're time's coming."

"Oh, wait," Clara said. "I've got something I want to give Tony." She disappeared into the next room and returned with a small package wrapped in green foil paper. "Our oldest daughter and her family won't be here for their Christmas until next weekend. I got this for my great-grandson. He's about your age, Tony." She pressed the box into his hand. "But I think you need this more than he does."

Tony looked at the package. A tag fluttered beneath the bright red ribbon. *To Keith from Gramps and Nanny.* "But what will you give your great-grandson for Christmas?"

"Money's always the right size," Clara said, winking at him. "He'd probably rather have that anyway."

Tony leaned over and kissed Clara's lined cheek. "Thank you."

In the Bronco, as Greg pulled out onto the road and headed back toward town, Tony unwrapped the box and pulled off the lid. Inside on a bed of white batting lay a silver cross and chain. It glinted in the weak winter sunlight, and he stroked it with his fingers.

"That was awfully nice of her," Greg said, glancing at it. "Looks expensive."

"Yeah."

"What did she mean, you needed it more than her

great-grandson?"

Tony looked at his father but couldn't meet his eyes. He shrugged. "Beats me."

But he knew she was probably right.

* * *

The winter wore on, dark and cold. Craig and Gabe were overwhelmed with senior activities – scholarship applications and financial aid forms and ordering caps and gowns – and Tony began to see less and less of them. Which meant, of course, that he had more time for Lori. His thoughts were filled with expectations for his sixteenth birthday in May, when hopefully he would get a car and some much longed-for freedom. And then maybe Lori would let him move a little farther along the bases. They had still not gone past a few tentative touches through their clothes, although during one sweaty, breathless make-out session in Lori's room he'd managed to work a finger beneath her bra and graze the supple flesh of her breast.

By March, talk about Melvin had died out around town. With no leads and no evidence of any foul play, the police seemed to drop the matter. Gabe's dad hadn't received any more official visits, although Gabe confided to Tony that he thought a deputy had been nosing around Sheila at the café. But that turned into nothing. The landlord had even cleaned out Melvin's trailer and rented it to someone else. It was as if Melvin had never existed.

One warm Saturday afternoon in early April when the trees had burst to life with green and the air was filled with birdsong and the smells of spring, Tony was surprised to see Craig's Camaro pull up in the drive.

Gabe was with him. Tony watched from his bedroom window as they climbed out and headed for the front door. He met them on the stoop, and the three of them stood looking at each other in awkward silence. Finally, Craig said, "Want to cruise around for a bit?"

They headed out of town and past the hole, and Tony felt a wave of unease as Craig turned onto 232 toward the quarry. The Camaro lumbered down the lane, which was rutted and muddy from the spring rains, and came to a stop at the turnabout. They climbed out and Craig leaned against the front of the car and stared over the cliff. Even in the bright daylight, the still water looked pitch black and cold, reflecting the sides of the old quarry like a perfect mirror.

Tony looked at Craig. "Why are we back out here?"

Craig continued to stare at the water. "I got the scholarship from Florida," he said. "I sign my letter of intent next Friday."

"Congratulations," Tony said. He clapped Craig on the back. "I mean it."

"Thanks." Craig looked at Tony, then at Gabe. "You guys probably won't see me much after graduation."

"I don't see much of you now as it is," Tony said. "Either one of you."

Craig nodded. "Yeah. Been so busy with stuff, we haven't had many chances to party, have we?" He looked back at the water. "We haven't hung out together much since. . . "

"Yeah," Tony said, following Craig's gaze.

"My promise still stands, you know," Craig said.

"Mine, too," Tony said.

Gabe nodded. "Yeah."

"You two are gonna have to watch out for each other," Craig told them. "I won't be around to keep you from freaking out."

"Nobody's gonna freak out," Gabe said, digging into the gravel with the toe of his boot. "We haven't freaked out so far, have we?"

"You've come pretty close," Craig said. He looked at them. "This scholarship is important to me. I want to get out of this town and forget all this ever happened."

Tony clenched his jaw. "We *all* want to forget it happened," he said. "This isn't just about *you*, you know."

Craig rubbed his temples. "Sorry. I didn't mean it like that."

"We're all in this together," Tony said. "You said so yourself. You can't put all this on Gabe and me."

Craig nodded, pinching the bridge of his nose. "You're right. I'm sorry."

"The Harper's Lake Three," Gabe said.

Craig looked at him. "What?"

"The Harper's Lake Three. Remember that night at the garage? We all swore we'd keep this a secret."

"But we've got to trust each other," Tony said. "Craig, that means you've got to trust me and Gabe."

Craig nodded, looking back at the water. "Yeah."

"Besides," Gabe said, "nobody's looking for him now. It's over."

But it wasn't.

Part Two:

December 1994

GABE

1

FOR THE BETTER PART OF AN HOUR, Gabe had watched the snow. It was coming down thick and heavy, illuminated by the canopy lights over the gas pumps and almost obscuring the Rite-Aid sign across the street. The snow plow had been down Lake Shore Drive once tonight, but already the street was covered again. He had put ice melt down along the walkway in front of the office, and so far the concrete was staying clear and wet. He hoped the temperature didn't drop too much or the granules would stop working and he'd have to start shoveling. He was *not* looking forward to that.

A white Cutlass with Georgia plates wheeled into the lot, its nose gray with dirt and road salt. It pulled up to the pump nearest the office and the bell dinged out in the garage. Gabe blew out a breath and grabbed his knit cap off the hook by the door, then trudged outside, shivering in his coveralls and pulling on a pair of thick, dirty gloves. The driver, a pudgy middle-aged man with salt and pepper hair, rolled down his window and smiled at Gabe. "Fill it, please. Unleaded."

Gabe set the pump and plugged the nozzle into the

Cutlass's tank. "You're pretty far from home, aren't you?"

The driver nodded. "Up here for Christmas. Just got into town. Thought I'd better fill up before I get snowed in."

"Visiting your folks?"

"My mother. Beulah Sparks."

Gabe nodded. He knew the name. She was a sweet old lady that drove a light blue Chrysler, and one of the few credit customers Mr. Anderson had left. "Nice lady," Gabe said.

The driver motioned to the snow. "How much we supposed to get?"

"Radio says about six inches." Gabe looked around. "I'd say we've got half that already."

"It sure is a mess for people traveling for Christmas. I've seen two or three cars off in ditches since I got off the interstate at Cedar Hill."

"Yeah," Gabe said. "First snow of the season. People forget how to drive in it."

"So, you ready for Christmas?"

Gabe hated people asking him that, like whether he was ready or not would keep Christmas from coming in a couple of days. He wished it were that simple. "Ready as I'll ever be," he said. He leaned back against the pump until it clicked off, then topped off the tank and racked the nozzle. "Twenty-three dollars."

The man in the car pulled a twenty and three ones out of his wallet and handed them to Gabe. "Merry Christmas, my man."

Gabe took the bills and gave the driver what he hoped looked like a sincere smile. "You, too. Drive careful."

The Cutlass pulled out onto Lake Shore and headed

toward the older residential section of town, leaving nothing but the sound of the wind whipping around the garage. Gabe could hear the snap hooks clanging against the flagpole at the bank down the street, which made the air seem colder somehow. He wished the old tower of St. Paul's still pealed out Christmas carols like it used to when he was a kid, but those bells hadn't rung in ages; no money to keep up the carillon these days. He pulled his collar up against the blowing snow and headed back to the office.

Inside, he hung up his cap and poured himself a cup of coffee. The pot had been sitting there cooking on the burner for about five hours now, so it should be good and strong. He blew on his cup and took a sip. Yep. That would put hair on his chest.

He flopped down into the folding chair behind the counter and hunched up against the space heater's glowing coils, swiping a hand across his bushy beard. Not much had changed here since he started working for Mr. Anderson all those years ago. The office was still cold as shit in the winter and hotter than hell in the summer, the guy still came to stock the Pepsi machine out front on Thursdays, and Mr. Anderson still walked down the street five days a week to make his bank deposit in person. But Gabe had grown ten years older, seeing his classmates leave Harper's Lake one by one, watching the seasons change from winter to summer and back again from this stinking little dump. He wondered if he would still be sitting here in another ten years, and if Mr. Anderson would still be in charge or if pervy old Gerald would be running things. He decided it didn't matter; it could be the queen of England and Gabe would still be pumping gas and checking oil. Maybe occasionally taking a turn behind the wheel of the tow truck. That's just the way it was.

Some Christmas special was blaring on the television. He didn't think he could take much more holiday cheer. He'd be glad when the holidays were over, when he could get back into his routine and not have to deal with people wishing him a Merry fucking Christmas twenty times a day. He reached up with his foot and turned the TV off with his boot. The office filled with silence. He leaned back in his chair and took another sip of his coffee, scalding his lips but drinking it anyway.

The snow had quickened outside. This was just like the big snow in 'eighty-four. The night Melvin died. It had come thick and furious then, too. And they had been grateful, the three of them.

But he wouldn't think about that now. It was a long time ago, and he had managed fairly well to keep it out of his head. Even during the couple of years with Julie. And Mikey.

He thought about Mikey often, especially around Christmas. He would have been eight now, the perfect age for Santa to bring him a BB gun or a BMX bike. He and Julie could have hidden the stuff in the outbuilding, then brought it in after Mikey was asleep and set it under the tree. Gabe would have eaten the cookies left for Santa and Julie would have scolded him and told him he was naughty, then led him to the bedroom to dole out some punishment. And then Mikey might have a brother or sister by next Christmas.

But that wasn't going to happen. Mikey was lying six feet underground in Oak Grove Cemetery and Julie was in Nashville, probably still shacked up with Damon Edmonds whom she'd run off with three months after Mikey's funeral. It was a sorry state of affairs. Merry

Christmas to all, and to all a good night.

He took another sip of his too-hot coffee and flipped the television back on. Even fake holiday cheer was better than letting his own thoughts drag him down.

* * *

At nine o'clock he shut off the sign and the canopy lights and placed his cash drawer in the safe in the back room. He had called Mr. Anderson at eight-thirty and got the okay to close early. The garage was supposed to be open until eleven, but fuck that. The whole evening had been dead. The guy from Georgia had been his only customer after five. He'd already written down the figures from the pumps at seven, not expecting any more customers in this weather, and he'd been right. Mr. Anderson had agreed. "Go on home, Gabe," he told him. "Nobody's gonna be out in this mess."

With the power to the pumps turned off and one lamp left burning above the desk, Gabe locked up the office and headed across the lot to his truck. It was a 1977 Dodge, two-tone green with rusting chrome trim. He'd bought it right after he'd turned eighteen from Harold Felter's lot, made every payment faithfully to the bank, and in two years it had been his free and clear. It wasn't the best-looking truck in town, but the engine was good and it had never let him down when he needed it. He slid in, brushing the loose snow from his coveralls, and the motor turned over on the first try. He let it sit idling for a moment, listening to Barbra Streisand singing "Ave Maria" on the radio. He punched one of the preset buttons and got Bing Crosby crooning "White Christmas." When he adjusted the tuner a third time and heard Bob Seger growling out "Little Drummer Boy," he snapped off the radio and climbed out to clear his windshield. By the time he was finished, the cab was just starting to warm up.

He rolled across the lot, crunched through the small mound left by the snow plow, and headed away from town toward Wickett Street and home. He passed the liquor store, which was completely deserted except for the lone clerk behind the counter reading a newspaper, and the old Princess theater, its marquee dimmed for some six years now. Everyone had been sad to see the Princess close up shop, even though no one ever saw movies there anymore at the last. Most everyone made the trek over the Cedar Hill or even Springfield to the new megaplexes. There had been talk of reviving the place, but so far it continued to sit empty and dark.

The sign in front of the bank said it was twenty-six degrees, and he actually shivered when he saw that. Maybe when he got home he'd take a hot shower and have some soup, then stretch out in the recliner under a blanket. He didn't used to mind winter, but now the closer he got to thirty the more he detested it. All that shoveling snow and de-icing and trying to drive through winter storms – it was too much damned work. And the cold! He could never get warm, no matter how many pairs of socks he put on or how close he sat next to the furnace. It was if the cold was coming from *inside* him somehow.

He watched as the turnoff for the old homeplace passed. It didn't look as though the snowplow had made it up Jones Street yet, and he wondered if he should give his mother a call when he got home. He hoped she was back from her shift at the café already, that she wasn't still hanging around helping wash dishes and mop up. He worried about her now that she was alone. Since Curtis had dropped dead of a massive coronary in 'eighty-nine, she seemed to have wilted a little. He would have thought she would be happy the bastard was gone, but with no one waiting for her at home, with Gabe moved out and her only grandchild dead and buried, nothing gave her a sense of purpose. She'd seemed tired and defeated when he phoned her the other day. Maybe he would call her after he got in and got settled. It was just three days before Christmas after all, and they still hadn't finalized any plans to get together.

To his right, the expanse of the lake was a black void behind the falling snow. He wondered if this winter the water would ice over. It never got cold enough to freeze, but old-timers sometimes talked about the days when the ice would be so thick on the lake that people would drive right out onto the middle of it in their Model Ts. He couldn't imagine it. And he couldn't imagine how cold it would have to be for the water to freeze up solid like that. He hoped he would never find out. One day he was going to head south. Maybe Florida. Anywhere to get away from this damned cold.

He slowed and made the left onto Wickett, feeling the backend of the Dodge fishtail in the snow. He eased off the gas immediately. The last thing he needed to do was meet up with a light pole. Along the street many of the houses were proudly festooned with colored lights and wreaths. Through the windows he could see trees aglow in living rooms and dens, and an ache burned in his chest as he again thought about Mikey and how it would be if things had turned out differently.

But there was no sense in dwelling on that. It would never – *could never* – be. He had to put it out of his mind. A man could drive himself crazy with thoughts like that.

A block away he could see the light above his stoop. Thank God he'd remembered to turn it on before he left. His trailer sat at the back of the small park, which he liked because it backed up to woods and a small creek. He had enjoyed taking Mikey back there to hunt for frogs and turtles a time or two, but he hadn't set foot in there since Mikey died. And Jesus, that had been four years now.

He slowed a little, feeling the brakes lock up and the front wheels slide before he could steer out of the skid. The snowplow hadn't made it to Wickett, either. He gunned the engine and managed to stop just shy of the row of multi-colored mailboxes at the entrance to the trailer park. He rolled down his window and checked his, pulling out a phone bill and a new issue of *Car and Driver*. No Christmas cards, although he couldn't imagine who would be sending him one anyway.

He pulled on into the park, heading down the short drive toward his trailer. Like everywhere else, the homes here were decorated for Christmas. Mrs. Frailley's mobile home on Lot 2 had strings of white lights outlining her doors and windows and a big wooden Santa and reindeer in the front yard spotlighted like a billboard. Big cut-out candy canes lined the walk to her front door, and a grinning light-up plastic snowman waved from her front window. He wondered why she even bothered; she had to be in her seventies and didn't have any family that he was aware of. But he knew the kids in the park enjoyed it. Probably most of the adults, too. Everyone except him.

He wheeled the Dodge into the drive and had just opened the door to climb out when he spotted something lying on the stoop by the front door. He squinted at it. Had UPS left him a package today? He didn't remember ordering anything. He stood by the truck and let the door slam behind him, staring, but not believing what he was seeing.

It was a chunk of driftwood. Weathered and gray. It lay atop the snow as if someone had gently placed it there deliberately. Yet there were no footprints through his yard or up his steps. And the wood had accumulated no snow. As if it was warm. As if it was generating its own heat. But the snow beneath it wasn't melting.

He continued to stare at the piece of wood. Snow landed on his eyelashes and he blinked it away. He stepped closer.

The wood was club-shaped, and the larger end was darker and stained. It looked like –

Gabe clubbed him like a goddamned fish!

He backed up against the truck.

No. That was impossible. It was just a dead limb off a tree. Had to be. There was no other rational explanation for it. It had come off one of the trees in the woods behind the trailer. Somebody set it on his porch as a fluke. He glanced around at the windows of the other trailers. Was someone watching him? Was someone playing a prank on him, trying to freak him out?

He looked again at the snow-covered steps and noted the lack of footprints. But the snow was coming down fast. It could have obliterated any prints in a matter of minutes.

So why wasn't the driftwood covered in snow?

2

H E ENTERED THE TRAILER through the back door. He didn't want to get anywhere near that piece of wood. He felt his way up the dark hallway to the living room and peered at the stoop through the front window.

The wood was still there. But now the white snow around it was spattered with what looked like blood. His breath caught in his throat. That hadn't been there before. Had it?

He sank into the recliner, still in his coat and hat. Somebody was fucking with him. Somebody that knew what happened with Melvin.

But who?

A noise in the dark room startled him until he realized it was the brown tabby cat leaping off the couch to come greet him. Gabe reached his fingers out and let the cat smell them, then gave it a scratch behind the ears. "Who's been sneaking around here, cat?"

Maybe one of the kids in the trailer park. Those Mitchell kids. But why? And how would they know? Melvin had died before any of them were even born. Besides, the Mitchell kids were friendly and had never given anyone a minute's trouble. It just didn't seem likely.

He stood and pulled off his coat and hung it over the back of a kitchen chair and tossed his knit cap onto the table. He suddenly had a desperate need to talk to Craig or Tony. He flipped on the light and grabbed the phone book from the top of the refrigerator. He had no idea where Craig was these days; his parents had split up not long after graduation and both had left town. Tony had stayed in Tulsa after he quit Oklahoma State, and Lori had moved there to be with him. Tony's mom and dad still lived here in Harper's Lake, though, and they came by the garage fairly regularly. They could get him in touch with Tony.

He flipped through the book until he came to the number, then dialed it, holding his breath as the phone on the other end began to ring. Tony's mom answered on the second ring. "Mrs. Sheldon, it's Gabe Devons, how are you?"

"Fine, Gabe, and you?" She seemed genuinely pleased to hear from him.

"Listen, I hate to bother you so late, but can you tell me how to get in touch with Tony? I need to talk to him." He realized his voice was quivering.

Mrs. Sheldon noticed it, too. "Is everything okay, Gabe?"

"Fine," he lied. "I'd just like to give him a call. Catch up. Wish him a merry Christmas. You know."

"Oh, sure." She rattled off the number and Gabe took it down. "He'll be glad to hear from you. I think he and Lori will get married soon."

"Really?"

"Hope so, anyway," she said, laughing. "We're ready for grandchildren."

Gabe winced at that and took a deep breath. "Well, thank you Mrs. Sheldon."

"My pleasure, Gabe. You have a good Christmas."

"Thank you. You, too."

He hung up the phone and looked at the note paper in his hand, then picked up the receiver and dialed the number before he could talk himself out of it.

"Hello?" The voice was familiar, yet distanced enough by time to be almost unknown.

"Tony? It's Gabe. Gabe Devons."

"Gabe! How are you, buddy?"

"I'm good. I'm okay."

He heard Tony pull away from the phone and say, "Lori, it's Gabe!" Then he was back. "So what are you up to these days? Last I heard you were still working at Anderson's."

"Yep. Still there."

"You must be running the place by now. Mr. Anderson put you in charge yet?"

Gabe gave a humorless chuckle. "Not yet." He pulled a bottle of Jack Daniel's from the cabinet and splashed some in a glass. "So what are you doing now?

"Working on my tool and die apprenticeship. I'm about two years in. Hope to be done by 'ninety-six. Lori moved down here last summer, and I think we're gonna tie the knot in June."

"That's what your mom said. Congratulations." He took a sip of the Jack and felt it burn in his chest. "Listen, I need to talk to you."

"Sounds serious."

"Yeah. It's about. . . about what happened. You know, at the lake."

Tony was silent for a moment. "Let me switch phones."

While he waited, Gabe downed the rest of the whiskey and steeled himself against the bite. He rarely drank hard liquor, but tonight he felt like he wanted to get really drunk. He went back to the front window, as far as the phone cord would stretch, and peeked around the edge of the curtain. The driftwood still sat at the top of the steps. Still not accumulating snow. Still spattered with blood. And now something else. Small gray clumps that looked like –

"I'm back," Tony said, and somewhere in the background a door closed. "What's going on?"

"I think somebody knows."

Tony drew in a sharp breath. "Why do you think that?"

Gabe told him about finding the driftwood on the front stoop, about the unmarked yet blood-spattered snow around it. About how even though the snow was thick and furious, none it seemed to land on the wood.

"You're seeing things," Tony said. "Maybe you're just tired."

"I'm looking at the goddamned thing right now," Gabe said. "I can see it through the window. There's no snow on it, Tony. Nothing."

"There's got to be some explanation for it," Tony said. "Maybe it's hot. Or wet. Feel of it and see if it's warm."

"I'm not touching it," Gabe said. "I don't know what it is, or who put it there, but I'm telling you somebody knows and they're screwing around with me."

"Okay, calm down, Gabe. Think back. Is there anyone you might have told? Anyone at all?"

"Nobody. I didn't tell a soul. I promised."

"Well, I never told anyone, either," Tony said. He lowered his voice. "Not even Lori."

Gabe looked at his empty glass. "Do you think Craig. . . ?"

"No. No way," Tony said. "Craig's got too much to lose."

"There's only one way to be sure," Gabe said, letting the curtain flutter down. "I want to talk to him. I want to ask him straight up if he ever told anybody."

"I can tell you the answer's no."

"I want to find out for myself. Do you have his number?"

"No, I don't. I don't even know where he ended up after college. Did he stay in Florida?"

"I don't know." Gabe rubbed his temples where a pain was beginning to throb behind his eyes. He sank into a chair at the kitchen table.

"You know," Tony said, "there's a chance maybe my dad can find out how to get in touch with him. He probably knows how to contact Craig's father."

"You think so?"

"I know Dad used to do a lot of legal work for the bank. I'm sure someone there has a phone number or something for where Mr. Marston ended up. I'll call him as soon as I get off the phone with you and see if he can make some calls tomorrow."

"You don't think he'll mind?"

"He won't care. I'll tell him we're planning a reunion or something."

"You won't forget, will you? It's important."

"I won't forget, Gabe. I promise."

"Thank you."

Tony blew out a breath. "Hey, you know, I meant to call you after your dad passed away and then after. . . after what happened with your son."

Gabe closed his eyes and twisted the phone cord

around his hand. "It's all right."

"I really hated to hear about it. I'm sorry."

"Thank you."

"And mom said you and your wife. . . "

"Yeah."

"Sorry, man."

"Shit happens," Gabe said. "That was a long time ago."

"So you making it okay?"

"I'm all right."

"Seeing anybody?"

"Not at the moment." Truth was, Gabe hadn't been interested in another relationship since Julie walked out. It seemed pointless. He had no desire to be locked in with someone again, not after what Julie put him through. All the sex in the world wasn't worth that.

"Someone will come along," Tony said.

"Yeah." Gabe rubbed the heel of his hand against his forehead. If only the damned headache would go away. "You and Lori have sure lasted a long time."

"Yeah, ten years now."

"Guess you finally got to third base."

Tony laughed. "Yeah, I hit that a long time ago."

"Listen, man," Gabe said, "I won't keep you. But if you could get Craig's number for me, I'd sure appreciate it." He gave Tony his own number and the number at the garage and waited as Tony scribbled them down. "I just want to talk to him. You know?"

"Sure."

"And Tony, you let me know if you see anything weird, all right?"

"Will do."

Gabe hung up the phone and stood looking at it for a moment before heading back into the living room and peering out at the front stoop.

He wasn't surprised to see that the driftwood was gone. The snow on the stoop was white and perfect.

3

GABE KNEW HE WAS DREAMING. He was dreaming because it was summer, and the sun was hot on his bare shoulders and his back. He was at the public beach area on the west side of the lake. Julie was beside him, sitting on a red towel. Her blonde hair was pulled back into a ponytail and she was wearing Wayfarer sunglasses, like in that old Don Henley song. The sand was scalding beneath his feet, and he shoved them down deeper where it was cooler. The beach was full of people. Families with little kids. Couples sharing blankets. Old men with hairy backs and paunchy bellies. The water was blue and shimmering – much bluer than he'd ever seen it, and boats were everywhere. A sailboat skimmed impossibly fast over the surface, its brilliant white canvas billowing in the breeze.

He glanced back at Julie. Her breasts were round and plump in her swimsuit, and tiny beads of perspiration trickled in the hollow of her throat. "Where's Mikey?" he asked her, and she pointed toward the lake.

"Hi, Daddy!" Gabe turned toward the voice and saw Mikey at the edge of the water, waving at him. His body was brown from the sun, and tufts of straw-colored hair stuck out from beneath the floppy white hat he was wearing. His swim trunks were navy blue with a white Mickey Mouse silhouette on them.

"Don't go any farther," Gabe called out to him. "Stay where we can see you."

Mikey continued to wave. He backed up a step into the water, and the waves enveloped his feet and ankles.

"Don't go any deeper," Gabe said.

Mikey was still waving.

A group of bare-chested teenagers, gangly and awkward, passed by on the beach. They were chatting loudly, giving each other high-fives and slapping each other on the back, talking about girls and "getting some" and kicking sand as they walked. They passed in front of Mikey. Gabe strained to see around the mass of bodies and legs, and then they were gone. So was Mikey. The stretch of beach was empty where he had just stood.

Panic seized Gabe's gut. In an instant, he was on his feet, running toward the water. "Mikey? Where are you?" People were watching him as he splashed through the shallow waves. "Did you see my son?" he cried at them, but their faces were blank and expressionless. "Where did he go?"

Julie still sat on the red towel where he had left her. Still staring straight ahead, her eyes invisible behind the sunglasses. "Did you see him?" he called to her. She didn't move.

He ran up and down the beach, calling for Mikey, dodging beachgoers and ignoring their stares. The water had turned icy cold, and he shivered.

Then he saw Mikey's hat floating at the very edge of the water. It was limp and covered with blood. He made a grab for it and felt the wet cloth in his fingers. The sunlight faded and the sky and water turned a dark gray. The wind blew off the lake, biting and cold and swirling with snowflakes. He looked for Julie but she had vanished. Everyone on the beach had vanished. He was alone.

Gabe opened his eyes in the darkness and felt the familiar surroundings of his bed. The wind was up; it howled around the air conditioner stuck in the window over his head, and though the unit was covered with thick plastic sheeting duct-taped to its sides, he could still feel an icy draft around his face. He glanced at the clock. 1:35. He buried his face under the covers and shut his eyes, trying to will sleep to take over. But the image of that blood-stained hat kept swimming up before him. And his bladder was full.

He swung out of the bed and felt his way to the bathroom, and after a minute or two of fumbling with the fly on his long underwear, he finally just slid them down his legs and sank onto the toilet, pissing silently into the bowl. He rubbed a hand over his face, stroking his beard. He couldn't get that hat out of his mind. And why the beach? That wasn't what had happened anyway. Gabe pulled up his underwear and stumbled down the hall toward the kitchen. If he was going to sleep tonight, he would need some more help from his buddy Jack.

He stopped in the living room. The front stoop light was still burning. He could see it behind the curtains. In the shadows, the cat stretched in the recliner and meowed at him. He reached down and stroked the cat along its back and felt it press toward his touch. He pulled the curtain aside and peered out at the stoop. The wood had not returned. The snow had stopped, and the white expanse beneath the light was still undisturbed. The wind rushed between the trailers, and the paneled wall around the window expanded and contracted. Like breathing.

In the kitchen he switched on the light over the stove and found his glass from earlier. The Jack was still sitting on the counter, and he poured a swallow, then added a bit more. The cat was not willing to move out of the recliner, so Gabe picked it up as he sat down and let it settle back into his lap. It purred and rubbed its face against his fingers. He took a sip of whiskey and ran his other hand along the cat's belly, grateful for the company.

Across the darkened room, sitting atop the television, he could see Mikey's picture grinning at him in the dark. Could see the blue and white stripes of the shirt. Could see the yellow truck emblazoned across the chest. He remembered going with Julie to the Kmart in Cedar Hill to have the portraits done, how Mikey cried when they got there and he realized he would have his picture made. Remembered telling him as soon as they were done they would go to the McDonald's across the street and he could get a Happy Meal and then run around outside in the play area for a while. How that had cheered him up. How he had laughed at the little feathery bird the photographer dangled behind the camera and how his big blue eyes grew excited when he was given a big red train to pose with.

How two months later he was dead.

It had been a Saturday in late September. The trees were a tired shade of dark green and the velvet air was filled with birdsong and the last taste of summer. It was a beautiful day for a walk. The three of them had headed down Wickett toward the corner convenience store.

Gabe and Julie were holding hands like high schoolers. Julie had just found a job as an admissions clerk at the clinic in town at twice what she'd been making at her previous job, and now they were looking at the possibility of moving out of the trailer park and into a real house. Maybe one with a garage and a fenced-in yard. Mikey was skipping ahead in front of them, turning back occasionally to make sure they were still following, and laughing when Gabe told him to slow down and wait up. To be careful because there were cars.

Gabe saw the blue Buick turn out of the convenience store lot and head toward them and had just enough time to realize the driver was bent over and not watching the road. Had just enough time to call out to Mikey to stop where he was and see Mikey whirl around, grinning and skipping and see his blond hair glistening in the sunlight. Had just enough time to scream out Mikey's name one last time before the Buick's tires hit the curb and the car jumped across the sidewalk and took Mikey down like a metallic whale swallowing him whole.

Gabe remembered the driver – a skinny high school junior named Toby Moore – spilling out of the door, his face ashen and panicked, screaming, "Oh, my God! Oh, my God!"

He remembered launching himself beneath the car and seeing Mikey's small hand stretched out in the shadows. Grasping it and pulling him out from underneath the Buick's frame.

He remembered Julie screaming and falling to her knees.

But he couldn't remember Mikey's face. As if some part of his brain wanted to spare him that, as if the memory had been cut. Edited for Television.

He knew the police had come, and he had a vague recollection of one of the cops – Robertson, maybe – talking to the Moore kid and as the ambulance took away Mikey's crumpled form beneath a white sheet Robertson asking Gabe if they wanted to press any charges. He remembered shaking his head no. For three days the sidewalk on Wickett Street was smeared obscenely with blood until Gabe called the fire department and asked them to come hose it off.

He had no memories of the funeral, but he clearly recalled the day after. He and Julie sitting on opposite ends of the couch. Both of them staring into space and drowning in the deafening silence. It was that moment, he thought later, that was the end of them. Damon Edmonds had been one of the ambulance drivers the day Mikey died, and he was often in the clinic where Julie worked, checking up on her and cozying up to her, and before Gabe knew it, the two of them were gone and Gabe was signing divorce papers.

And just like that, everything changed.

When Julie left, Gabe started out taking a day at a time. It was the only way he could cope. And now he had taken a day at a time for four years and he felt he was still no closer to healing. He'd tried various churches in town – the Baptist, the Methodist, even the Catholic – hoping to make some kind of sense of his life, but the juxtaposition of damnation and Pollyanna bullshit only drove him into a deep depression. Who was this God who promised great things on one hand while snatching away a little boy with the other? It made no sense. And after a while, Gabe stopped trying to understand it.

And now, sitting in the dark of the living room with the cat purring contentedly in his lap and feeling the whiskey burn through his gut, he didn't figure any of it would ever make sense. God had abandoned him the moment the driftwood connected with Melvin's skull. There would never be any healing for him.

He unfolded the recliner and leaned back. The cat stretched out along his side and reached a paw toward his face. Gabe closed his eyes. Maybe he would just sleep here the rest of the night.

He had just begun to drift off when a loud thump shook him awake. He strained to see in the darkness. His first thought was that the cat had jumped out of the chair. But no, it was still curled up against him. It, too, had been jolted awake by the noise.

Heart pounding, Gabe sat up in the recliner.

The thump came again. Maybe the wind had picked up his trash can and was throwing it around the yard. But the sound had come from above him. There was another and another. It sounded like. . . *footsteps*. Like someone pacing back and forth on the roof. Was someone up there fucking around? Maybe the same someone who had placed the driftwood on his front stoop? He pushed himself out of the chair and stood staring up at the ceiling. "Who's up there!"

The clomping continued. It moved away from him toward the far end of the trailer, then back toward the front directly over his head.

He'd had enough of this. He wasn't going to be terrorized in his own home.

In the kitchen, he grabbed the flashlight out of a drawer, pulled on his coat and stepped into his boots by the front door. He was going to put a stop to this, whatever the fuck was going on up there. He unlocked the door and stepped out onto the snow-covered stoop, flicking on the flashlight and bracing himself against the icy wind. "Who's up there?" he said again.

He flashed the beam up and down the length of the trailer. There was nothing. The wind caught a sprinkling of loose snow and it hit his eyes, icy and stinging.

"You've got ten seconds to show yourself before I come up there after you."

He stood still as a stone, straining to hear the tiniest noise, but was greeted only with the rush of the wind whispering through the bare trees. He shivered in the brisk air, wondering why he hadn't thought to grab his cap off the table. His ears were already burning with cold.

He stepped off the stoop down into the yard. Snow spilled over the tops of his boots against his feet. He swept the flashlight up and down the trailer once more, but he could see nothing. Whoever it was must have climbed down the other side. Or maybe it was a *what*. An animal could have made those noises. A raccoon maybe.

Gabe made his way around to the far side of the trailer, but the snow on the ground was perfect and smooth in the glow of the flashlight.

No. This was crazy. Something was up there. Had to be.

Behind the trailer stood his shed. Inside was an extension ladder. There was only one thing left to do. He had to see what was on the trailer's roof.

The door to the outbuilding was braced with snow, and with some effort, Gabe managed to get it open. He realized he was making a great deal of noise, and he wondered if the Carsons next door might wake up and see him outside in his long johns and boots climbing up a ladder at two o'clock in the morning. Maybe they would call the police. Let them. Maybe the police could help catch whoever had been prowling around his house all night.

He located the ladder and pulled it out of the shed, extended it up the side of the trailer and locked it into place. His bare hands were nearly frozen now, his fingers like meaty icicles. He grabbed the flashlight where he'd set it in the snow and started up, aware of how his boots clanged on the metal. Even if whatever had made the noise was gone, maybe he could tell by the tracks what had been up here. At the top he shined the light across the roof.

The roof was free of snow. The wind had swept it clean.

4

WHEN HE AWOKE IN THE MORNING in his bed, he first thought he had dreamed the whole episode. Surely he hadn't been freaked out enough to venture out into the winter night in nothing but his underwear and a pair of boots to check a noise on his roof. But his boots sat on the rug by the front door and the flashlight lay beside them, right where he had left it.

He pulled on some clothes and ventured out into the crisp morning. The sky was overcast with the threat of more snow later, but the wind had stopped and the air was still. He could hear traffic moving down on Lake Shore, so the snowplows must have been going all night long.

He located his tracks from last night and followed them around to the end of the trailer, then walked all the way back around to the stoop, but there were no tracks other than his own.

But something had been here. Something or someone.

The ladder still leaned up against the side of the trailer. He looked at it for a moment before starting up.

He didn't really want to do this. He topped the ladder and stared out across the roof. Nothing.

But *something* had been up here making that noise. Something had been banging around on the roof. Something heavy. Could it have been an owl? Or a hawk?

"Something wrong?"

Gabe looked down to see Mr. Carson from next door staring up at him from the foot of the ladder. "No," Gabe said. "Thought I heard something on the roof last night. Just checking things out." He started down the ladder.

"You know these old trailers make a helluva noise when the wind blows like it was last night," Mr. Carson said. He smoothed down his bushy white mustache with his finger and thumb. "Banging and popping. Sometimes it sounds like a clown tap dancing in tin shoes."

Gabe stepped off the ladder. "That's what it sounded like, all right."

"Sure," said Mr. Carson. "You think your whole roof is gonna rip off like a can of sardines."

Gabe laughed in relief. "Yeah, I guess. I've just never heard it that loud before."

Mr. Carson shrugged and headed back toward his own trailer. He looked around at the ground. "Think we got that six inches they were calling for?"

"Every bit of it," Gabe said. He started to take down the ladder and remembered the driftwood. "Hey, Mr. Carson, you happen to see anybody prowling around my place yesterday?"

Mr. Carson stopped and turned, one hand stroking his chin. "Not that I recall."

"Any of the neighbor kids or anybody?"

"Nope. The Mitchells left the other day for Penn-sylvania. Told my wife they wouldn't be back 'til after New Year's."

Gabe nodded. "Thanks."

Mr. Carson threw a hand up and disappeared around the corner of his trailer.

* * *

Back inside, Gabe fixed a pot of coffee and waited for it to brew. There was nothing on television – there never really was during the day – and he'd already watched both the tapes from the Video Barn. He need-ed to drop those off on his way to work or he'd have late fees. Again.

He wondered if Tony would remember to get in touch with his dad and whether they'd be able to get a phone number for Craig. He wasn't sure he wanted to call Craig. It had been almost ten years since they'd seen each other, after all. He couldn't imagine what he was going to say to him. Gabe had followed the Semi-noles all while Craig played, and the team had done really well, winning the Sugar Bowl and the Fiesta Bowl while Craig was with them. Craig had even ap-peared with some of his teammates on the cover of *Sports Illustrated*. Gabe had always known he would do well. He had drive. He was "ruthless," as their old high school coach had said. Whatever he was doing since he left college, Gabe was certain it was something important. And not anything he would want tarnished by the discovery of what had happened that night in 'eighty-four. The more Gabe thought of Craig spilling his guts to someone about Melvin, the more absurd it seemed.

The coffee maker gave one last heaving gurgle, and Gabe pulled a cup from the cabinet and poured it full. The bottle of Jack Daniel's still sat on the counter, and Gabe looked at it, remembering the awful dream he'd had about Mikey. The hat covered in blood. Julie's indifference as she sat motionless on the sand.

Hi, Daddy!

He carried his coffee down the short hallway to the door of Mikey's tiny bedroom and slid the pocket door aside on its track. Except for the layers of dust, nothing in here had changed in four years. Bright, colorful dinosaurs of impossible hues decorated the paneled walls. A shelf beside the tiny toddler bed held Mikey's books and his collection of rocks. He had forever been picking up rocks everywhere they went; Julie had said he would be a geologist when he grew up. A plastic tote full of cars and Ninja Turtles and cheap toys from Happy Meals sat in the corner. And atop the built-in dresser was a framed photo of the three of them – Mikey, Julie and Gabe – all dressed in their Sunday best and smiling into the camera. Mikey was three in this picture, laughing with his mouth open and showing his perfect baby teeth. Julie held him in her lap, and her blue eyes sparkled. Gabe himself looked awkward in a light blue suit and tie, and he remembered Julie fussing at him that day because he hadn't trimmed his beard. He still had that suit in his closet. He'd worn it to Mikey's funeral.

Gabe had met Julie in a bar in Springfield. He'd barely been nineteen, and had expected to be turned away at the door, but no one had questioned his age, not even the bartender who kept supplying him with bottles of Budweiser. Julie had come in with some friends when he was just starting to feel a good buzz. She was tall and muscular – had been a pitcher for her high school softball team he found out later – and her blonde hair, blue eyes and black dress had really stood out in the sea of cowgirl wannabes with their plaid shirts and tight jeans. She had looked *sophisticated.* He could still remember the song that was playing in the jukebox: Alabama's "Touch Me When We're Dancing." And somehow he'd worked up the courage to go ask her to dance. And apparently, she'd seen something in him, too, because she ditched her friends and spent the rest of the evening with him at a tiny table in a dim corner. And suddenly, they'd been an item, seeing each other a couple of times a week. She was his first, and somehow she made him feel okay about that, never mind the fact she was two years his senior and a lot more experienced than he was. And when they discovered after a couple of months that she was pregnant, there was no hesitation when he asked her to marry him. And when Mikey had come along, everything seemed perfect. Even Gabe's dad had mellowed out some with a baby in the picture, and though Curtis never said it, Gabe sensed a spark of pride in him whenever he was with Mikey, something that had lasted right up until Curtis' death. And then a year later Mikey was gone, too, and everything changed.

The phone jangled in the kitchen. Gabe stepped out of Mikey's room and slid the door closed, surprised to find his eyes were watering. The cat regarded him from its spot on the recliner as he passed. "Why don't you get that?" Gabe asked it. He set his cup on the counter, sloshing coffee over the rim, and grabbed the receiver. "Hello?"

"Gabe Devons, you old son-of-a-bitch!" cried a male voice.

Gabe stiffened, his fingers tightening around the phone. "What?"

The voice laughed. "Gabe, it's me. Craig."

The relief he felt came out as a nervous chuckle. "Craig!"

"How're you doing, man?"

"Okay. I'm. . . okay."

"That's good, that's good. So you're still in town. You still at Mr. Anderson's?"

"Yep. Still there. Where are you now?"

"Still in Florida. Working as lead credit analyst at a bank down here. They hired me right after I graduated from FSU. Got me on some kind of management track."

"Hey, that's great."

They chatted a bit more, catching up on the events of their lives over the past decade. Craig gave his condolences about Curtis and Mikey, telling him he hadn't known about either until way afterward, and Gabe lied about how many of Craig's football games he'd caught. They talked about Tony and Lori and their upcoming marriage, and Craig joked that Tony would finally be getting some.

"So what's up?" Craig asked. "My dad called this morning and said you were trying to get in touch with me."

"Yeah," Gabe said, "about that." His fingers were suddenly ice-cold, as cold as they had been in the icy wind the night before. He sat down at the table and cupped his hands over the coffee mug, shrugging the receiver between his shoulder and cheek. "Something weird's going on here." He told Craig about the driftwood, about his frantic call to Tony and the noises on his roof, ending with his excursion up the ladder that morning. "I think somebody's screwing around with me. You haven't had anything weird like that happening to you, have you?"

Craig's voice was low and guarded. "No. Hang on a sec." Craig was gone for a moment, and the background noise quietened. "I needed to shut my office door." He blew out a breath. "So what do you think is going on?"

"Somebody knows," Gabe said. "Somebody knows and they're playing games."

"Nobody knows," Craig said.

"You never told anyone, did you Craig? Just tell me if you did. I won't get mad, I just need to know." He was aware of the desperate tone in his voice and hated himself for it.

"I've never told anyone, buddy," Craig said. "You know that. We made a promise."

"So how do you explain the driftwood in front of my door?"

Craig sighed. "I can't. Maybe Tony's right. Maybe you imagined it."

"I swear it was there, Craig. I'm not crazy."

"I know you're not crazy, man. I'm just saying, maybe you were stressed out or something. People see and hear all kinds of shit when they've got a lot on their minds. I know you've been through a lot the past couple of years. Maybe it's just catching up to you."

Gabe felt a knot of anger in his stomach, tempered by the thought that maybe Craig was right. Maybe he *was* just imagining it all. Maybe he had truly lost it. That terrified him almost as much as the thought of some anonymous person knowing about Melvin.

"Listen," Craig said, "I've got to get back to work. Let me give you my number, and you call me if you start freaking out again." He rattled off the number and Gabe scrawled it down on the same scrap of paper beneath Tony's. "You're making too much out of this," Craig told him. "A piece of wood, some banging around on your roof. . . It's nothing."

"I hope you're right."

"Of course I'm right," Craig said. "Just keep hold of yourself. Everything will be all right." Someone said something in the background, and Craig said, "I've really got to go, my boss just walked in. You have a good Christmas."

"Yeah, you, too," Gabe said, but he was talking to a dead line.

5

A T TWO HE LEFT THE HOUSE and headed to his mother's. He didn't have to be at the garage until three, but he wanted to stop and check on her on her day off and make sure everything was still on for Christmas Day. The roads were much better than the night before, and even Jones Street was mostly clear.

Nothing had changed much at the old house since he'd moved out with Julie. He'd finally begged his mother to let him haul off all the junk on the porch after Curtis died, and now two large rockers occupied the space, gliding lazily in the crisp breeze. He knocked lightly on the door, then stepped inside, knocking the snow off his boots on the worn mat. "Mom?"

Sheila sat on the sofa in a pink sweatshirt and jeans, smoking a cigarette and watching some Christmas movie on the television. She blew out a plume of smoke and gave him a smile. "Hey, sweetie."

He bent down and gave her a kiss on the cheek, noticing the dark circles under her eyes. "You feel all right? You look tired."

She stubbed out her cigarette in the ashtray on the

coffee table. "I didn't sleep good. Tossed and turned all night."

He pulled off his knit cap and sank into the recliner. He had never felt quite comfortable in it because it was where Sheila had found Curtis' lifeless body. It seemed tainted somehow, and he wondered why his mother had never thrown it out. "You work last night?"

She nodded. "We closed early. Because of the snow."

He looked at the tiny Christmas tree where it sat in front of the big picture window on a small table. The multi-colored lights blinked on and off, and all he could think was that constant flashing would drive him insane if he had to look at it all the time. "You still want me to come over Christmas morning?"

"Of course I do!" She leaned back into the couch and pulled her dark hair behind her ears. "I'll fix us a good dinner. Got a ham I'll cook in the Crock Pot. And I'll fix mashed potatoes and gravy and green beans, and whatever else you want."

"Chocolate pie?"

She smiled. "Anything you want."

He noticed suddenly how much she had aged since his father and Mikey had died, how tiny lines had begun to appear around her eyes and across her cheeks like fractures on fine china. "I don't want you to go to a lot of trouble."

"Nothing's too good for my boy."

He smiled and twisted his cap in his hands. "I just meant, if you don't feel like it. . . "

"I'll be all right," she said, holding up a hand. "Besides, it's Christmas. And I can't wait for you to see what I've got you."

"I hope you didn't spend much," he said, thinking

of the toilette set he found for her down at Rite-Aid. "I know you can't afford it."

"Oh, hush. You're all I've got. If I can't spend my money on you, what good is it?"

He shrugged. He knew there was no arguing with her. He looked about the house, at the tired but clean furniture, at the hardwood floors that badly needed refinishing. "You know," he said, "I've been thinking. What would you say about me moving back here? Helping you out with the bills. Getting you caught up."

"I'm all right, Gabe," she told him. "Really, I'm fine. And you need your own place. You're gonna meet a sweet girl someday, and you don't want to be bringing her back to Mama's."

"Yeah, you're right," he said. "Although I don't know if I really want to get back into that scene again."

"Well, sure, you do," Sheila said. "It's not good for a young man your age to be alone. You need somebody. Somebody that will help you forget Julie."

He was surprised at how her words stung him. He would never forget Julie. He had truly loved her, and in some small way he supposed he still did. She had given him Mikey, and he could never let go of that. It wouldn't be fair to Mikey's memory. He wanted somehow to tell her this, to tell her she was wrong, that no one could ever erase Julie, but he found himself simply nodding and saying, "Yeah."

"I thought about Mikey yesterday," she said suddenly, staring at the TV. "Little boy came into the café with his dad. Curly blond hair and big blue eyes, just like Mikey had. He was a little older, about six, I think. I looked at him and thought Mikey would have looked just like that." She looked at him. "You ever think about Mikey?"

He stared at her. What the fuck kind of question was that? "Of course I do. I think about him every day."

"I still miss him," she said.

He felt the hurt balling up in his chest and closed his eyes so he could push it away. "Me, too."

"I still miss your father, too. Five years since he's been gone, and sometimes I still expect to come home from work and find him sitting there in that recliner watching TV."

"And most likely liquored up," Gabe said.

She gave him a hard look. "You know he wasn't always like that."

"I don't remember him being any different."

"Well, he was young and handsome in his day, coming back to town after the army and strutting around. Stole me away from Melvin Hart."

He felt a jolt through him, like grabbing a live wire. "M-Melvin?" he stammered.

"Yes, you remember Melvin Hart. I dated him in school. He shipped off to Ford Hood right before your dad came back to town and swept me off my feet. Melvin used to come around here and play cards on Friday nights with Curtis. He ran off to Mexico or something. I think it was your senior year of high school."

Gabe felt his face flush and hoped his mother didn't notice. "Yeah, I remember him." He again felt the driftwood in his hands, heard Melvin's garbled screams, smelled the stench of burned flesh.

Gabe clubbed him like a goddamned fish!

"He was still sweet on me, even then," she said. "Always said he was going to steal me back from your father. I wonder whatever happened to him?"

Gabe thought back to seeing Melvin and his mother holding hands and whispering in the café, and a wave of nausea swept over him. He stared at the braided rug on the floor, following the pattern with his eyes. "Guess we'll never know."

Sheila pulled another cigarette from her pack and fumbled for her lighter. "I had a dream about him the other night."

Gabe looked at her. "What?"

She lit the cigarette and crossed her legs. "Yeah, it was the strangest thing. I hadn't thought about him in forever. Don't know what made me dream about him."

Gabe pulled his knit cap tight around his knuckles. "Dreams are funny things," he said, his mouth dry.

Sheila took a draw off the cigarette, and smoke curled from her mouth. "I dreamed I was in bed, and I woke up. He was standing in the doorway to the bedroom. I couldn't see his face, but I knew it was him. He had this funny posture, you know? I could always spot him a mile away. He had a way of cocking his hip and tilting his head back. Anyway, I sat up in bed and looked at him, and he said, 'I'm back, baby girl.' And that's when I woke up." She put the cigarette to her lips and the tip bloomed red and bright.

Gabe stared at her. "Are you sure it was a dream?"

She laughed. "Well, of course it was a dream. Nobody's been sneaking around my house in the middle of the night. Leastways, nobody that looks and talks like Melvin Hart. Don't be silly."

Gabe forced a laugh. "Yeah. You're right. What was I thinking?"

6

GABE ARRIVED AT THE GARAGE a little before three. The lot had been cleared, and now waist-high mounds of ice and snow circled the garage like the walls of a fort.

Jeremy, the high school kid who had started back in the summer, was kicked back in the office with the sports section of the paper. He threw it down on the counter when he saw Gabe. "Hallelujah," he said. He adjusted his ball cap and swiped a hand through his greasy dark hair. "Didn't think three o'clock would *ever* get here." Jeremy was usually part-time, working on Gabe's nights off, but Mr. Anderson had him working days during Christmas break.

"Been busy?" Gabe asked, hanging his knit cap on the hook by the door.

"Not really. Same old shit, different day." He stepped into the back room and Gabe heard him punch his timecard with a mechanical *chunk*. He stuck his head out. "You want me to clock you in?"

"Sure."

Chunk.

Jeremy zipped up his jacket and headed out the

front door. "Later."

Gabe watched him saunter across the parking lot toward his car, a beat-up 'eighty-three Camaro. The same model Craig used to have. He despised Jeremy, hated his teenage cockiness and the never-ending stream of words that flowed from his mouth. Gabe was actually stunned that today he'd left so soon without talking his ear off for half an hour. But it was Friday; maybe he had a hot date.

Mr. Anderson came in through the garage door, wiping his oil-stained hands on his khaki coveralls. He was a big bear of a man, intimidating to most people, but he liked Gabe and treated him fairly, and that's all Gabe could ask of anyone. "Hey, hoss," Mr. Anderson said. "Whistlebritches already left?"

"Yep. Seemed kind of in a hurry today."

Mr. Anderson shook his head and poured himself a cup of coffee from the pot on the back desk. "I don't know about him," he said. "I may not keep him on much longer."

Gabe leaned against the front counter. "Really?"

Mr. Anderson blew on his coffee and took a small sip. Grimaced. "Yeah, he's not really working out. Had a couple of. . . complaints. I won't go into details, but let me just say the young ladies of the town don't like to fill up when he's on duty."

Gabe snorted. "Yeah, he's a horndog, all right."

Mr. Anderson looked at him. "You know, I hired you while you were still in high school. You never acted like that. You were always respectable. People like you. Still do."

Gabe nodded, feeling his face flush. "Thanks."

"What would you think about moving to days?"

He thought about that for a moment. He'd been

working the evening shift for ten years now. He liked the garage being quiet at night and no one else around after the others left at five. Going to days would change his whole routine. It would almost be a different lifestyle. "Gee," he said, "I don't know, Mr. Anderson. I've been working nights for so long. . . "

"I could use somebody good. I'd have you work Monday through Friday, and you could have your weekends free."

"Let me think about it."

Mr. Anderson nodded. "Sure. Let me know something next week." He leaned closer. "There might even be a raise in it for you."

"How much?"

"Enough so's you'd notice."

Gabe smiled. He liked the sound of that. "Let me think about it over Christmas."

Mr. Anderson winked at him and took another sip of his coffee.

* * *

When everyone else had gone and the light outside was dimming to a deep blue, Gabe bought a Clark bar off the rack and sat crunching it next to the space heater. A raise. He surely could use one. Even though his bills were caught up and the only debt he had was his account with the auto parts store, it would be nice to have a bit extra. Even if all it did was buy him a dinner out once in a while. And it sure would be something to be off on weekends for a change. He hadn't had a Saturday night off in years.

Below the counter, the news was droning on the television, and that son-of-a-bitch Mark Evans with his blow-dried blond hair and perfect white teeth was grinning like a possum while he read a story about third graders at Lake County Elementary meeting Santa and having a canned food drive. Evans had come by the garage once a couple of years ago when he was just a beat reporter traveling the countryside in a banged-up news van with nothing but a video camera and a microphone. And though it had been in the sweltering days of August, Evans had only cracked his window enough to tell Gabe to fill his tank, then snaked his twenty-dollar bill through the opening like he was afraid Gabe might reach in and grab him. And when Gabe thanked him, Evans drove off without so much as a "kiss my ass" or a "toodle-loo." Gabe wondered what the viewers would think if they knew what a jackass he was in real life.

When the news ended and *Wheel of Fortune* came on, Gabe turned the TV off and switched on the radio by the cash register. Jeremy had been fucking around with it again and tuned it to some top forty station, and now All-4-One or Boyz II Men or one of those other black vocal groups came blaring out at him. He turned the dial to the country station in Cedar Hill, hoping to hear some Garth or George Strait, but instead they were playing Christmas music – the old twangy stuff. Tammy Wynette. He couldn't handle that.

He twisted the dial and picked up an old-time preacher on the little gospel station over in Fairdale. His voice was high-pitched and strong. "Friends, the Devil is never far. He watches you all the time. Day and night. Waiting for you to slip up."

Gabe's fingers froze on the knob.

"You may think you're safe, but you're not. No matter where you are. You're not safe in your home.

You're not safe in your place of business. You're not even safe sittin' on the church pew on Sunday mornin'. Because he's *watchin' you*. He's watchin' you *right now*. Just waitin'. And when you feel that moment of weakness, that's when he reaches in and *grabs you!*"

The service bell rang in the garage, sending a shockwave through him. He whirled toward the front of the office, peering out the window to see who had driven up to the pumps. But no one was there. But the bell had gone off. He had heard it.

"The devil is spyin' on you every minute of every day. You think old Santy Claus knows when you're sleepin' and when you're awake? So does the devil. And he knows when you've been good, and he wants to make you bad."

Ding-ding.

Gabe froze, his hands on the counter. The lot was empty. Something must be messed up. Some wires crossed or something. He looked toward the garage door. It was pitch black in there behind the glass.

"Satan is a conniver! Satan is a liar! Satan is a cheater! He knows your weaknesses, and he knows how black your heart is deep down inside. He knows the true you, the one you don't ever show in public. He knows your sins. Oh, yes, brothers and sisters, he knows them. And he wants you to sin again. He wants you to sin and like it."

Ding-ding.

Gabe's feet were made of lead. He shuffled over to the garage door and peered inside, but he could see nothing but blackness. He eased open the door with a creak, and a rush of cold air blasted him. "Somebody in there?"

"And you *will* like it. But just remember, brothers

and sisters, the wages of sin is *death*. And not the death of the body, but eternal damnation of your *soul*."

Gabe felt along the wall for the bank of light switches and flipped them on. The fluorescent fixtures blazed to life, filling the garage with brilliant light. A gray Chevrolet Cordoba sat in one of the bays, but otherwise, the place was empty. Tools were hung neatly in their spots on the wall, hoses coiled and stored away.

Ding-ding.

His gaze shot to the red painted bell attached to the wall near the ceiling. It still hummed like a tuning fork. Gabe stepped over the corner and looked at it. Maybe the cold had got to it. Or maybe mice had chewed a wire somewhere. He reached down and unplugged it, then flicked out the lights and headed back to the office.

"But stay on your guards, soldiers of Christ. For rest assured, your sins will surely find you out."

Gabe snapped off the radio. That was enough of that bullshit.

Light flooded the office and Gabe looked up to see a shiny red pickup wheeling into the lot. Harold Felter. He pulled up next to the garage and climbed out of the cab, leaving the engine idling, then limped toward the front door, raising his hand in greeting. "What'cha know, Gabe?" Harold said, pulling off his hat. His gray hair splayed on end with static electricity all over his head.

"Not much. What can I do for you?" He chucked a thumb over his shoulder. "Want some coffee?"

Harold shook his head. "I was just coming down 232, passed that old road that goes off to the quarry. You know where I'm talking about?"

Gabe's mouth went dry. "Yeah. I know it."

"There's a truck stalled there. The guy says he was

headed into town and his engine cut out on him."

"Who is it? Somebody local?"

"Naw. Never seen him before. Plates are Indiana or Illinois or something. I offered him a lift to town, but he said he wanted to stay there with his truck. Asked if I could send a tow truck back for him. Says he's got Triple-A."

Gabe nodded. "Sure, Mr. Felter. I'll give Mr. Anderson a call and we'll go get him."

"I know he'll appreciate it." He turned to leave, then nodded toward the outside. "I see you're still driving that old Dodge I sold you."

Gabe smiled. "Yes, sir. She's been a good one."

"Well, you come see me when you get ready to trade. I'll make you a good deal."

"All right. Thanks, Mr. Felter."

"Merry Christmas, Gabe."

"You, too."

Harold climbed back into his truck and pulled away.

Gabe watched him wheel out of the lot, then picked up the phone and dialed Mr. Anderson's house. Mr. Anderson answered on the fourth ring, and the background was full of talking and laughter. "Hey, sorry to bother you, Mr. Anderson, but we've got a tow out on 232."

Mr. Anderson sighed. "Ah, boy. I got a house full of company right now. The daughter's here and the grandkids. I'm not sure I can get away."

"What about Gerald? You rather I call him?"

"Gerald's out of town 'til after Christmas. Looks like you'll have to take it, Gabe. You been busy tonight?"

"Nope. Not as slow as last night, but we're not setting the world on fire here."

"Just close the place up then. Shut everything down and lock up. You won't be gone long. Be sure you get cash or a credit card if they're from out of town."

"Says he's got Triple-A."

"That works, too. Remember to call that eight-hundred number and make sure his account's paid up."

"Will do. And hey. . . " He glanced back at the door to the garage. "Something's up with the signal bell. It was ringing like crazy earlier and nobody was on the hose. I unplugged it."

"Must be a short. Keep it turned off and I'll see to it Monday."

Gabe hung up the phone and shut down the pumps and locked the cash register, then grabbed the keys to the tow truck and headed out. He'd only been on tows three or four times, and always with Gerald or Mr. Anderson, but they'd shown him how to operate the wench and position the vehicle. And this might be just the chance he needed to show Mr. Anderson how valuable he was. The more he thought about it, the more he liked the idea of working days. Maybe he was spending too much time by himself. Maybe working around other people would be good for him for a change.

He climbed into the cab of the truck and the diesel engine started on the second try, snarling and snorting like a pug. He shifted into first and eased off the clutch, then headed toward the street. At the last minute he remembered the warning lights and flipped them on, sending out pulses of yellow light as he made his way out of town.

He hadn't been out this way in forever. He supposed the last time he'd been on this side of the lake was before Julie left, when they'd driven the loop around the lake one Sunday afternoon. But that was when they still did things together and acted like a husband and a wife. Before that horrible day in September when Mikey was taken away. Before that dark cold night in December when she told him she was leaving. Four years now. Four years since his life had changed forever.

No. He would not do this now. It wasn't fair to himself to wallow in self-pity like this. He had a future now. Even if it meant nothing more than a few extra dollars in his pocket and weekends off, it was something. It was at least a reason to keep going. A purpose for living. And maybe he could talk his mother into letting him move back home. It would be good for her. Good for both of them. He could help her fix up the old place. There were repairs that had been needed ever since Curtis died. And if Gabe started making more money, if he didn't have to pay rent on his own place, he could get them done. He might even hire somebody to do it right. He might even take up Mr. Felter on his offer of trading in his old truck. Maybe he'd even get something cool like a Mustang or a T-Bird. Maybe he'd get chrome wheels.

He passed the turnoff to the old fishing hole and once again thought of the horrible night Melvin had died. He hadn't been back there since, and as far as he knew, neither had Tony or Craig. He noted with satisfaction the turnout was grownup and weedy. It didn't appear that anyone had been there in a long time.

He blew out a breath and stared ahead. The whirling yellow lights bounced off the snow-covered pines like disco lights. Mesmerizing and nausea-inducing. He was glad he didn't have to go far because looking at that very long would give him a sick headache. He was already jittery enough from the events of last night and the lack of sleep, and the road to a migraine wasn't very far away.

He made the turn onto 232, passing a couple of sprawling farmhouses with Christmas trees in the front windows, and slowed as he neared the gravel lane to the quarry. The lights glinted off a blue pickup where it sat just off the highway. He could barely see a figure sitting behind the wheel through the steamed-up windows. He hoped the guy didn't try to pay with a check and that Mr. Felter had been right about his having Triple-A. He didn't like the idea of a confrontation.

The gravel crunched beneath the wheels of the truck as he turned off the pavement and glided past the truck. Even this close with those damn warning lights blazing he couldn't see the guy through the windows, just a shapeless lump. Those windows were so foggy it was like sneaking up on two horny teenagers on a date. He shifted into reverse and the transmission whined in protest as he backed toward the pickup, the warning beep drilling through his head. He would have to haul the pickup down to the turnabout above the pit before he could get it back onto the highway. Mr. Anderson or Gerald might have been able to back it out, but they weren't here, and Gabe didn't want his first solo tow job to end in a mess. When he was close enough, he put the truck in neutral and engaged the handbrake, then climbed out of the cab.

It was colder out here in the dark away from town. He pulled on his gloves and walked toward the pickup. The guy inside hadn't moved. That was odd. Was he asleep or something? "Sir?"

There was no response. A light breeze played through the pines on either side of the lane, a whispering that sent chills through him. The yellow lights continued to swirl and pulse.

He knocked on the glass. "Sir? I'm from the garage in town. You needed a tow?"

Nothing.

He put his face up to the glass and peered in. He could see the shape inside but it wasn't moving. "Sir, are you all right?"

There was a trickling sound, and he felt more than heard something dripping on the toes of his boots. He looked down. Water was running from beneath the truck door. It had already puddled in the snow beneath the truck. What the hell? Was something leaking?

Gabe backed away from the truck. Something wasn't right. The person inside the truck had to be either dead or unconscious. And where the hell was the water coming from? He was suddenly afraid.

The tires and sides of the truck were covered in mud and muck, as if it had been stuck in a bog and pulled out. Why had he not noticed that before? Even the bed of the pickup was full of slime and silt.

His legs buckled, and he went down on his knees. He knew this truck. Recognized it even through the dirt and grime.

But that was impossible. That pickup was sunk at the bottom of the quarry. Had been for ten years. This all had to be part of some sick, elaborate joke, tied in with the driftwood and whatever had paced across his roof. This wasn't real. It wasn't.

The shape inside the truck's cab was moving now. The driver's door unlatched and muddy water poured out like thick coffee. A leg appeared, sodden and dripping and clothed in dark pants that ended in a rotted black boot.

Gabe was rooted where he kneeled. He was no

longer aware of the cold, of the whirling lights, of the knock and ping of the tow truck's diesel engine. He could only stare as a second leg appeared, and then a skeletal hand at the edge of the door.

"You're not real!" he shouted at it, his voice cracking. "You can't be real!"

The door swung wider, revealing the tattered jacket.

"You're not real," he said again, his voice fainter this time. "You're dead!"

And then the pulsing yellow lights were upon the thing's face. Its charred skin had shriveled and hung in tatters from the moss-covered skull. A skull that was cracked and sunken just above the left temple where a piece of driftwood had connected with it years before. Strips of flesh that might have once been lips stretched over blackened teeth. It was smiling at him. Empty sockets seemed to lock directly on him, as if it could still see even though its eyes had been eaten away years ago. And when it spoke, its voice was like the rotted, fetid leaves in the mud of an old creek bed. *Say hi to your mama for me.*

Gabe screamed. But even then he couldn't move. Couldn't make his arms and legs work. Even as the thing drew closer, close enough for Gabe to smell its decayed flesh, a stench of dead fish and dirt and rot. Even as it reached out and stroked his face with fingers colder than ice, fingers that closed tight around Gabe's throat.

And then the screaming stopped.

The yellow warning lights continued to throb and swirl, and the snow that had threatened all day began to drift down from the muddy sky.

Part Three:

December 2004

CRAIG

1

CRAIG STIRRED IN THE EARLY MORNING LIGHT as the radio blared on the nightstand by the bed. It couldn't be six o'clock already, it just couldn't be.

He sat up in the bed and snapped off the alarm, his eyes bleary and dry. He hadn't closed the blinds all the way before he went to bed, and now a single beam of sunlight pierced through the darkness of the room. The brightness stabbed at him and he rubbed his stubbled face with the palms of his hands. Beside him, Jessica continued to snooze, her blonde hair spilled across the pillow. He nudged her. "Hey. Time to get up."

She groaned. "Just a few more minutes." She rolled over and glared at him. "Wait a minute. I don't even have to get up. I'm off today, remember?"

"Yeah, I remember," he said. "Just seeing if *you* did."

She turned away from him. "Going for a run?"

He stretched. "Yep."

"Have fun."

Naked, he slipped from the bed and crossed the room to his closet and pulled out his running clothes. "So what're you going to do all day?"

"Thought I might do a little last-minute shopping. I still don't have anything for Charles yet and Christmas is the day after tomorrow."

He laughed at the irony of that as he stepped into his shorts. Here she was, fucking around with him and she was still planning to buy her poor husband a Christmas gift. He wondered, as he had many times, what she told Charles on the nights she didn't go home, on those nights she stayed here with Craig. Did she tell him she was working late? Staying over at a girl-friend's? Going out of town on business? Maybe Charles knew the truth and played along with it. He decided it didn't really matter in the end. Jessica was never going to leave Charles, no matter what. Craig had given that idea up a long time ago.

"I'll probably be gone by the time you get back," she said, still facing away from him. "I want to get an early start before the stores get crazy, and I need to go home and get ready."

"Sure," he said. "Just lock up when you leave."

"I always do."

He had met Jessica at a seminar in 'ninety-nine, a last-minute Y2K fearfest for bank executives on how to deal with customers who were insisting on withdrawing all their funds in anticipation of Computer Armaged-don. His marriage had been failing since the birth of his daughter Ella the previous year, he was anxious and stressed over being recently appointed as president of the bank, and he was ripe to let off some steam. He and Jessica had been seated together at lunch. She was tall and blonde and perfectly poised. She told him that she, too, had recently been promoted to president of her own bank, that she wasn't too worried about this whole Y2K thing because she thought it had been way overblown, that she was confident the operations team at her bank had everything under control, and how did he feel about blowing off the rest of the seminar and going to grab a drink somewhere? As it turned out, he felt very good about it, and he surprised himself by ducking out of the conference center and meeting her across the street at an Applebee's.

He learned she was very unhappy in her own marriage, that her husband was fifteen years older and resented the fact she made more money than he did, and that she was only staying with him because a divorce would be messy and expensive and she really didn't have the time for it. That they had slept in separate bedrooms for five years and hadn't made love in three. And about halfway through her third Jack and Coke, she put a hand on his thigh and asked him if he was up for a little fun. He'd always known he was good-looking, but no one had propositioned him outright since the drunken parties at college. He was both flattered and surprised. And within an hour they were fucking frantically in a bed at the Holiday Inn Express by the interstate. It was sweaty and exciting and better than any sex he'd had in the three years since he'd been married to Kristin, and he realized how bland his life had become in such a short period of time.

He and Jessica met frequently after that, and after about a year, he decided it was time to end things with Kristin. By that time, he really didn't want to fight for much. Not the house. Not the vacation home in Gatlinburg, Tennessee. Not the cars. Not even the share of his retirement funds Kristin was asking for. His and

Kristin's lawyers battled over terms and money and property, and in the end all that mattered was that he would still see Ella on a regular basis. He hadn't cared that he was stuck still paying for most of the stuff from his former life, or even that he was trapped in a five-year lease for this apartment, nice as it was. He still had a vague notion then that Jessica would divorce Charles and the two of them could pursue their relationship freely, but that had never come about. And now it appeared it never would.

He really had no idea why he continued this relationship. Jessica, when she was sober, was cold in her lovemaking. Almost clinical. They never went to dinner or a movie unless it was out of town, where she wouldn't be known. "I have to think about the best interest of the bank," she told him once. "I know you understand." And indeed he did. Talk of an adulterous affair would not have a positive impact on the bank's board of directors. But that didn't keep him from feeling second-class.

* * *

Outside the apartment building, the Jacksonville streets were already bustling, even though the sun was barely up. The air was warm for December, even for Florida, but he shivered when he thought about all the snow blowing through the Midwest right now. He'd seen it on the news last night – huge drifts as high as a man, cars and trucks frozen on interstates, icy winds howling through the streets of Chicago. It made him grateful he'd stayed down here after college.

He headed down toward the Riverwalk, and within a couple of blocks he'd found his pace. He passed another runner, and they nodded in greeting. It was the red-haired guy with the bushy beard and the sleeve tattoos. He didn't look like a runner. He was stocky, and he reminded Craig of Gabe. But then lots of things reminded him of Gabe this time of year, and he had to fight to keep those things from his mind.

He reached the boardwalk and headed east. Gulls soared overhead and boats that were docked along the Riverwalk rose and fell lazily with the water. Across the river, the glass and steel towers of the city caught the early sun like pillars of crystal. Behind the Modis building, which rose up majestically from its squat base, he could barely see the modest concrete façade of his bank, still in shadow at this early hour. He loved this time of the day. Nothing to distract him but the cry of gulls overhead and the rhythmic thump of his footfalls on the wood of the boardwalk. He passed a couple more runners and a few walkers. Lots of the same people he saw every day. Track Suit Lady, her gray hair perfectly coiffed. Military Dude, his black hair cropped close and even. Long-legged Brunette, always wearing sunglasses. And Coffee Guy, a pudgy man with a white mustache who sat outside one of the cafés two or three days a week reading a newspaper and sipping from a tall foam cup. Just the usual cast of regulars. There was comfort in this sameness, in seeing these same people every day. He wondered sometimes about them, about their private lives and whether he had anything in common with them besides these early mornings. He'd never seen any of them anywhere else, and it seemed that for a few minutes every day they all occupied a space and time that was all but invisible to everyone but them. Their own world with its own citizens, its own history and landscape.

He laughed at himself. Boy, that was deep. He was always amazed at the crazy thoughts that hummed through his brain while he ran. Sometimes it was music – loud and clear as if he were actually hearing it. Other times it was thoughts of Ella. Or Kristin. Or Jessica. Most days he struggled to keep out the invasive concerns of work. His morning run was his own time, and he refused to clutter it up with business.

When he reached the River Taxi landing near the Main Street Bridge, he circled around and headed back the way he had come. A cold breeze stirred off the water, and the light sweat across his face and arms seemed to freeze. He had gone just a few more steps when he saw the dark figure in a group of trees near the parking structure. A man in a jacket and cap. He couldn't see the face, just a black shape looming among the shadows. But it was enough to turn his blood to ice.

At that moment, the toe of his shoe caught the edge of one of the boards in the walk and he went sprawling forward, landing on his knee with a bone-crunching thud. He rolled over onto his backside and brought his knee to his chest. The pain was so sudden and so fierce it nearly took his breath.

"Hey, buddy, you all right?" He looked up to see Military Dude peering down at him, his chest heaving from exertion.

Craig massaged his kneecap, gingerly feeling to make sure it was still intact. The skin was scraped and oozing blood, but nothing seemed to be broken. "I think so."

"Pretty nasty spill you took there." He extended his hand and helped Craig to his feet. "You sure you're okay?"

Craig blew out a breath. "I'm fine. Thank you."

Military Dude nodded and headed back into his run.

Across the walk, the shape had disappeared from the shadows.

* * *

He walked the rest of the way back to the apartment building, and by the time he got off the elevator at his floor, his knee was swollen and purple and he was hobbling down the hall.   Great.   Just great.   He was supposed to have lunch today with the board chairman and a prospective customer at the River Club.   The customer was looking for a young, dynamic bank to take care of his equally young, dynamic technology company.   How was it going to look if Craig showed up walking like an eighty-year-old man?

He rounded the corner, fishing his key out of his shorts pocket, and stopped dead in the hallway.

Something was hanging from the knob on his door. Something red and white and tattered and smeared with dirt and grime.

No.   That was impossible.

But even as he wondered at how implausible it was, he could still see the grubby white letters spelling out his name across the back of the jacket.

M-A-R-S-T-O-N

He closed his eyes.   Opened them.

The jacket still hung there.   Taunting him.

He glanced up and down the hall, expecting to see someone waiting in a corner, laughing at him and satisfied with themselves that they'd pulled off such an elaborate joke.   But there was no one.   The hall was empty.

He limped toward the door and reached his hand out

to it. His fingers, he saw, were trembling, and that angered him. Surely he was imagining this. But the wool he touched was very real. As were the white leather accents, now cracked and dull with age and decay. He lifted the jacket off the door knob and felt its heft. Smelled the odor of rotted leaves and fish from the lake. If this was a prank, it was a fucking good one.

Jessica. Had she done this? If so, how the hell did she get it? He thought back to that night at the hole, of burying the jacket beneath the riprap. She couldn't have known about it. Not without some help. And the only other person left alive who knew about it was Tony. Had Jessica talked to Tony? How the fuck did she even know who he was? Or *where* he was?

Gabe's voice drifted into his head from ten years ago. *Somebody knows. Somebody knows and they're playing games.*

Gabe had told him that over the phone the day he was found dead.

A shudder passed through him. He unlocked the door and slipped inside, bolting the door behind him. Had someone been watching him? That figure he'd seen in the shadows. The one that looked like. . . But he couldn't bring himself to finish that thought. Had someone followed him to the Riverwalk this morning, then rushed back here to leave the jacket? And was Jessica really behind it or involved with it somehow? And if so, *why?*

He looked closer at the jacket. Was it even really his?

He felt inside the right-hand pocket and pulled out a navy blue tag sewn into the lining and saw his name embroidered on it in fancy gold thread. He remembered the enlarged loop at the top of the "C," how it always annoyed him that it made the letter look like a lowercase "E." It was his jacket, all right. He dropped it to the floor.

He grabbed his phone off the console table by the front door and flipped it open, then dialed Jessica's number. It rang four times and went to voicemail. And after the beep, he stood there in silence for a couple of seconds, unsure of what to say. "Jessica. . . " He took a deep breath. "Call me back when you get this. I need to talk to you about the *gift* that was left on my door this morning." He disconnected the call and closed the phone.

He gave the jacket one last glance and headed down the hall toward the bedroom. He needed a shower, and then he needed to get some ice on his knee.

Half an hour later, after he had taken some naproxen left over from a muscle tear last year, he called Ashley his secretary and told her he would be in later. And as he sat on the sofa with his leg propped on the coffee table and a bag of crushed ice resting on his knee, his cell phone rang. Jessica. He grabbed the TV remote and turned down the *Today* show, then unfolded his phone. "So what's the deal?"

She took in a surprised breath. "Well, 'hello' to you, too."

"Where did it come from, Jessica?"

"What are you talking about? Where did *what* come from?"

He looked at the thing, now draped casually over the back of a chair in the dining area. "The jacket. My old high school letter jacket. How did you get it?"

Jessica blew out a breath. "I don't know what the hell you're talking about, Craig."

Rage was building up inside him. "I came back

from my run and it was hanging on my front door. That jacket's been lost for twenty years. I haven't seen it since my senior year of high school."

"Well, maybe somebody found it for you. God, I would think you'd be happy about it."

"No, you don't understand. . . " And then he realized he couldn't tell her. If he said anything more about it, she would start asking questions. And he wasn't prepared to answer them. "It surprised me is all."

"There wasn't a note with it or anything?"

"Nothing. It was just hanging there on the knob."

"Well, I'm sorry to disappoint you, Craig, but it wasn't me. And it wasn't there when I left your apartment. Sounds like somebody went to an awful lot of trouble to get it back to you, though."

"Yeah," he said. "Yeah, they did."

"Check with your neighbors. See if they saw anything."

"Yeah. I might do that."

"Look, I've got to go. I'll talk to you later. Let me know what you find out."

He hung up the phone and sat looking at the jacket. Jessica didn't have anything to do with it. Or if she did, she was a damned good actress. And that only left one person. Tony. He had to get in touch with Tony. He had an email from a year or so ago saved at work with Tony's phone number. Hopefully the number was still good. And hopefully Tony could give him some answers.

If not, it only led to more questions, and he didn't like any of them.

2

A LITTLE AFTER TEN he was finally seated behind his desk. No one had asked about his limp, and he volunteered nothing. He'd told Ashley to hold all calls, that he wasn't feeling well and that he needed to go over some information before his lunch meeting. In reality, he wanted some time alone to think.

He found Tony's email from last October; he'd put it in a "Save" folder. There was the phone number. "Call me," the email said. "I'd love to hear from you."

Craig picked up the handset and punched in the number, and his heart drummed in his chest as the phone on the other end began to ring. Once. Twice. Three times. And on the fourth ring a machine picked up. Tony's voice – slow and stilted. "You've reached the Sheldon residence. We can't come to the phone. Please leave a message."

Beep.

Craig took a breath, but his mind suddenly went blank. He sat staring at his desk, fumbling for words, but nothing would come out of his mouth. Finally, he gave a disgusted sigh and hung up.

He swiveled around and stared out the window behind the desk. Beyond the Modis building, the blue steel of the Main Street Bridge stretched across the St. John's River. A few sailboats dotted the indigo water and the sun glistened off the surface like diamonds. He remembered how he had fallen in love with this view when he first saw the office. Bringing Kristin up here one evening and hearing her exclaim over the lights of the city, trying to talk her into making love on top of the desk, only half-seriously, and the way she cut her eyes at him and told him he was crazy. How the Hispanic cleaning lady had barged into the office a little while later, not knowing they were there, and how Kristin had said, "See? What if she'd caught us?" And he'd told her, "Then she would have had some juicy gossip about the new president."

He still loved Kristin. He always would. There were nights, especially lately, when he lay in bed staring at the ceiling and wondering why he had been so stupid. He had chucked it all for Jessica. And Jessica didn't really care about him; he could see that now. She had only wanted something to spice up her miserable life with Charles. She'd used him, strung him along for five years, just keeping him around for sex, the same way she'd used Charles to help maintain her lifestyle and image. A user. That's all she was. And he and Charles were both fools.

The more he thought about it, the more he realized Jessica couldn't have had anything to do with the jacket. What motive could she possibly have? Blackmail? Not likely. She didn't need any money, and even if she did, she knew he had little to give her. Everything he owned was now tied up in the divorce, his cash in alimony and child support. It just seemed unlikely.

But Tony didn't know his financial situation. Tony might think Craig was still rolling in dough. And Tony, as far as Craig knew, was still the only person who was aware of that awful night back in high school. Unless, of course, he'd blabbed. Maybe he had told Lori about it. Maybe the two of them had hatched a plan to get some cash out of Craig. Money for their silence.

But why? Tony couldn't implicate Craig without implicating himself. It made just about as much sense as Jessica trying to blackmail him.

Somebody knows, and they're playing games.

He swiveled around to this desk and grabbed up his phone, then punched Tony's number back in. And this time when the machine picked up, he left his cell number and told Tony it was urgent. He had to talk to someone. He would go crazy if he didn't.

* * *

Jason Bates was just a kid. At twenty-six he was the CEO of his own communications company that had made monumental leaps in the amount of digital data that could be handled by cellular equipment. Verizon and AT&T were courting him. So were Motorola and Nokia. Craig had seen Bates' financial data and had been impressed. And who wouldn't be? The kid was worth almost two million dollars in personal assets. That didn't even count the business side of things. Bates Communications was hot, and its stock was flying across the NASDAQ at ninety-three dollars a share. At a time when most tech companies were flatlining from the dot-com bust, Bates' company was thriving.

Craig watched across the table as the kid sipped on a Bud Light. His hair looked as though he'd only given it a rudimentary hand-combing, and he sported a three-day growth of dark stubble. He was wearing a navy sports jacket and a white shirt open at the collar. No tie. Khakis that looked in need of a good pressing. Leather Italian loafers with no socks. But Jason Bates had style. And nerve. He would have looked equally at home in the middle of a frat party as he did here among the rich décor and sweeping city views of the River Club.

Beside him, Arnie Shoemaker, chairman of the bank board, looking quite professional in a light gray suit and a maroon tie, stirred his bourbon and soda and wore a plastered smile on his face that told Craig he had no idea what any of this techno-jargon meant, let alone what services the bank could offer Bates' company. He was strictly along for the ride, to show Bates that his company was so important the bank sent the board chairman out to meet him. It was all a show. Arnie was pushing eighty, and he had neither a cell phone nor a computer. But he was a likable guy, and he could bullshit his way through most anything. Even discussions about bandwidth and data communications.

"So here's where we are," Bates said, pouring the last of the beer from the bottle into his glass. "In a few years, the advances we've made in digital signal processing will make it possible for people to do all their web surfing with their cell phones, even hook up computers and TVs so that old landline internet services will be obsolete. DSL? Cable? You can kiss that stuff goodbye. Even satellite services. The cellular technology will be faster and cheaper. But it will take some time. We're pouring everything we've got into this idea. But it's going to be a long-term payout, no getting rich overnight. The big three – Verizon, AT&T, Sprint – they're watching us closely, and it's just a matter of time before one of them makes an offer. Then, with our technology on their communication systems, it will be a smooth ride."

Craig nodded, trying to look interested. Damn, his knee hurt. He rubbed it through his slacks. The swelling seemed to have subsided, but it still throbbed. "So when do you expect this big revolution to take place?"

"I'm guessing eight to ten years. Like I said, we're in this for the long haul." He lifted the glass of beer to his lips.

Arnie rattled the ice in his drink. "What'd you major in at college, Jason?"

Jason grinned and dabbed at the foam on his upper lip with his cloth napkin. "Beer and women." He let Arnie and Craig laugh at that politely, then laid his folded napkin back on the table. "I started out in economics, but I got bored with it pretty quickly. Technology had started its big boom then, and another guy and I decided to drop out and form our own company. After a couple of years, he decided to sell out to me and go back to school. I took it from there, and here we are."

Craig looked at him. "So you never finished college?"

Jason smiled. "There was no point by that time."

Arnie slapped Craig on the shoulder. "Craig here went to FSU. Played football for the Seminoles."

Jason's eyebrows arched. "Really?"

Craig smiled and took a sip of his old-fashioned. "Back in the 'eighties. Ancient history."

Arnie laughed. "He's modest, but he played with

Deion Sanders. How many times was it you guys went to the Fiesta Bowl? Three?"

Craig stared at his salad fork. There was a water spot on one of the tines. "Just once while I was playing."

Jason looked at him with genuine interest. "What position did you play?"

Across the crowded dining room, something caught Craig's gaze. Someone was sitting alone at a table. A man, his back to them. He was wearing a dark blue jacket and a cap. The kind of cap truck drivers wore.

No. That couldn't be. He was seeing things. The River Club would never let someone in dressed like that.

A hand snaked out from beneath a sleeve and reached for a glass of water. The skin was charred, and where it was cracked, the bright red of seared flesh showed through. As Craig watched, the hand lifted the water glass to an unseen mouth, then set it back on the table. And then the figure shifted. The shoulders began to rotate as the form began to turn toward them, and all Craig could think was *I don't want to see its face, please GOD I don't want to see its face!*

"Craig, are you all right? You're white as a sheet."

Arnie was staring at him. And Jason, too. Arnie's eyes were round with concern.

Craig's gaze darted back to the table across the dining room. It was empty. He blew out a breath. "Yeah. Yes, I'm sorry. I'm just not feeling well today."

Arnie looked at Jason. "Craig fell on his run this morning. Banged up his knee." Arnie elbowed Craig. "You sure you didn't hit your head?" He laughed – a little too loudly – and Jason chuckled with him.

Craig gave them a weak smile. He suddenly felt

dizzy. He shouldn't have had a drink on an empty stomach. Not after that naproxen. He rubbed his temple with his fingertips. That was it. The alcohol and the pill. He was just seeing things. He was all stressed out about the jacket and now he was half-lit and just seeing things.

Someone knows and they're playing games.

He realized Arnie and Jason were both staring at him. "I'm fine," he told them. "Really." He opened his menu and spread it out on the table. "Who's hungry?"

* * *

"I think we got him," Arnie said as they walked back toward the bank. "In spite of you. . . zoning out for a minute."

"Yeah," Craig said, "sorry about that. I took a pain pill and that drink on top of it. . . "

The street was frenetic with traffic and the sidewalk teemed with pedestrians. Overhead, the sun was hot and relentless, and a light sweat had broken out on Craig's forehead. He couldn't wait to get back to the cool quiet of his office. Maybe he would have Ashley hold his calls for the rest of the day. Maybe he would even cut out early.

"How's the knee?" Despite Arnie's age, Craig was having a difficult time keeping up with him. Arnie was robust and active, and even on a bad day he could outpace many men half his age.

"Better," Craig said. The pain had eased and the swelling was down, but it was still sore. He was going to have a hell of a bruise.

Arnie squinted against the mid-day sun. "I don't

have to tell you what landing Bates Communications would do for us."

"Yes, sir, I know."

"I mean, he can go to any bank and get anything he asks for."   Arnie looked at him.   "But if he does, he won't have you or your staff.   I want you to convince him that he needs our bank.   That he needs *you*.   And I'm giving you authority to do whatever it takes to land him.   Even if we have to, shall we say, bend some rules."

"I think we can accommodate him without bending any rules," Craig said.

"Well, give him a premium rate on his deposit accounts.   Waive fees.   Whatever you have to do. Develop new products if you have to."

"We can do that."

They reached the front doors of the bank and Arnie stopped.   "You're a smart man, Craig.   That's why you're in this position.   You have the support of me and the rest of the board.   I know you'll figure it out."

"Thanks, Arnie."

Arnie glanced at his watch.   "Well, I've got to get to the jeweler's.   Picking up my wife's Christmas present today, and I want to get it under the tree before she gets back from the hairdresser's."   He shook Craig's hand. "Merry Christmas, Craig."

"You, too, Arnie.   Give your wife my best."

Inside the bank, the air was close and thick.   The drone of customers and telephones seemed to eat at him, and the club sandwich he'd had for lunch seemed stuck in his gullet.   He hoped he still had that bottle of Tums in his bottom drawer.   The Christmas tree, shimmering with white lights and gilded ornaments, towered in the center of the marble-tiled lobby.   Beneath it lay a bounteous array of perfectly wrapped packages, all of them empty but artistically arranged on a snow-white blanket. It really *was* beautiful, and the decorating firm they'd hired had outdone themselves this year.

He hadn't even bothered setting up a tree in his apartment, and the gifts he purchased for Ella and had wrapped in the mall at a fund-raiser booth sat in a corner of his living room. He and Jessica wouldn't exchange gifts. They never did. And suddenly he found that odd. She would spend probably a thousand dollars on Charles but not one penny on the man she claimed to love. He really was a fool. But why had it taken him five years to figure it out?

He stepped onto the elevator and pressed the button for the executive floor. The elevator was original to the building, decorated in white marble with brass accents, and lovely he guessed for its intended purpose, but he didn't trust it. He had wanted to replace it for years, but the board wouldn't hear of it. That was fine for them, since they only had to use it one day a month, but for Craig and everyone else who rode it daily it was a crap-shoot. Sometimes it would stop on random floors; at other times it would glide up and down the shaft by itself. The rumor was that it was haunted by the bank's first president, Victor Herbert, and that he liked to visit each floor and see how things were progressing in the institution he had founded in the mid-1920s. "Old Victor's riding the elevator again" was a fairly common saying among the bank staff.

The elevator door slid open and Ashley glanced up from her computer monitor. She gave him a smile. "How was lunch?"

"Fine," he said. "I think Jason Bates was impressed with us."

"That's great," she said. "You want me to start your afternoon pot of coffee?"

His stomach lurched at the thought. "No, thanks. That club sandwich is fighting back." He started into his office, then turned back. "In fact, why don't you hold all my calls the rest of the afternoon. I really need to get some stuff done."

"Sure, Mr. Marston." She looked at him. "Oh, I almost forgot. Your father called while you were out. I put him through to your voicemail."

His father? What the hell did *he* want? "All right, thanks."

He closed the door behind him and sank into his chair. The red "message" light on his phone glared at him. He pressed the voicemail button. "Merry Christmas, Craig," said his father's voice over the speaker. "Just wanted to touch base with you. I know it's been a while. Denise and I are spending the holidays in Arizona. Lake Havasu. It's beautiful here, you'd love it. Give me a call when you get back from lunch. I'd really like to talk with you. Call me on my cell. You know the number."

He deleted the message and sat staring at the phone. He hadn't heard from his father in several months and couldn't imagine what had prompted the bastard to call out of the blue. The spirit of Christmas, he supposed. Good will toward men and all that shit. The last time Craig had talked to him was in April, when Jeffrey had called to let him know he'd moved to Denver and re-married. Denise Something-or-other. She was a thirty-four-year-old divorcee and had been running an ad agency there in Colorado. How his dad had met her, he didn't know. Didn't really want to know. This would be, what, his fourth marriage since he and Celia had split up? He had lost count.

He remembered his father had just married Evelyn when Celia passed away six years ago. Craig and Kristin were still together then, and the two of them had journeyed to St. Louis to take care of his mother's arrangements and settle her affairs. She'd died suddenly in her sleep – a brain hemorrhage, he'd been told. It had taken weeks to close out the estate, involving numerous trips from Jacksonville and countless long-distance calls. In the end, he'd taken only a few small keepsakes and left everything else in the hands of an attorney and an auction house. But he still resented how he'd been forced to deal with it all on his own while his father cavorted with his new bride. Not that Jeffrey still had any obligations toward Celia, but Craig needed some support, and his father hadn't been there to provide it.

But that wasn't anything new. Craig had seen less and less of his father over the years and had lost more and more respect for him. He'd never made it to one college football game. Not one. Hadn't come to Craig's graduation from FSU in 'eighty-nine. Or to his and Kristin's wedding. He'd sent a card with a fifty dollar bill tucked inside when Ella was born, but he had yet to actually see her. And the kid was fucking six years old.

And now the old man was married to a girl younger than Craig. It was disgusting. She had to be a gold digger. There was no other explanation that he could imagine.

Against his better judgment, he thumbed through his Rolodex and found Jeffrey's cell number, then punched it into his phone and waited. Jeffrey answered after the second ring. "Jeffrey Marston speaking." His voice sounded thick.

"Hey, Dad."

"Craig! Great to hear from you! How are things going?"

"Pretty good. Staying busy."

"That's great, that's great. How's Ella?"

Craig swiveled around and stared out the window. There were more boats on the water now. He could see one decorated with garland and a big wreath on the stern. "She's great. Gonna see her tomorrow."

"Bet she'll have a big Christmas. How old is she now? Four?"

"Six." Craig rubbed his chest. His lunch was burning from his stomach to his throat. He reached down and grabbed the Tums from the drawer.

"Six years old," his father mused. "Well, you tell her Grandpa says 'Merry Christmas.'"

"I'll do that." He shook two white tablets out of the container and popped them into his mouth. Why couldn't the selfish bastard call her himself? "So. . . Lake Havasu, huh?"

"Oh, it's wonderful here," Jeffrey said. "Sitting out on our hotel balcony now looking at the water. Bluest I've ever seen. How's the weather there in Jacksonville?"

Craig crunched the tablets and swallowed them down. They were like chalk. "Hot. I think we'll set a record today."

"Banking business still treating you well?"

"Yep. Still is. We've had a good year."

Jeffrey grunted, and Craig could hear ice rattling in a glass. "I'm glad as hell to be out of that rat race. I tell you, son, you need to retire early. Life's too short to spend it locked up in a glass tower."

"Yeah." He thought about his mountain of debt, of how he'd be lucky to have it paid off in time to retire in thirty years, of the struggle to come later when it would be time to send Ella to college. He would like nothing better than to be able to run all over the country with a sexy new wife, but it didn't look likely anytime soon. "So how is Denise?" He asked not because he really cared, but because he felt obligated, and as much as he disliked the idea of his father with a much younger woman, he didn't want to be rude.

"She's great. You'd like her. In fact, I'd really like the two of you to meet."

Holy Christ. Craig pinched the bridge of his nose; his knee and stomach felt better, but now his head was beginning to throb. "That would be nice."

"I was thinking," Jeffrey went on, "maybe she and I could swing through Jacksonville next week before we head home."

"Little out of the way for the return trip to Colorado, isn't it?"

Jeffrey chuckled. "You might say that. But I'd love to see you. It's been a long time. And I'd like to see Ella, too. Hell, she's my only grandchild and I've never laid eyes on her."

Something in the way he said that made it sound like Craig's fault. "Yeah, I'd like that. Maybe the four of us could meet up for dinner or something."

"Maybe you and I could squeeze in a round of golf. You still play?"

"Sometimes. It's been a while."

"Hell, we can just make a day of it. Golf, dinner, whatever. Maybe New Year's Day. You got any plans for New Year's?"

"Not really."

"Well, it's settled, then. I'll give you a call next week and we'll make everything definite."

"Sure."

"Hey," Jeffrey said, his voice quieter, "look, I know I haven't been around much since your mother and I split up. And I know I probably wasn't the best father when you were younger. And I regret that now. I'd like us to see each other more often. Maybe next summer you and Ella can come out to Denver and stay with us for a few days. Has she ever seen the mountains?"

"No, she hasn't." He couldn't imagine where this sudden sentimentality was coming from. Maybe Jeffrey was mellowing out in his old age. Or maybe he was just drunk. "She hasn't ever been out of the state."

"Then it's time she did some traveling. And you, too. I'll bet you didn't even take all your vacation days this year, did you?"

Craig laughed in spite of himself. "How did you know?"

"I've been there, son. I know what it's like, trying to keep a board of directors satisfied. You need to take care of yourself. You want to be around for Ella as she grows up. Don't do like I did." The ice rattled again. "Well, I think Denise is ready to go grab some lunch. I'm looking forward to seeing you next week."

"Yeah, same here," Craig said, suddenly meaning it. "Maybe I can take a couple of extra days off. We could take out a charter boat or something."

"I'd love that," Jeffrey said. "See what you can arrange."

"I'll do it."

"Well, Merry Christmas. I love you, son."

The words hung thickly in the air. He couldn't remember the last time he'd heard Jeffrey say them.

"Love you, too."

He hung up and sat staring out the window for a while, unsure of what to think of the conversation. He'd always known, of course, that deep down his father cared for him. It was just another thing entirely to have it spoken aloud. But Jeffrey was almost seventy now, and he probably didn't have many good years left; maybe he was realizing that. Maybe he wanted to reconcile things with Craig before he got too old or sick. Maybe Denise had pushed him to do it. If so, Craig applauded her; she would be the first person to push Jeffrey Marston into doing anything.

At three o'clock he told Ashley to go on home, and since tomorrow was Christmas Eve and a Friday, he gave her the day off and told her he would see her Monday. She seemed grateful, and gave him a small Christmas gift – a yellow coffee mug with "26.2" emblazoned on it. "It's the distance of a marathon," she said. "I know you like to run. I thought it might encourage you to train."

He massaged his knee. "Thanks. That's very thoughtful."

"You can't use it until after you finish your first marathon. And no, two half-marathons don't count."

He chuckled. "I'll make note of that." He handed her a small envelope. "Merry Christmas," he said. "I hope what's in there makes up for all the crap you had to put up with all year." Ashley was a single mother, raising two teenage boys with little help from her ex, and he knew the ten crisp hundred-dollar bills in the card would go a long way toward their Christmas.

The tears that welled up in her eyes when she looked at the money said it all. "Thank you, Mr. Marston." She raised up on her tip-toes and gave him an awkward kiss on the cheek. "Merry Christmas."

3

ALL THROUGH THE DRIVE HOME he wondered about the letter jacket. He really hoped Tony would call him back, even if he was behind it. But after the episode at the River Club today he was doubting his earlier suspicion that Tony had somehow cooked up an elaborate blackmail plot. He still saw that burned hand protruding from the singed sleeve and reaching for that glass of water. Still felt the hammering in his chest as the thing began to turn toward him.

Somebody knows and they're playing games.

But it wasn't a game. It had been a hallucination, pure and simple. It had to be. Pain medication and alcohol and stress and guilt and the memories stirred up by that fucking jacket. There had been nothing at the Club. At least nothing real.

He remembered Gabe calling him just before he died, the panic in his voice as he rattled on about driftwood and noises on his roof. And Craig's own voice, hollow with cockiness, telling Gabe he was imagining things, that it was nothing, that he was stressed out from his shitty life and his mind was tricking him. And how Gabe was dead within a few hours.

And if Gabe *had* been imagining things, what else had he seen? Figures lurking in the shadows? Apparitions in the light of day, crystal clear and unwavering? Was the driftwood Gabe saw as tangible and real as the jacket hanging on Craig's door?

He wanted to look at that jacket again. He had been in a rush this morning. Maybe there was clue somewhere as to where it had come from. Maybe Jessica was right, that there was a note with it somewhere and Craig in his panic had simply overlooked it.

But when he reached his apartment and came through the front door, the jacket was gone.

At first he thought it had simply slipped off the back of the chair. But it wasn't in the floor. Did he hang it in a closet somewhere without remembering it? But after a quick search through the apartment, he came up empty-handed. The jacket had vanished.

The sky outside had turned orange, and the skyline across the river was dotted with lights. He poured himself a small glass of bourbon and sank onto the couch, staring out the window. The room grew darker, and he still he sat, sipping the bourbon and watching the skyline. Had Jessica come back and retrieved the jacket? He called her cell and again got her voicemail. But even if she had something to do with it, she would never own up to it. And worse, if *she* had nothing to do with it, who did?

A thought struck him. Building security. It was tight as a drum, one of the reasons he'd chosen to live here. There were cameras on every floor, in the elevators, on the front door, everywhere. And the lobby desk was manned by an attendant twenty-four hours a day.

Surely the cameras caught something. Maybe they caught Jessica leaving the jacket in the morning and sneaking back to take it later in the day. Or someone else.

He made his way down to the lobby, his heart in his throat. If it was Jessica he would have the bitch's head on a platter. She'd already played him for five years, and he would be goddamned if she would do *this* to him.

Steve was on duty tonight, and Craig didn't like Steve. He was new and fresh-faced and always friendly and ready to help. Too ready, almost like a dog waiting to pounce on a bone. He smiled now as Craig strode toward him across the lobby, his teeth brilliantly white and his blond blow-dried hair perfect above his tanned face. "Good evening, Mr. Marston. How are you?"

Craig nodded at him. "Well, I have a problem, Steve."

Steve's face showed mock concern. "Oh, no! What's the trouble?"

Craig hesitated. Now that he was down here, he wasn't sure what he would say. "I think," he said finally, "that someone came into my apartment while I was out today."

Steve's head tilted. "Is something missing? Do we need to call the police?"

Craig shook his head. "That's not necessary. I just think. . . someone was messing around."

Steve's lips became tight. "That is truly disconcerting, Mr. Marston. How can I help you?"

"You have security cameras on my floor, don't you?"

"Yes," Steve said slowly.

"And they record everything that goes on, correct?"

"Yes, sir."

"Can I take a look at the tape from today? I want to see whoever might have come to my apartment while I was out."

Steve gave a sympathetic smile. "I'm sorry, Mr. Marston, but I'm not allowed to do that. Privacy concerns, you know."

Craig sighed. He was afraid it would come to this. He pulled out his wallet and slid a twenty across the counter. "I'll make it worth your while."

Steve looked at the bill, then back at Craig. "I'm sorry, Mr. Marston. I can't do that. Company policy."

Craig added another twenty. "How about now?"

Steve scowled. "I'm sorry, Mr. Marston. . . "

Craig placed a third twenty on the counter. It was all the cash he had. His face had begun to flush; he could feel the heat on his ears.

Steve looked at him. "Mr. Marston, I really can't let you see those tapes. If anyone found out – "

Craig leaned forward and Steve's eyes grew wide. "Look, you little shit, I don't give a good goddamn about your company policy. Somebody was in my apartment today, and I want to know who the *fuck* it was. If you can't do it on your own, then call somebody to give you the okay."

"But Mr. Marston – "

"I'll wait."

Steve blew out a breath and picked up the handset and punched in a number. Craig heard him speaking very quietly, only catching a few words. ". . . Craig Marston. . . wants to view the security tapes. . . told him it was company policy. . . very insistent. . . yes, sir, I understand. . . very good, sir. . . yes, sir. . . Goodbye, sir." Steve hung up the phone and looked at him. "My supervisor gave me permission to show you the tapes, Mr. Marston."

"Thank you, Steve."

Steve looked at the twenties on the counter. "You should put away your money, sir."

Craig raked up the bills and stuffed them back into his wallet, avoiding Steve's eyes. "So where do we go?"

Steve motioned behind the desk. "Just come back here and we'll take a look."

Craig stepped around and gazed upon a row of computer monitors, each displaying the color video feed from several cameras. The feeds were labeled by floor and camera number. At the top of the left-most monitor he spotted the view of the lobby and himself standing behind the desk.

Steve opened a program on the computer and began scrolling down a list of icons. "There are actually no 'tapes' involved," he said. "The video's all stored on hard drives now." He clicked on one of the icons and brought up another list. "You're on the sixth floor, is that correct?"

"Yes." Craig watched him, fascinated.

"What times do you want to look at?"

Craig drew up an empty chair and took a seat beside Steve. "Can we just look at the whole day?"

"Sure." Steve studied the screen and punched some keys. "Now the video recording is only triggered when the cameras detect motion, so we won't have to look at a whole day's worth of empty hallways."

The monitor showed the recorded feed broken into four separate angles, with each camera capturing a different view of the floor. He saw Mrs. Jepson next door emerge with a white bag of trash and carry it down to the rear elevator; the cameras captured her from the time she opened her door until the elevator doors closed behind her.

Next was the blonde girl from 6A; she was in running clothes, and she was holding something in her hands. A phone? A music player? He couldn't tell. She punched the button for the front elevator and waited for it to arrive. The door slid open and she stepped inside.

Then he saw himself exit his apartment and head in the same direction as the blonde. He, too, waited for the elevator. The door opened and he disappeared inside. "What time does that show?" Craig asked.

"Six-twelve."

Next came Mrs. Jepson out of the rear elevator, this time without the bag of trash. She unlocked her door and slipped into her apartment.

The older gentleman in 6B came out with his small terrier and made his way down the hallway to the front elevator. At the same time, Jessica emerged from Craig's apartment and shut the door behind her. She appeared to double-check to make sure the door was locked, then headed toward where Mr. 6B and his dog waited for the elevator.

"Do you know her?" Steve asked.

"That's my girlfriend," Craig said. "What time is that?"

"Six-forty."

Jessica and Mr. 6B chatted for a moment. Jessica reached down and gave the dog a pat on its head. The elevator door opened. Mr. 6B made a great pretense of allowing Jessica inside first, then he followed with the dog. The door slid closed.

At 6:55 the blonde from 6A returned from her run,

her hair and clothes damp with sweat. Craig watched her closely. It *was* a music player she was holding, and she appeared to be having some difficulty with it; she jabbed at it repeatedly with her index finger as she made her way down the hall. But she never went near his door.

At 7:04 the front elevator door opened and Mr. 6B and the dog exited and headed back toward their apartment. They, too, gave Craig's apartment a wide berth.

Next, the front elevator opened again, and Craig saw himself hobbling out into the hallway. "Wait, that can't be right. What time does that show?"

"Seven-twenty-two."

"Are you sure there's nothing between the man with the dog and me getting off the elevator?"

Steve shook his head. "Nothing that recorded, Mr. Marston."

Craig watched as the recorded image of himself stumbled toward his apartment door. A door, he saw with growing horror, that had no jacket hanging from the knob. That was impossible. In the video he stopped and stared at the door, then looked up and down the hallway. He inched toward the door and reached out his hands, clutching something only he could see. Something that was not visible to the camera.

"Um, what exactly are you doing there?" Steve said.

"Nothing," Craig lied. "I fell on my run. I was just. . . stretching."

On the video, he unlocked his door and disappeared inside the apartment.

"I think I've seen enough," Craig said.

"But that's not all," Steve said. "Don't you want to look at the rest of the day? There's still several hours to go."

Craig looked at him. "No."

Steve shot him a puzzled glance. "No?"

"No." There was a sick feeling in his gut. His hands and feet were numb. "Thank you."

He stood and made his way around the desk. Outside, night had fallen in earnest, and his own reflection stared back at him in the glass of the front doors, hollow-eyed and pale-skinned. And frightened as hell.

4

IS CELL WAS RINGING IN HIS POCKET as he entered the dark apartment, and he fumbled to open it while reaching for the light switch. A 918 area code. Tony. "Hello?"

"Craig?"

"Yeah, it's me. How are you, man?" He loosened his tie and pulled it from around his neck.

"I'm good. What's going on? You said it was urgent."

Craig flopped down on the sofa. His half-finished drink was still on the coffee table, sitting in a puddle of water. "Something's happened," he said. "Can you talk in private?"

"Yeah, of course I can. Lori's at work. Nobody here but me and Colton."

"Colton?"

"My son."

"I didn't know you had any kids."

"Yeah. But it's okay. He's five. He's parked in front of the Disney Channel right now." Tony lowered his voice. "Are you all right? Are you in some kind of trouble?"

Craig took a deep rattling breath and sipped on the watered-down bourbon. "Tony, who have you told about Melvin?"

He sensed rather than heard Tony's gasp. "Nobody, Craig. I swear. I've never told a living soul."

"Not even Lori?"

"No. Now what's going on? You're starting to freak me out."

Craig found himself rattling on about what he'd seen, starting with the shape looming in the shadows on the boardwalk, finding the jacket at his door, the vision in the club, and ending with the footage from the surveillance cameras. "At first I thought somebody was trying to blackmail me. I even thought it might be you."

"Craig, I – "

"But now I know it wasn't. I think I'm truly going insane. Either that, or. . . "

"Or what?"

But he couldn't make himself say what he was thinking. It was just too crazy.

"Or what, Craig?"

"Maybe Melvin. . . "

"You know that's bullshit. It's impossible. Listen to yourself. You're sounding like Gabe right before he died."

"Yes," Craig said. "And now he's gone. He was seeing things, too. Experiencing things. I told him he was imagining it all. That he was stressed out."

"Maybe he was," Tony said. "Maybe you are, too."

"The jacket was *real*, Tony. I held it in my goddamned hands. I could see it. Feel it. Hell, I could fucking *smell* it."

Tony sighed. "Craig, I don't know what to tell you. Maybe your fall this morning – "

"How much do you know about Gabe's death?"

"Probably no more than you do. I just know they found him on the road to the quarry."

"Don't you find that ironic, Tony? Of all places."

"He was attacked, Craig. Somebody lured him out there and robbed and killed him."

"Somebody they never caught. What if it really *was* Melvin? What if he came back for revenge?"

"Craig. . ."

"You didn't see him, Tony. Sitting across from me in the club today." He knew he was starting to sound hysterical, that Tony would think he had lost it, but he didn't care. "These aren't just visions. Hallucinations. Whatever you want to call them. Something is going on and I'm scared, man. I'm scared shitless."

Tony's voice was suddenly hard. "You're not doing any drugs are you?"

Rage pressed in on him, tempered by sadness. "No. I haven't done anything since college. I haven't even smoked a joint since then. Look, I know you don't believe me, but it's real, Tony. It's fucking *real*."

"Maybe you need to go to a hospital," Tony said. "You could have, I don't know, some kind of head trauma from your fall that's making you experience these things."

"I didn't hit my head."

"Or maybe you just don't remember hitting it. You told me yourself it happened really quickly. You could have bleeding on your brain or something."

"There's nothing wrong with my head." He was starting to get angry now. "Just do me a favor."

"Of course."

"If you see something, anything weird or unusual, call me. I don't care what time of the day or night it is. You let me know."

"I will," Tony said, "if you promise to get yourself checked out."

"Of course," Craig lied. He had no intention of going to a hospital and letting them milk him out of hundreds of dollars for a scraped knee. "But you be careful."

"I will," Tony said. "Merry Christmas."

"You, too." He snapped his phone shut and downed the rest of the watery bourbon, then crunched the remaining ice with his teeth.

So Tony thought he was seeing things. And why not? It was the same thing Craig had thought about Gabe. He knew how crazy it sounded. How crazy Gabe had sounded. The whole idea was ludicrous. And if he hadn't seen it himself – that blackened hand reaching out for the glass of water, that rotting letter jacket he had held with his own fingers – he would think himself crazy, too. It was more than he could comprehend.

He poured himself another bourbon and stood looking out at the city lights across the river. The red lights blinked atop the Modis building, slowly and steadily like a heartbeat. He hadn't smoked since high school, but now he found himself wanting a cigarette. Something to keep his hands occupied. Something to keep his mind off the fact that he was being stalked by a ghost.

* * *

At nine, drowsy from the bourbon and exhausted from worry, he took another naproxen and went to bed. His knee was bothering him again, and maybe he just needed some rest. But he found himself unable to sleep. Instead his mind kept wandering back to that night at the hole. Melvin wallowing in the flames. Craig and Gabe dragging him to the water. The hollow thud of the wood smacking against bone. Hauling him out to the truck. Sending it over the edge into the quarry. Gabe's face, ashen and hollow-eyed. And Tony's, tear-streaked and flushed.

And Gabe's trembling voice over the phone: *Somebody knows and they're playing games.*

He'd left the blinds open – on purpose this time – and he watched the dim light of the traffic play across the textured ceiling. Tonight he didn't want to be in the darkness. If something was coming for him, he wanted to see it.

If something was coming for him.

He sat up and switched on the bedside lamp.

There was nothing in his room but the chest in the corner, and in front of the bay window the chair with a shirt draped across it. The doorway to the bathroom yawned like a black hole. Anything could be in there. He strained to listen, imagining that he could hear something moving. Something wet and heavy.

Before he could stop himself, he whipped off the covers and staggered to the bathroom, feeling desperately for the light switch. The lights above the mirror blazed on. There was nothing there. Water dripped from the shower head, and he tightened the handle. It had been dripping for days now, and he kept meaning to call maintenance.

Alone. He was alone in the apartment. He had to

keep telling himself that.

Leaving the lights burning, he crawled back into bed and rolled over onto his left side, keeping his face toward the door to the hallway. The jacket. He had seen it. Had *held it*, by God. He couldn't have imagined it. The vision in the club he could chalk up to hallucination. But not the jacket.

So why hadn't he seen it on the video?

Maybe Tony was right. Maybe something was wrong with his brain. Maybe he *had* hit his head when he fell.

He ran his fingertips across his scalp, feeling for any place that was tender or swollen, but there was nothing. The only part of his body he had hurt was his knee. The pill had killed most of the pain, but it was still sensitive to his touch. He still counted himself lucky that he hadn't broken anything.

And then he remembered. He'd seen the shape in the shadows *before* he tripped. Before he could have hit his head. If it were hallucinations they had started before his accident. And if that were so and it was all in his head, it could be something else. A brain tumor. Some kind of psychosis. And the thought of that was almost as scary as the idea of Melvin coming back from the dead.

* * *

At some point he fell asleep, because the next thing he was aware of was the warmth of the sunlight on his face as it streamed in through the windows. He stirred and stretched, amazed that he'd been able to get any rest at all. The lamp on the nightstand still burned, and now seeing its pale light in the bright room, he felt foolish. His knee was throbbing again, and he pulled back the covers to look at it. It was dark and purple, and the scrape had scabbed over. He should probably put some Neosporin on it to keep it from getting infected.

He sat up and swung his legs over the edge of the bed, then stared at the sight before him. His bowels turned to acid, and he had to grip the side of the mattress to keep from falling over.

There were boot prints on the carpet. Dark and muddy. They entered the room from the hallway and stopped just beside the bed, as if whoever made them had stood watching him sleep and then disappeared into thin air.

He slipped from the bed and sat cross-legged on the floor, staring at the stains on the tan carpet. He reached out and felt the cold, damp mess. Brought his hands to his face and looked at the grit. Slid his fingertips together and watched the gray dirt smear on his skin.

Not a hallucination. This was real. It was fucking real.

And he knew without a doubt who had been in his room.

5

WHEN THE ELEVATOR REACHED the top floor of the bank, he thought at first that something was wrong. The lights were still out and the office was deadly silent. Then he remembered he'd given Ashley the day off.

He made his way to the kitchenette and started a pot of coffee, then headed into his office and placed the phone on "Do Not Disturb." Since Ashley wasn't here, he would just let all his calls go to voicemail. He was only planning on working until about noon. But with no interruptions he should be able to put together a proposal on the Bates project in no time.

Provided, of course, he could keep his mind focused.

For a brief moment this morning he'd thought of trying to scrub the boot prints out of the carpet, of grabbing a bucket of soapy water and a brush and going at it. But he figured it would be pointless. They would probably be gone by the time he got home anyway.

He sat at the desk and watched the river through the

window. A lone sailboat skimmed over the water surrounded by a flock of gulls. It seemed odd to be sitting here in silence, with not even the normal everyday office noises around him. He was used to the ringing phone, or the ding of the elevator as it reached the floor, or the sound of Ashley clacking away at her keyboard. But today there was nothing. It was silent as a tomb.

He wondered how long this would continue. How long would Melvin continue to play with him? How long would he hide in the shadows and lurk about the house just outside of Craig's vision? How long would he leave reminders of that night at Harper's Lake, reminders that would disappear like fragments of half-remembered dreams?

How long until Melvin finally came for him?

His cell phone vibrated, startling him. He looked at it. Kristin's number. "Hello?"

"Hi, Daddy."

Sweet Ella. He pictured her curly dark hair and her large brown eyes and felt a desperate ache in his chest. "Hey Punkin. What'cha doing?"

"It's Christmas Eve!"

"I know. Are you excited?"

"Yes! Santa comes tonight!"

"He sure does. And I'm bringing you some more presents after lunch today."

"I know. And I've got a present for you, too."

"You do?"

"Yeah, but I can't tell you what it is."

"Well, I'll bet it's going to be the best present I ever got."

"Mom wants to talk to you."

"Okay. Put her on. And I'll see you in a little while."

"'Bye, Daddy.'"

There was a thunk as the receiver was set down, then a rustling as it was picked up again, and Kristin's voice came on the line, soft and warm as velvet. "Hey."

"Hey. I think she's ready for Christmas."

Kristin laughed. "Oh, my God, she has been bouncing off the walls for a week."

"You got the doll, right?"

"I've had it for a month. And thank God she didn't change her mind about which one she wanted. The last time we went to see Santa at the mall I was terrified she would suddenly decide she wanted a Nintendo or something."

He sat up in his chair. "Yeah, you remember that year she wanted the kitchen set and – "

"And on Christmas Eve she decided she wanted that ride-on car!" They both laughed, remembering. "I still don't know how we managed to get it in the house without her seeing it," she said.

He smiled. Just hearing her voice stirred up a hollow ache within him. If she were still around, he could tell her about Melvin. He would confide in her, despite his promise to Gabe and Tony. She would know what to do. She would know how to handle it. "I've missed you," he said suddenly, not really knowing where the words came from.

"Craig. . . "

"I don't know what really happened with us, and I wish. . . I don't know, that I could take back the last five years."

She sighed. "I miss you, too."

Tears stung his eyes. "Really?"

"Even after all this time. I still sleep on the same

side of the bed. Still sit at the same place at the kitchen table. It's like I'm still waiting for you to come back."

He closed his eyes. The sunlight on the river was suddenly blinding. "What happened, Kristin? What happened to us?"

"You cheated on me, Craig. You know what happened."

"No. I mean before. We drifted apart long before that. From the time Ella was born."

She was silent for a moment. "I don't know," she said finally. "I was fat from the pregnancy, and hormonal, and depressed. I remember those days, how awful I felt. And I've thought a lot of times that I drove you away. It's like I could see it happening but I couldn't stop it."

"You didn't drive me away. Not entirely. I was going through a rough patch, too."

"Yeah, I know. I don't think either one of us really knew what we were doing then."

"Well, we were younger. We had a new baby. I think we were both just stressed and maybe taking it out on each other."

"Yeah."

And suddenly he wanted her back. He wanted to be rid of Jessica and back at the house and waking up tomorrow morning beside Kristin and sharing Christmas with her and Ella. Jessica had been bad for him. He saw that now. He couldn't believe he'd wasted five years on her. Five years he could have been with Kristin and Ella, watching Ella grow and nurturing his and Kristin's love back to where it had once been. "You got any plans for later tonight?" he asked.

"Not really. Probably just trying to get Ella to bed and asleep by a decent hour."

"How about the three of us go out to dinner? Somewhere really nice."

"I don't know. . . "

"Come on, Kris. I'd like to take you and Ella out. It's just dinner."

She took a deep breath. "I'll think about it. We can discuss it when you bring Ella's presents over later."

Hope bloomed within him for the first time in months. "We can go anywhere you want. Even that Italian place I hate."

She laughed. "The place with the watery marinara sauce? No thanks."

He pressed the phone tightly to his ear, as if he could pull her closer. "Well, think about it. I'll see you after lunch. I'm only working until noon, and then I'm taking the rest of the day off. I want to spend some time with Ella."

"Ella will like that," she said. "She's missed you."

"Yeah," he said. "I've missed her, too."

"How about I fix a pot of coffee and the three of us can play some games this afternoon?"

"Sounds fun."

"Ella and I made some cookies, so don't eat too much at lunch. She'll be disappointed if you don't have any."

"I couldn't turn down Ella's Christmas cookies."

"Okay, then. Well, I'll see you later."

"Yep. See ya."

He closed up the phone and marveled at how for a brief moment he'd forgotten all about Melvin. And he wondered if meeting up with Kristin and Ella during all this was such a good idea. What if he was putting them in danger? But maybe he would be safe if he could be with them. Maybe they could ward off whatever evil had been stalking him the past few days. In any event, he knew he didn't want to be alone any more than he had to. Maybe he would discuss it with Kristin this afternoon. Maybe he would come clean. And maybe they could get through it together.

The elevator in the front office dinged and he heard the door slide open, then close gently. Then the car whirred back down. He swiveled around and waited for someone to appear in his doorway. And waited.

"Hello?" he called out.

Nothing. It must be old Victor again, come to say Merry Christmas.

"What's the matter? Am I not working hard enough to please you?"

And then he heard it, almost imperceptible at first. The soft, wet sounds of footsteps on the marble tile. The sound muddy boots would make. Boots that might have lain at the bottom of a flooded quarry for twenty years.

His gaze was frozen on the office doorway. "Who's there?"

A shadow slid across the tile. The footsteps continued, louder now. Coming closer.

Squish. Drag. Squish.

Craig was vaguely aware that he had stood up. "What do you want?"

Squish. Drag. Squish.

He glanced at the phone. He could dial the security officer. And he could be up here in five minutes. And –

A shape loomed in the doorway. Something dressed in a navy blue jacket and rotted, sodden trousers. He could see the water dripping onto the tile, could hear it, a steady trickle like rain. It raised a hand,

and the remaining charred skin hung in strips from the gray bones. It was then that Craig saw its face – hideous and eaten away, the teeth black and the crushed skull green with mold. Empty holes where eyes had once been, now filled with mud and muck and, as Craig saw with horror, wriggling with worms. It took another step toward him.

Squish. Drag.

Craig knew he was screaming, knew that the sounds were coming out of him even as they sounded foreign and distant. He couldn't tear his gaze away from the thing's eye sockets. The worms continued to writhe. The shape continued to move closer.

Squish. Drag.

Somehow he had backed up against the window. He held the chair between him and the thing, as if he could ward it off. As if he could stop whatever demon from hell was now advancing toward him. He could smell it now. The odor of fish left to rot in the hot summer sun.

It was mere inches from him. The water continued its steady drip. He could see it coming off the tattered sleeves of the jacket, could hear it flat and dull as it hit the carpet. The skeletal hand reached for him. He could see what remained of the nails clinging to the withered strips of skin.

His back pressed against the glass of the window, and his fingers were numb from gripping the chair. He was no longer aware of his screams, no longer conscious of anything but the sight in front of him as it continued to draw closer.

The decomposing hand grabbed the chair, and with an impossible strength, wrenched it from Craig's grasp. It clattered to the side.

Now there was nothing between him and the thing. The putrid, skeletal fingers reached toward Craig's face. He pressed harder into the glass behind him. Harder.

With a deafening crack, the window gave way. He felt himself in mid-air before he realized he was falling.

Down. Down. Watching as the concrete below flew up to meet him.

Part Four:

December 2014

TONY

1

ALL THE WAY ACROSS TOWN Tony's gaze darted from the road to the mood ring where it lay on the dash rattling and sliding with each little bump in the pavement. He had always known this day would come eventually, that sooner or later whatever had gotten Gabe and Craig would come for him. He remembered Gabe's panicked voice on the phone that night as he described the piece of wood on his front porch; Craig's equal distress ten years later as he recounted finding the letter jacket hanging on his front door. He remembered telling them they were imagining it. Seeing things. And, guiltily, wondering if Craig was on some kind of bad drug.

But both of them had been adamant. The things they had seen were *real*. They were sure of it. And if what they had experienced was as solid as the ring he was looking at now, then he had been a fool to doubt them. And now both of them were dead.

A car honked behind him, and he realized he had crossed over the center line. He could feel the panic rising up inside him like lava. He forced himself to take a deep breath, forced himself to ease off the accelerator. He would be of no use to Lori or Colton if he crashed his truck head-on into a semi.

He wheeled into the hospital parking lot and threw the Ford into park, grabbing the ring and heading for the front doors. He slipped it on his finger as he crossed the lobby to the elevators, noticing how icy cold the metal was against his skin.

One of Lori's co-workers – Cindy? Sandy? He couldn't remember– stepped onto the elevator just as the doors started to close. "Hey, Tony."

"Hey," he said, punching the button for the fifth floor.

"Here to see Lori?"

"Yeah." He stared at the indicator above the door, hoping he could stave off any further conversation.

"You guys got all your Christmas shopping done?"

He glanced at her, bleached blonde hair pulled back into a ponytail. Her scrubs had kittens on them. "Yeah," he said. "Yeah, we're ready."

"I've got just a few last-minute things to pick up, but then I do this every year. My husband makes the biggest joke out of it." Cindy/Sandy tapped her pen against the clipboard in her hand. "Can you believe Christmas is only a week away?"

"Yeah," he said, looking back at the floor indicator. "We're running out of time."

With aching slowness, the elevator finally reached the fifth floor. The door slid open and he bolted out, ignoring whatever Cindy/Sandy was calling after him.

Several people meandered through the hallway. Patients in gowns with IVs in tow, nurses flitting in and out of rooms, visitors looking lost. No sign of Lori anywhere. He would have to go to the nurses' station and ask for her.

"Tony!"

He turned and saw her coming toward him down the hall. He rushed to her and grabbed her hands. "Is there some place we can talk?"

Lori's face turned ghostly white. "What's the matter? Did something happen to Colton?"

"No – "

"Is my mom okay?"

He squeezed her fingers in his. "Everybody's okay. I just have to talk to you. Some place private."

She looked at him doubtfully, then pulled him toward a linen closet. "In here." She flipped the light on and he saw shelves of folded bleached white sheets, blankets, and pillows. They smelled of bleach and disinfectant. She nudged him in and closed the door gently behind them. "What the hell is going on?"

He held onto her hands again and tried to meet her gaze. "I've got something I have to talk to you about. Something that happened when we were in high school. Something terrible."

Her eyes were round and frightened. "What's wrong, babe? You're shaking like a leaf."

He looked down at his hands. The mood ring he had slipped on just a moment before was gone. He scanned the floor, knowing he wouldn't find it but looking anyway. A trickle of sweat crawled down his forehead.

"Tony! What's wrong? What's happened?"

He took a deep breath and looked into her brown eyes. "Do you remember a man back home in Harper's Lake named Melvin Hart?"

A look of confusion crossed her face. "Melvin

Hart. No. I don't remember anyone by that name."

"He disappeared. We were sophomores. Everyone thought he ran off to Mexico or something."

She shook her head. "I don't remember. What's all this about?"

His breath rattled in his chest. "We killed him, Lori. Me and Gabe and Craig."

She looked at him for a moment and then laughed. "What?" She continued to stare at him, and when he didn't return her smile, her eyes grew round again. "Oh, my God, you're. . . you're serious, aren't you?"

He told her all of it. Everything he could remember about that night at the hole. The bonfire. Melvin showing up drunk, then falling into the flames. Gabe and the piece of driftwood. Hauling the body out to the quarry and running the truck over the cliff. He told her of the years of guilt and shame, and of the frantic calls he'd received from Gabe and Craig just before they died. And of today – finding the mood ring on the front stoop and it disappearing off his finger somewhere between the lobby and here on the fifth floor. And when he was done, when his throat was raw and dry as sand from talking, he finally looked at her and saw tears spilling down her face.

She stared at the floor, not meeting his gaze, and wiped her eyes with the back of her hand. "I don't know what to say," she told him. "All this time. And you never told me."

"I couldn't," he said. "We promised we'd never tell anyone. I thought it was all in the past. I never wanted to. . . to burden you with it."

"Burden me with it?" She gaped at him. "Tony, you helped hide a body! A *body!* People go to jail for that! What was wrong with you? Why didn't you go to the police when it first happened?"

"We were kids. We were scared. We didn't know what we were doing. We thought if we went to the cops we'd go to jail."

"But you said yourself it was an accident. You were good guys. They would have believed you."

"Not after Gabe hit him with that piece of wood. It wasn't an accident after that."

She wiped her eyes again. "But I still don't understand why you have to tell me this now."

He grabbed her hands. "Don't you see? The same thing is starting to happen to me that happened with Gabe and Craig. Gabe saw the driftwood. Craig saw his jacket. I found the ring. And now both of them are dead. They're dead, Lori. And I think. . . I think Melvin had something to do with it."

She shook her head. "Are you saying he's still alive?"

He looked at her. "No."

"What, a ghost? You think a ghost killed Gabe and Craig?"

"I don't know."

"Tony, Gabe was robbed and killed by some drifter. Everybody knows that. And Craig killed himself by jumping out that window. And if you're standing here thinking somebody that's been dead for thirty years came back and killed them. . . I don't know what to say." She sighed and looked at her watch. "Look, I've got to get back to my patients. We'll talk some more when I get home tonight." She opened the door and stepped out into the hallway. "Don't forget to pick Colton up from basketball practice."

He followed her out and watched as she walked away. "I can't do this on my own, you know."

She turned back to him. "You're not on your own, babe." She gave him a weak smile. "We'll talk more tonight."

2

COLTON CLIMBED INTO THE TRUCK and collapsed on the seat, pulling off his Raiders cap and swiping a hand through his mop of sweaty dark hair. "What's for dinner? I'm *starving*."

Tony pulled away from the curb and headed down the street. The gloomy afternoon had given way to a black, blustery night, and the lighted snowflakes attached to the light poles swayed in the stiff breeze. "How about Jack in the Box? I don't feel like cooking anything tonight."

"Sounds great. I want one of those ultimate burgers with bacon." He blew out a breath. "Coach Davis had us running suicides at the beginning of practice *and* after it was over. My legs are killing me."

"Exercise is good for you," Tony said absently, pulling up to a red light.

"Yeah, well, if you ask me there's a reason they're called 'suicides.'"

"Didn't you have a history test today?"

"Yep. I think I did pretty well on it. It was over the

French revolution. It was pretty easy."

"That's good." They sat in silence until the light turned green and Tony pulled through the intersection. "How was practice?"

He felt Colton glare at him. "I just told you. We ran all those suicides?"

"Oh, yeah, I'm sorry."

"You okay?"

Tony glanced at him. "Yeah. It's just been a long day."

"Yeah, well *I* had a long day, too."

Great. It was going to be one of *those* nights.

Tony pulled into the Jack in the Box and waited in line behind a white Yukon. Did people who drove Yukons actually eat at Jack in the Box?

Colton continued to prattle on about his day. Derek Something-or-Other was giving him a hard time in civics class and Colton had asked his teacher if he could be moved. There was a new girl in school and she was *so* hot, but she might be a junior or maybe a senior and he was sure he wouldn't have a shot with her, and besides, Tim Doyle had already asked and she had a boyfriend back in her old hometown. The astronomy teacher said they would be going to the planetarium when Christmas break was over and it was going to be twenty dollars and she didn't know the date yet but she wanted to give everyone a heads-up.

The Yukon pulled forward and Tony advanced toward the menu board. "You said you want bacon on your burger, right?"

"Yeah. But make it two burgers and I want large fries and an Oreo shake."

Jesus, where did the kid put it all? Even when Tony had been fifteen he didn't think he'd ever been able to

down that much food at one time. He gave his order
and pulled forward behind the Yukon. Now Colton was
talking about getting his driver's license, how he
couldn't wait until April when he could get his learner's
permit and he wanted a cool car, like a Pontiac G6 or
maybe even a little Toyota truck, but he didn't want
some lame color like white or blue. Tony leaned his
head out the window into the cool night air, but the Yukon's exhaust wafted back in his face. He was close to
telling Colton to shut the hell up.

"What kind of car did you have when you turned
sixteen, Dad?"

"Chevy Cavalier. 'Eighty-four model. And it was
white. You've seen pictures of it, I'm sure."

"I don't remember. Jason Murphy's getting a Tun-
dra pickup. His parents already got it for him and it's
sitting his driveway. I don't want anything that big,
though. And besides, I know we can't afford it."

Tony glanced at Colton and felt a wave of guilt. In
all honesty he wondered how they could afford to get
the kid *anything*. Tony made decent money at the tool
and die shop, but there was a rumor that the company
might close within the next couple of years and all their
jobs would be shipped south to Mexico. Tony's supervisor had neither confirmed nor denied the rumor,
which led Tony to believe it was true. Lori's pay would
be enough to keep them afloat for a little while, but not
if they had to look at another car payment. And then
there was the cost of adding Colton to their insurance.
Jesus Christ. If he lost his job, he might have to ask for
help from his parents, and that was something he'd only
done once, right after Lori came out here to join him
when he quit college. There were Lori's parents, of
course, but he really hoped it wouldn't come to that.

He didn't want to think about being in his forties and still asking for financial help.

The Yukon pulled away, and Tony eased up to the window, handing over his debit card to the pimply young man at the register. "We'll get you something," he told Colton. "It may not be exactly what you want, but at least you'll have a way to get around." He looked at him. "After a while, you may want to get a job and try to get something nicer."

Colton seemed to consider this for a moment. "Yeah, I could do that. I might even get a job here at Jack in the Box."

"I'm sure you could flip burgers with the best of 'em."

He heard the drive-through window slide open. "Your food, sir." He turned to grab the bags and froze.

Melvin Hart stood grinning at him in the window. The charred face. The crooked cap atop his head, its bill melted and fused to his forehead. Eyes red and glassy, teeth hideously white behind cracked blistered lips.

No. *No!*

The blackened hands thrust the paper bags toward Tony. He could smell the singed skin. Sweet. Like barbecued pork.

"Sir?"

Tony blinked and the vision was gone. Instead, the pimple-faced teen was staring at him with an impatient frown. "I'm sorry," Tony said, reaching for the bags. "Long day."

The teen grunted and slid the window closed.

Beside him, Colton was already digging into one of the bags, shoving fries into his mouth. He hadn't noticed a thing.

* * *

After they had eaten and Colton had retreated to his room, Tony grabbed a beer from the fridge and flopped down at the computer desk. While he waited for the Dell to boot up, he grabbed one of his old yearbooks off the shelf and thumbed through it. 1985. Craig and Gabe's senior year. He found Gabe's portrait and stared at it. He couldn't help but smile at the tuft of scruff on Gabe's chin, how Gabe said his mom had fussed at him for not shaving it off before senior pictures. Tony flipped over a few pages to the photo of Craig. He already looked comfortable in a suit and tie, his expression one of confidence and privilege. "What happened to you?" Tony whispered.

In the sophomore section, Tony looked at his own portrait, marveling at how much Colton looked like him at that age. He'd always hated this picture – his feathered hair and that stupid purple oxford with the button-down collar. But he noticed something. Yearbook pictures were taken in the fall not long after school started. He and Craig and Gabe – they all looked carefree and happy. Like kids were supposed to.

He flipped to the back of the yearbook, to a section of candids. Somewhere there was a photo of the three of them sitting on the bleachers in the gym. He remembered that day, and he remembered the picture being taken. It was only about a week after Christmas break, and the three of them had met briefly to discuss things before Tony had basketball practice. They were discussing things often during that time, and keeping their ears open for any news pertaining to Melvin's disappearance. They were all three scared and on edge, and were meeting to commiserate more than anything.

But that day some jackass from the yearbook staff had come upon them and snapped the photo before any of them could protest. Craig had blown up at the kid – a scrawny little senior named Kevin White – and threatened to smash the camera. But of course nothing happened. The kid slinked away, the three of them went back to talking, and the image of their meeting was preserved forever in the yearbook.

He located the picture and stared at it. All three of them caught with a look of surprise on their faces. And guilt. And for the first time ever, Tony noticed their eyes. Older, sadder. He leafed back through the yearbook and compared the expressions to their portraits taken earlier in the year. There was a definite difference. The boys on the bleachers looked. . . *haunted.* As if whatever last vestiges of childhood innocence that remained had been torn away, leaving three souls older beyond their years.

Tony closed the yearbook and shelved it, then took a sip of his beer. It tasted good after that greasy burger and fries. In fact, when he finished this one, he might have another. And if he couldn't get that image out of his head of Melvin Hart standing in the drive-through window of Jack in the Box, he might need a third. But right now he had some snooping around to do.

He opened up Google and ran a search on Gabe's name. He wasn't surprised that nothing showed up. He knew the Harper's Lake weekly didn't have an online presence, and even the daily papers in Cedar Hill and Springfield didn't have internet archives that went back to 'ninety-four. He'd saved a clipping about Gabe's death, but there was no telling where it was now. Probably moldering away in some cardboard box in the attic.

He cleared the search and typed in Craig's name. After looking at it for a couple of seconds he added "suicide" and hit enter. The first search result linked to a story on the Jacksonville newspaper's website from December 25, 2004. He clicked on it.

Jacksonville Banker Falls from Twelfth Story Window

Police were called yesterday to First Jacksonville Bank's main office on East Forsyth Street to investigate an apparent suicide.

Authorities say Craig Marston, 38, First Jacksonville Bank president and CEO, fell from his office window on the twelfth floor. Lead investigator Troy Clark said the bank's windows are reinforced glass made to withstand hurricane force winds. "Right now it doesn't look like an accident," he said. "A person would have to deliberately break the window to fall through it."

Arnold Shoemaker, the bank's chairman of the board, issued a statement saying, "Craig was loved by bank staff and customers alike. The city has lost a wonderful man. Our condolences go out to his family. It's especially tragic at this time of the year."

Marston is survived by his father and a six-year-old daughter.

Tony read the article through a second time, then clicked back to the search results. Farther down the page he found a link to another story, this one dated February 23, 2005.

Case Closed in Jacksonville Banker's Suicide

Authorities have ruled the death of 38-year-old Craig Marston in December a suicide, stating there is "no evidence of foul play or anything that would lead us to believe it was an accident."

This news doesn't sit well with Marston's father, Jeffrey, who has been in Jacksonville since his son died last Christmas Eve. "I still don't believe it," the elder Marston says. "I talked with Craig just minutes before he died. He didn't say anything that led me to believe he was depressed or contemplating suicide. He was looking forward to seeing his daughter for Christmas that afternoon, and he and I had made plans for New Year's Day. Either he tripped and fell or someone was in that office with him and pushed him out that window. His desk chair was on its side. Something happened in there."

Lieutenant Troy Clark, who led the investigation into Marston's death, says there can be no other explanation. Video from the bank's security cameras show no one other than Marston was on the twelfth floor at the time of his death. As for the idea that Marston tripped over his desk chair and fell through the window, Clark says "The glass in those windows is hurricane-resistant. Even if it wasn't, the height of the window would make it nearly impossible for a person to accidentally fall through it unless he was standing on the sill. Even then it would take a lot of force to break it."

But Marston's family remains uncon-
vinced. Jeffrey Marston says he can think of
no reason why his son would want to take his
own life. "My son did not commit suicide," he
says.

Marston has offered a $50,000 reward for
any information leading to the conviction of
someone in his son's death.

Tony closed out of the article and entered Jeffrey
Marston's name into the search bar. Maybe Jeffrey
could give him some insight into what else might have
happened with Craig. Maybe other information had
come to light since that article had been published. But
a quick glance at the results confirmed his worst fears.
Jeffrey had died in 2010. Probably still telling anyone
who would listen that Craig had not jumped out that
window.

Tony drained the rest of his beer and headed toward
the refrigerator. It was still early, and he had every intention of getting very, very drunk.

3

WHEN LORI CAME IN AT MIDNIGHT, he roused himself from his drunken stupor long enough to kiss her as they climbed into bed. She made no mention of their conversation at the hospital, and he saw no sense in bringing it up before they both went to sleep.

He'd spent the rest of the evening drinking beer and surfing the internet. Once out of curiosity he even Googled Melvin's name, but that had turned into a dead end. He found nothing else on Craig's death and no mention of Gabe anywhere. There was nothing that was going to help him in all this. And if it really was Melvin coming after him, well, God help them all.

He lay awake long after Lori was snoring, listening to every creak and groan of the house, watching every shadow for some furtive movement, some indication that something else was in there with them. But there was nothing, and finally the beer took over and he drifted into oblivion.

* * *

He dreams of Harper's Lake. Of the fishing hole. Of a dark winter's night and a bonfire. Craig and Gabe are there, both of them still eighteen, looking exactly as they did that night. The three of them sit on the log before the fire drinking beer. Craig turns to him and says, "You know you're going to die, right? He's going to kill you just like he killed us. It's our punishment, Tony."

And Gabe sits staring into the flames, his fingers idly pulling at the downy whiskers sprouting from his chin and saying, "You can't stop him. You can't run away from him. He'll find you wherever you go. Just like he found us."

"Just like us," Craig says.

And suddenly something is moving in the woods just above the shoreline. Something big. Tony can hear branches breaking and the crash of something heavy trudging through the underbrush.

Craig and Gabe are looking at the treeline. "He's coming," Gabe says.

"No," Tony says, his voice dull and lifeless. "He isn't real." And words drift back to him from a conversation from long ago. "He's a moon shadow."

"Oh, he's real," Craig says. "He's fucking real, Tony."

Whatever is in the woods is coming closer. Tony wants to run, but he is rooted to the spot. His father would say he's a literal bump on a log, and he finds that hilarious.

But even as he is laughing, something is looming out of the infinite blackness of the woods. Something in a navy jacket and a trucker cap. Something long-dead and rotted and dripping the muck from the bottom of a quarry where it has waited for thirty years. . .

"Tony!"

He opened his eyes. Back in his bed, back in his house. Thank God.

Lori was shaking him, her eyes round with fright. The bedside lamp was on, filling the room with soft yellow light.

He sat up. "What is it? What's wrong?"

"I think someone's in the house," she whispered. "I heard someone walking in the kitchen."

He rubbed a hand across his face. "It's probably Colton."

Lori shook her head. "I don't think so."

They sat in silence, holding their breath, straining to hear.

Then Tony heard it. The squelch of wet shoes on the kitchen linoleum. Someone was moving through the house.

As silently as he could, he reached into his bedside drawer and pulled out the Glock he kept there. It was cold and heavy, and he could feel his palm sweating around the grip. He slipped from beneath the covers and crept toward the half-open bedroom door, peering down the hall toward the living room. The rest of the house was like a cave, devoid of light or movement.

He stepped into the hall, cursing the creak of the bedroom door as he did so, and slid along the wall toward Colton's room. He turned the knob and eased the door open. In the half-light from the window he could see Colton on his back in his bed. His breathing was steady and deep.

He crossed the hall and looked in at Lori. "Call the police," he whispered.

She nodded and grabbed her phone off the

nightstand.

Tony headed toward the living room, feeling his way down the hall. His fingertips brushed a picture frame and it came down onto the hardwood floor with a crash. He felt splinters of glass hit against his bare legs and feet. "Fuck!"

The footsteps in the kitchen had stopped. Now they came again, moving closer, heading into the living room.

"You might as well leave," Tony called out. "I've got a gun and my wife is on the phone now with the police."

Someone laughed, a gurgling sound like stirring the mud in the bottom of a creek.

Tony's blood turned to ice. He backed up toward the bedroom. "I'm warning you," he said, angered at the tremor in his voice.

"They're on their way," Lori said. He could tell she was scared.

"You hear that?" Tony called. "The police are on their way. You might as well leave."

The door to Colton's room swung open, and Colton stood in the doorway in his underwear, his hair tousled and his eyes round. "Dad?"

"Get back in your room," Tony said. "Lock the door."

"What is it?"

"Get in there!"

Colton shut the door, and Tony heard the lock turn.

A hand touched his shoulder, and he nearly squeezed the trigger of the Glock. Lori had come up behind him. "What are you doing?" he whispered to her. "Get back in the bedroom."

She gasped, staring down the hallway, and he followed her gaze.

Something was moving toward them. It was blacker than the darkness around it. And although Tony couldn't make out a definite shape, he could hear the wet footsteps across the floor. And he knew what it was.

"Stop right there," he said, the Glock pointed in front of him. "I *will* shoot."

"You won't shoot me," came the gurgling voice. It sounded like rot and fishy muck. "You ain't got the balls, boy."

Tony backed up a step, forcing Lori back into the bedroom doorway. "You sure you want to find out?"

The darkness advanced, and now Tony could make out the form of a man. Could see the outline of a jacket. The cap atop the misshapen head.

Before he could think, he squeezed the trigger. The shot exploded in the close hallway, leaving his ears ringing. He fired again.

The hallway blazed with light. Lori stood at his side, her hand on the light switch.

The hall was empty. Tony could see two holes in the far wall where the bullets had entered.

Colton's voice came from behind his door, muffled and shaky. "Dad?"

"It's okay, son," Tony said. "Everything's okay."

* * *

They told the police the intruder had run off when Tony fired the shots, that there was no sign of forced entry because they must have left the front door unlocked. That it had been too dark to get a look at the person's face or see any other features. One of the cops shook his head grimly, telling them they needed to be more diligent about checking their locks, especially this close to Christmas when burglaries were usually on the rise. And Tony nodded in agreement, saying it must have just slipped his mind before he went to bed. That he had been tired and would be careful in the future. And the cop wrote something down and the other one told them Merry Christmas as they left. They watched them drive away, knowing that whatever happened now, they were beyond the help of the police or any kind of brute force.

After the police had gone and the house was quiet again and Colton was back in his bed, the two of them sat at the kitchen table, not at all sleepy, staring at the coffee maker as it brewed, knowing they were up for the day even though it was only four in the morning. Neither of them spoke. Instead, Lori squeezed his hand and dabbed at her eyes with a tissue. His stomach felt heavy and sick, and he forced himself to concentrate on the feel of Lori's hand in his, of the smooth wood of the tabletop, of the firmness of the chair under his buttocks. Anything that was tangible and solid. Because what they had seen could not have been real.

The coffee maker gave one more heaving sigh and the last few drops of coffee trickled into the pot. Lori pulled two mugs out of the cabinet and filled them, stirring creamer and sugar into hers, then setting them on the table. "Maybe we just imagined it."

Tony watched the steam rise from his coffee, and a laughed escaped him. "Both of us?"

"It could have been mass hysteria. We saw what we *expected* to see."

Tony looked at her. "Do you really believe that?"

She frowned. "No." She laced her hands around

her mug. "But I don't believe in ghosts, either."

"Then what do you call that?"

She picked up her coffee and blew on it, then took a quick sip. "I don't know."

Tony reached out and took Lori's hand again. "You know, I remember telling Gabe and Craig they were both seeing things, too. And I remember both of them insisting – *insisting* – that what they experienced was real." He leaned across the table toward her. "We didn't just see something, we heard it, too. We heard it talk to us. *You* heard it."

Lori shook her head. "I don't know what I heard."

"It was him, Lori. It was Melvin. I don't know how, and I don't pretend to know, but he was here in this house tonight." He let go of her hand and leaned back in his chair. "I want you and Colton to go stay somewhere else for a while."

She looked at him, alarmed. "No. Absolutely not."

"I think it's dangerous for the two of you to be here."

"I'm not leaving you alone," she said. She rubbed her temples. "Look, I don't know if what I saw was a ghost. I don't know what it was. But I'm not leaving you to face it by yourself." She reached out and squeezed his forearm. "Maybe Colton could stay with a friend for a few days. At least until we get something figured out."

"Or until I'm dead," he said, trying to force some humor.

Lori's expression remained severe. "You're not going to die."

"Gabe and Craig are both dead."

She leaned over and kissed his cheek. "They weren't married to me."

4

FOR THE FIRST TIME IN THREE YEARS, Tony called in sick, and as soon as Lori left to drive an agitated Colton to school, he was searching the internet for spiritual advisors. His first thought was to go to a local minister, but he and Lori had never made any kind of connection with a church in the twenty years they had been out here, and he felt awkward about asking for this kind of help out of the blue. He even thought about going down the street to St. John's to talk with Father Martin, and while he and Tony knew each other as acquaintances, Tony wasn't Catholic and he wasn't sure the priest would talk to him on this level. So instead he was trawling the web, trying to sift through the profusion of local psychics and ghost hunters. He wasn't even sure what kind of help he needed at this point.

So when he saw the listing for Shinko Taguchi, he felt more than a little foolish for picking up and dialing her number. Even more foolish for making an appointment with her at ten that morning. But when Lori returned to the house and Tony told her about the planned meeting, she insisted she was going as well. "No husband of mine is going alone to see a woman he met on the internet," she said. "She might offer you some other kinds of services."

But Tony wasn't fooled by her demeanor. What they had seen the night before had shaken her up. Badly.

Shinko turned out to be a middle-aged Japanese lady who lived in a quiet community behind a strip mall. Her street wound cozily through a neighborhood of well-kept duplexes, many of which were festooned with Christmas lights and giant Santas. Shinko's house was a small, neat brick home with no decorations, and when Tony pulled into the drive, he was sure he'd made a mistake, even more so when she answered the door. Her dark hair was perfectly styled, and she wore a simple white frock. She was, for her age, still an attractive woman. But it was her eyes that held his interest. They were green. Vividly green, as if she wore colored contacts, although Tony was sure she didn't. He had never before seen a Japanese woman with green eyes.

She showed them into her tiny living room and motioned for them to take a seat on the sofa. "Make yourselves comfortable," she said with hardly a trace of an accent. "I will be back in shortly with some tea." Tony started to tell her they didn't want anything to drink, but she had already disappeared through the far doorway.

The room was light and airy, and the bay window that overlooked the street was full of plants – ficus and ivy and two bonsai trees. Two large Japanese symbols made of black painted metal hung on one wall, flanked on either side by two multi-paneled screens showing geishas in gardens. The room smelled faintly of lemons.

A petite Siamese cat appeared in the doorway and made its way toward them, arching its back and rubbing itself against the side chair, purring loudly. Tony reached his fingers out to it, and it smelled him, its nose quivering.

"I see you've met Suki," Shinko said. She held a tray with a silver teapot and tiny cups and a plate of almond windmill cookies. "She must like you. She's very particular and doesn't usually show herself to visitors."

"I like cats," Lori said. "I had several growing up."

Shinko set the tray down and poured the tea. "Do you have any now?"

"No," Lori said. "Our son's allergic."

"That's a shame," Shinko said. "Cats are excellent companions. They resonate with humans on a much higher spiritual plane than dogs do." She set the teapot down. "And when you tire of them, they make an excellent meal."

Tony and Lori looked at each other, unsure if they had heard correctly.

Shinko smiled. "I'm kidding." They all laughed then, and Shinko plucked her teacup from the tray and took a seat on the edge of the chair facing them. "So what can I help you with?"

Tony glanced at Lori, then back at Shinko. "Well, first of all, I don't know what you charge for your. . . services and – "

Shinko stopped him with a wave of her hand. "I don't charge anything."

Lori raised her eyebrows. "Nothing?"

"Mrs. Sheldon, I wouldn't know where to begin to charge for what I do. It's not a business. It's not even,

as your husband says, a 'service.' It's a calling. I help
people. It would seem wrong to charge people money
for that."

Lori nodded, and Tony saw her visibly relax. "I
thought we should get that out of the way first," he said.
"Before we. . . get into it."

Shinko smiled. "Mr. Sheldon – "

"Tony."

"Tony. Have some tea. Tell me what's troubling
you."

He found himself telling her the whole story. It
seemed easier now that he had already told it to Lori.
He started with the night of the bonfire, not meeting
Shinko's eyes when he described placing Melvin's
body in the truck and sending it into the quarry. He
took her through Gabe and Craig's deaths, ending with
what had happened at home the previous night. He left
out nothing, and by the time he was done, Lori was
flushed and crying. Shinko produced a box of tissues
and set them in front of her.

"So," he said, "I really don't know what to do at his
point. I wasn't even sure who I should talk to. We're
not particularly religious so we don't have a minister to
call on. And getting 'ghost hunters' involved seems a
little ridiculous." He took a breath. "I guess I was just
hoping for some kind of advice. Somebody completely
removed from the situation that could tell us what we
need to do."

Throughout his story, Shinko had sat unmoving on
the edge of her chair, her back perfectly straight. Now,
she leaned forward and poured herself another cup of
tea. "Your problem is actually very simple," she said.
She picked up one of the windmill cookies and bit off a
tiny corner. "You're being attacked by a *yūrei*."

He watched as she followed her bite of cookie with a sip of tea. "A what?"

"A *yūrei*. A vengeful spirit. Someone who was wronged in his earthly life and now seeks revenge against those who harmed him."

Tony glanced at Lori, then back at Shinko. "So. . . what do we do?"

Shinko folded her hands in her lap. "The spirit must have some kind of closure. The wrong must be righted."

"But how do we do that?" Tony asked. "The man's dead. Believe me, if I could take back that night, I would." He reached for a cookie and broke it in half. "I don't know any way of changing that."

"There are two ways to defeat the *yūrei*. The first is to recover the person's remains and give them a proper burial."

Tony took a bite of his cookie and shook his head. "That would mean going to the cops. I'm not sure I'm ready to do that."

Lori placed a hand on his arm. "Tony. . . we may not have a choice."

"But think what that would mean," he said, looking at her. "Think of what that would do to you and Colton. And our parents."

"But Tony, if it would end all this – "

"No!" He looked back at Shinko. "What else?"

Her gaze was steady. "You won't like it."

"*What?*"

She took a sip of tea. "Allow the spirit or the person's family to exact their revenge."

Tony blew out a breath. "Well, that's not going to happen."

Lori frowned. "Maybe there's a way of. . . of recovering the body without involving the police."

"How do you figure that?" Tony said. "The truck's under a hundred feet of water. Maybe more. I don't know how to dive, do you? And we can't very well just hire somebody to go down there and bring him up for us, now can we?"

Lori glanced away, tears brimming in her eyes.

Tony looked squarely at Shinko. "There's got to be something else."

Shinko sighed and set down her cup. "There is. . . one way. But there's no guarantee it will work. And it could do more harm than good."

"What is it?"

"First you will need three objects — something owned by each person involved. Things of importance. You must return to the place where the incident occurred. At midnight, draw a circle on the ground with salt. Ordinary table salt will do. Place the objects within the circle." She paused and looked toward the bay window.

Tony waited a moment. "Then what?"

Shinko looked back at him. "You said you have a son, correct?"

Tony nodded. "Yes."

"Your firstborn child?"

"Yes." He leaned forward. "What are you getting at?"

"Your firstborn child's blood must be added to the circle."

Tony's heart sank in his chest. "What do you mean?"

"You must spill his blood on the objects. Each one. Just a spattering."

"But why does it have to be Colton's blood?" Tony

asked. "*I'm* the one responsible, not him."

"It must the blood of one you hold most dear."

"Then use me," Lori said. She looked at Shinko. "He can use *me*, then, right?"

Shinko shook her head. "You don't understand. It must be someone connected to Tony by blood – his progeny. Your son is the only choice."

Tony bowed his head, staring at the broken cookie in his hands. "You said, 'just a spattering.'"

"That's right," Shinko said. "The prick of a pin, a small cut. Just enough to stain each object with a droplet of blood."

Tony took a deep breath. "So then what? Is that it? Will that end it?"

"You must summon the spirit. It shouldn't be difficult if it is following you as you say. Calling out to it should be enough. Then you must set the objects aflame. They must be burned to white ash. No trace of them can remain."

"So the objects have to be things that can be set on fire."

"That's right. No jewelry or coins. Nothing that cannot be destroyed by the flames. As the objects burn, the spirit will dissipate."

Tony leaned back on the sofa. "And you said there's no guarantee."

"None." She broke off a piece of her cookie and placed it in her mouth. She followed it with another sip of tea. "It's not something I condone, Mr. Sheldon. It's a black magic spell, and a primitive one at that. Keep in mind, you could be opening a door to something much worse."

Tony stared at the Japanese screens across the room, studying the images of the geishas. And then he realized that what he had first took to be an idyllic, peaceful setting was actually a scene of horror. Instead of bowing in humility and servitude, the geishas were slumped over, their hands still grasping the daggers they had plunged into their own abdomens. What he had thought were red silken sashes tied around their kimonos were actually rivers of blood flowing across their white garments.

He looked back at Shinko. Her face was serene as she watched him.

Three options. Not one of them good.

COLTON SAT AT THE KITCHEN TABLE, staring at them, his mouth open and slack. "Is this some kind of joke?" he said.

Tony shook his head, staring at the bottle of beer in front of him. "I wish it was, son."

He had picked Colton up from basketball practice as usual, but Colton was astute enough to realize something was amiss, especially when they arrived home and Lori was waiting for them instead of being at work. Colton gave them both an alarmed look, and after they assured him no one was dead or dying, he took his spot at the table and listened to what they told him, his expression one of incredulity. Tony felt as if he were telling Colton a story, something made-up and ridiculous. Lori interjected at points, reminding their son that Tony had just been a kid – the same age as Colton in fact – when it all had taken place. They told him about Gabe's death. And Craig's. They told him about everything, including their meeting with Shinko. And when they were done, Tony slumped back in his chair, completely and utterly exhausted.

Colton sat up straight. "So. . . you're saying that what was in our house last night. . . was a *ghost*?"

Tony nodded. "That's right." He gave a humorless laugh. "I know how it sounds, believe me. If I were you, I'd think dear old Dad had finally gone over the edge, too."

"It's true, Colton," Lori said. "If you could have seen it. That thing in the hallway. How it just. . . *disappeared* when Dad shot it."

Colton frowned. "But you told the police the guy ran off, that you fired at him and scared him away."

"What else were we supposed to say?" Tony said. "I couldn't very well tell them I shot a ghost, now could I? They'd think I was crazier than you do right now. And they probably would've cited me for bringing them out on a prank call."

Colton blew out a breath and shifted his gaze between Tony and Lori. "You know how demented this sounds, right?"

Tony reached out and squeezed Colton's shoulder. "Of course I do." He looked at him. "But you know we've never lied to you. We'd never make up something this crazy."

Colton gave him a crooked smile. "I know that." He laced his fingers behind his head and leaned back. "So what's the plan?"

Tony swirled the beer in his bottle. "If we leave tonight, we can be in Harper's Lake in time for breakfast."

Lori looked at him. "Tonight? What do I tell the hospital?"

"Tell them we've got a family emergency." He met her gaze. "Well, it's the truth." He took a sip of beer.

"The tool shop shuts down next week for the holidays anyway. I wish I could just go alone. I wish I didn't have to involve the two of you, but I need you."

"You're not going back there without me," Lori said. "We need to stick together. All three of us. Tomorrow's the last day of school for Colton until after New Year's. I can call them from the road if I have to. And I don't think it'll be a big deal with my shift supervisor. I've got about a month's worth of personal leave time saved up."

"I hate the idea of putting you two in danger."

"We're already in danger," Lori told him. "And I'll feel a lot better being with you than just Colton and me on our own." She reached out and took his hand. "We'll get through this, babe. Together."

* * *

While Lori talked to her shift supervisor at the hospital, Tony called his boss at the tool and die shop to tell him he wouldn't be in the next day. A family emergency back home in Harper's Lake, he told him. No, he couldn't really say what was going on, but yes, it should be over in time for him to return to work when the shop reopened the Monday after Christmas. He wondered fleetingly if he would even come back from Harper's Lake, but he decided that was a worry he couldn't spend much time on right now.

He called his parents and told his dad they were surprising them and coming in for Christmas, forcing his tone to be light and cheery. His dad was genuinely happy, and he heard his mother squeal with delight in the background. This would be the first time in a couple of years they had gone back home during the holidays, and he found himself wishing more than anything that it was just another Christmas, just another annual overindulgence of yuletide cheer. It was snowing in Harper's Lake right now, his dad told him, and the weather was expected to get worse. Didn't they want to wait a few days until the weather cleared up? No, Tony said, they would drive Lori's Outback; it was all-wheel drive and they wouldn't have any problems. And besides, maybe if they left early they would beat the worst of it. He hung up, hoping and praying he wouldn't have to tell them the real reason for his visit.

Lori was throwing clothes into a suitcase back in the bedroom. She glanced up as he entered. "I called my mom," she said. "She says it's snowing up there."

"Yeah," he said, "Dad told me that, too. He wanted us to stay put." He opened the top drawer of the chest, pawing through his underwear and socks. In the back of a drawer was a small wooden box holding his keepsakes. He pulled it out and lifted off the lid.

"What are you looking for?"

"I need something for the ritual," he said. "Shinko said it has to be meaningful."

He sifted through the trinkets in the box – old ticket stubs, photos of half-remembered friends, folded love notes he'd kept from Lori. Nothing significant. Until he found the mixtape. It was an old Maxell cassette he'd loaded up with love songs by Foreigner and Atlantic Starr and Lionel Richie – songs he'd known Lori would like. It had been in his tape player the night he and Lori fumbled through their first lovemaking, and he had kept it because it reminded him of those early days together when all he could think about was being with her, when she was his whole world. It represented everything he loved about that time, everything that was good and decent, everything that had ignited their life together. When he looked back on the thirty years he had spent with her, he knew this tape had started it all. This was it. This was the most important thing he had held onto.

He pocketed the tape and started to close the lid when something shiny in the bottom of the box caught his eye. He pulled it out. It was the silver cross old Mrs. Henderson had given him during that black Christmas of 'eighty-four. He had worn it for years, relegating it to the box not long after he and Lori had married. He let it dangle from his fingers for a moment, and then on a whim fastened it around his neck and dropped it down the neck of his shirt. It was cold against his chest, but somehow reassuring. And he had a feeling he would need all the help he could get.

In thirty minutes, the car was loaded and ready to go, and as they drove down their street toward the interstate, Tony couldn't help but wonder if he was doing the right thing. Maybe once they were back in Harper's Lake he would change his mind. Maybe he would go to the police after all. He'd been a scared teenager for chrissakes, a snot-nosed kid. Surely they wouldn't punish him too severely for what he'd done back then. He was only an accessory. But then, he realized, everyone else involved was dead. There would be no one to back up his story, no one who could testify that he was telling the truth.

But was going through this harebrained ritual a real alternative? What if Shinko's fears were realized, and instead of defeating Melvin he called forth something worse? What if he summoned up some demon from hell? He fingered the cross through his shirt. No. That couldn't happen. He would see Melvin sent back to where he came from or he would die trying. But if the ritual didn't work, he'd have no choice but to go on to the cops. One way or another, this trip was going to end it. And if he had to go to prison to save Lori and Colton, that's what he would do. Letting Melvin win was not an option.

About an hour out of town, when all the lights of the city were behind them and there was nothing but the endless ribbon of interstate stretching into the black night before them, Lori rested her hand on his thigh. "What are we going to do about the other objects?"

"What do you mean?"

"Well, you've got your tape. But there's nothing from Gabe or Craig."

"I'm not sure," he told her. "Maybe I can get something from Gabe's mother."

"What are you going to tell her?"

"I have no idea. I don't know that I can tell her the truth. I mean, how do you tell a person their kid killed someone?"

"And Craig?"

Tony shook his head. "Craig doesn't have any family left in Harper's Lake."

"What about his daughter?"

"I don't know where she is or how to get in touch with her."

"So what are we going to do?"

He glanced at her and gave her what he hoped was a reassuring smile. "I'll think of something by the time we get there."

* * *

Just outside of Joplin, Missouri, they hit the snow. It was thick and wet and reflected back the headlights in a wall of blinding brilliance. In spite of the Outback's all-wheel drive, a thin layer of ice under the snow made driving treacherous. Tony slowed down to thirty-five, but he could still feel the wheels slipping on the pavement.

Lori checked the weather radar on her phone, which showed they were just reaching the edge of a massive storm. Winter storm warnings covered sections of five states with upwards of ten inches expected. "I think we should stop for the night," she said.

Tony gripped the wheel. He didn't want to stop. Not now. He wanted to keep going toward Harper's Lake, keep moving toward an end to all this craziness. But he knew Lori was right. It was already after midnight, and at this rate they wouldn't get there until after lunch. And he was already exhausted and drained from fighting the weather.

At the next exit, he pulled off at a Super 8 that was packed with travelers waiting out the storm. They were lucky to get the last available room. It had one queen-sized bed and a ratty chair and a bathroom that smelled of cheap cleaners. But at least it was warm and they would be able to get some rest.

Colton volunteered to sleep in the chair, and Tony didn't argue with him. His head and back had begun to ache with tension and he just wanted to lie down. They stretched out in their clothes, not even bothering to turn down the covers, and Lori and Colton were both snoring in minutes. Tony lay in the darkness, staring at the too-bright LED on the smoke detector and wondering whether this was all going to be for nothing. What if the ritual didn't work? And what if he went to the cops and Melvin's body was pulled from the quarry and that didn't work either? What if Melvin came after him anyway? What if Melvin got to him before they even reached Harper's Lake?

He decided he could only deal with *right now*. There were too many what-ifs, too many scenarios that could play out, and he would go crazy trying to plan for them all.

Tony fingered the cross against his chest, trying to remember how to pray, wondering if he should even attempt it. Maybe what Craig had said in the dream was right – that Melvin had been sent to punish them. And if that was what God had chosen, there was no changing His mind.

He closed his eyes, trying to force his mind to go blank, breathing deeply to calm his pounding heart. Eventually, sleep came, deep and blessedly dreamless.

* * *

He awoke with a start. The room was still dark. He checked the clock on the nightstand and saw that he had only been out for a couple of hours. Beside him, Lori continued to snore; she hadn't even changed positions.

The chair beside the bed was empty, and at first Tony thought Colton must have gone into the bathroom. But as the time passed and Colton didn't return, worry started to gnaw at him.

He sat up and cocked his ear toward the bathroom door. Nothing.

He climbed off the bed, careful not to wake Lori, and felt his way through the darkness across the room. The bathroom was open, and there was just enough ambient light for him to see it was empty.

He glanced about the floor, wondering if Colton had decided to stretch out beside the bed. But even in the darkened room he could see the floor was bare.

"Colton?" he whispered, and his throat was tight and dry.

Maybe he had gone out to the vending machines. They'd only had a rushed fast food dinner, and with Colton's appetite he was probably already starving. But Tony didn't like that. Colton shouldn't be going off anywhere by himself. Not now.

He stepped into his boots and quietly slipped out of the room. A seemingly endless row of doors lined the hallway. Halfway to the elevator he found the vending area, but Colton wasn't there.

Panic clawed at his gut. He took the elevator to the first floor and made his way across the empty lobby to the front desk. A wall-mounted television was blaring a commercial for a mini-blender, and the blonde girl behind the counter sat slumped in her chair, eyes closed and oblivious to the noise. Tony banged on the countertop, and the blonde jumped, then blushed and clambered to her feet. "Sorry, I guess I dozed off there for a moment."

"Have you seen anyone come through here in the last little bit?"

She shook her head. "No, sir. Of course I've been doing paperwork, and I can't see a whole lot when I'm sitting back here."

Tony blew out a breath. "I'm looking for my son. He's about five-six, slim, dark hair. Maybe wearing a Raiders cap."

"I'm sorry, I haven't seen anyone in here since before midnight."

He thanked her and retraced his steps across the

lobby. Would Colton have gone out to the car for something? His phone perhaps? But Tony distinctly remembered him using it to check Facebook in the room right before they all crashed. There was no reason for him to leave the hotel.

He pushed the button for the elevator, but as the doors opened, something urged him to look around a bit on the first floor. He meandered down a side hall, passing the fitness room with its dilapidated treadmill and weight machine and a couple of darkened meeting rooms. He wondered what kind of forlorn company would choose to hold a corporate function in a meeting room at a Super 8, and then realized he'd been to worse places.

At the end of the hall was the heated indoor pool, and what he saw behind the steamy glass door looking in on it turned his blood cold.

Colton was standing on the concrete deck, his sock-clad toes just over the edge above the deep end of the blue water. He stared straight ahead, his face expressionless.

Tony grabbed the door, but it was locked tight, and he would need his room keycard to open it. He felt his pockets and realized he'd left it behind.

He banged on the glass. "Colton!" Was he sleepwalking or what? Colton couldn't swim; if he fell in on that side of the pool he would drown.

Colton didn't move. He continued to stare into nothingness.

"Colton!" Tony tugged on the door handle. Surely there was a safety release somewhere.

Colton's foot stretched out over the water as he took a step in slow motion.

Tony banged on the door again. "Get back!"

He could only watch as Colton fell face-first into the water. He didn't even blink.

"No!"

Tony lunged toward the glass door, throwing all his body weight into it, but he bounced harmlessly off. He hit it again, and this time he felt something pop in his shoulder. Pain radiated down his arm like electricity.

Colton was under the water now. Tony could just barely see him through the ripples. He appeared to be sinking to the bottom.

Tony stepped back and kicked desperately at the door with his boot, and a crack appeared in the glass. Hope surged through him. He kicked again, and the panel shattered, showering the concrete on the other side with shards of glass.

He ducked through the door and plunged into the water. Though heated, it was still cool enough that the shock nearly took his breath. He could see Colton sitting on the bottom, his eyes still open and unseeing. Tony dove for him. Wrapping his arms around Colton's middle, he used his feet to propel them off the pool floor and kicked for the surface.

As he broke through the water, he was vaguely aware of the front desk clerk entering the pool area. "What's going on in here?"

"Help me!" Tony called to her. "Help me get him out of the water!"

"Oh, my God!" She ran toward them, her heels clopping on the concrete. "What happened?" She knelt and helped pull Colton from the pool. "Is he all right?"

Colton was coughing and gagging, struggling to sit up. His terrified eyes locked with Tony's. "Dad?"

Tony climbed from the pool and threw his arms around him. "It's all right, son. You're okay now."

"There was a man," Colton said. "He was telling me to follow him."

The desk clerk looked from Colton to Tony. "Man? What man?"

Colton began shivering. "He was in my dream. He was wearing a dark jacket. And a blue cap. And. . . something was wrong with his face."

The desk clerk grabbed a dry towel from a nearby shelf and draped it over Colton's shoulders. "Do you want me to call the police? Or an ambulance?"

Tony shook his head. "We're okay now." He glanced behind him. "Sorry about the door."

She shook her head. "Don't worry about it. We can fix it."

Moments later, Tony was banging on the door to their room. Lori opened it, looking disheveled and bleary-eyed, but when she caught sight of them she appeared to come fully awake. "What's wrong? What happened?"

Tony led Colton into the darkened room. "Melvin tried to get to Colton," he said.

Lori flipped on the bathroom light, and Tony blinked in the sudden glare. She placed her hands on Colton's face and drew him close. "Oh, my God, baby, are you all right?"

"I'm okay now," he said.

Lori glanced up at Tony, her eyes wide.

Tony looked at her. "We're gonna have to stay on our guard every minute."

6

I N THE MORNING, they set back out on the interstate. The snow had stopped, and although the plows had evidently been going all night, the pavement was still covered and slick. Tony kept his speed down, not daring to go over fifty, muttering curses every time an eighteen-wheeler or a maniac in a four-wheel-drive pickup flew past them and doused them with ice and slush. They left the interstate for a four-lane highway, less traveled and more snow-packed, but Tony felt safer not having to dodge so much traffic.

They stayed quiet, watching the unending white landscape as it crawled by, measuring their progress by the passing exits. Even Colton was uncharacteristically reserved; his encounter the night before seemed to have left him stunned and shaken. He reclined in the Outback's rear seat, his cap pulled down over his eyes. He was pretending to sleep, but Tony knew otherwise.

Lori, her eyes hidden behind her sunglasses, kept her gaze on the rolling snow-covered hills and tree-lined valleys, the occasional shack in the woods just visible from the road. Tony wondered what she was thinking. Wondered if her image of him had changed now that she knew the truth. Wondered when all this was all over if their relationship would be stronger for it or whether it would crumble. He reached out and took her hand and she gave him a quick smile.

When they stopped for lunch at a truckstop just outside of Poplar Bluff, Tony called his parents and told his mother they should be home in time for dinner. It was still snowing in Harper's Lake, she said, and the town had come to an absolute standstill. "Eight inches so far," she said. "The plows are doing their best to keep the streets clear, but they're having a tough time keeping up. Maybe you should wait and drive the rest of the way in tomorrow."

"We'll be all right," he told her.

"They say this is the biggest Christmas snow since 'eighty-four. You remember that?"

Tony closed his eyes and rested the phone against his forehead. "Yeah," he whispered.

"What's that?"

"I remember," he said. "Look, Mom, don't worry, we'll be careful."

"I'll have a big pot of chili for you when you get here."

Just across the state line, the divided highway again became interstate. The sky to the east was dark with the burden of snow, but amazingly none was falling. And by the time they turned off onto the highway that led to Harper's Lake, the last weak beams of the winter sunset had broken through from the west.

The closer they got to town, the stronger the thudding in Tony's chest. Even though he'd been back here several times over the years, nothing so far had prepared him for this. They passed the Route 232 junction, still snow-covered and untouched, and in a few moments the old turnout at the fishing hole. The yellow crossbars still blocked the way, though now they were nearly hidden by brown brambles and saplings.

They descended the hill into town, and the lake came into view beyond in the dusk – flat and gray and lifeless. Waist-high piles of snow lined the streets where the plows had deposited them. A single vehicle – a Toyota pickup with unbelievably monstrous tires – crawled along beneath the yellow streetlamps, which Tony was amused to see were adorned with the same giant snowflake decorations he remembered as a kid. His mom had been right – the town was completely shut down.

They passed the old Anderson's Garage – now a Chevron with modern pumps and a brightly-painted façade, and Tony felt a sting in his chest as he thought about Gabe.

Something must have shown on his face, because Lori was watching him. "You okay?"

He nodded. "Just. . . tired."

She surveyed the street. "Not much has changed." She pointed to the lit marquee of the Princess. "Movie theater's back open."

"Yeah," Tony said absently. "Dad told me some rich banker from Springfield bought it. Probably as a toy he can use for a tax writeoff."

Lori watched it pass by. "We sure have a lot of good memories of that place. Maybe. . . "

"What?"

"Maybe when this mess is over we can go there one night. Just like old times."

He squeezed her hands and met her gaze. "I'd like

that."

He turned onto Lakeview and just around the bend the house appeared. He was pleased to see his dad still outlined the roof with lights, though these days they were the glaring LED variety that shone coldly and a little too bright. He wondered about his seventy-year-old father climbing around on a ladder and then figured Greg Sheldon was still fitter than most men half his age, including Tony. He pulled into the drive and switched off the engine, and they sat looking at the house in the mounds of snow. Like a gingerbread house, he thought. As if he could reach out and pull off one of the shutters and start nibbling on it. So calm. So peaceful. He hated the thoughts of what might happen to the serenity over the next few days.

Colton leaned forward in the back seat. "So are we getting out?"

They climbed out of the warmth of the Outback and stepped into the bitter breeze that blew off the lake. Tony shivered, and he knew it was from more than the cold. There was something about being back here, being back in Harper's Lake and knowing what they had to face that chilled him to the bone. But he wouldn't think about that now.

He couldn't, because the front door was flying open and his parents were bustling down the steps and his mother had wrapped her arms around him, smelling of too-strong perfume and chili powder and cinnamon, and his dad was kissing Lori on the cheek and slugging Colton playfully on the arm and telling him he'd grown a foot since they'd last seen him. And everyone was carrying bags and packages into the humid golden cocoon of the house and locking away the winter outside.

At least for the time being.

* * *

Colton scraped the last of the chili out of his bowl and licked his spoon. "Can I please have some more, Gran?"

They all sat around the small table in the kitchen. The remains of half-eaten chili and cracker crumbs littered their places. They'd eaten in near silence, hardly stopping to speak, relieved to be off the road and in for the night.

Kathy smiled at Colton and gave Tony a glance. "Don't you feed this kid back home?"

"I don't know where he puts it," Tony said. "If I ate as much as he does I'd weigh three hundred pounds."

Kathy ladled more chili into Colton's bowl. "I remember you having a pretty healthy appetite at that age."

"Seriously?" Tony looked at the beer bottle in his hand. Heineken, his dad's beer. The good stuff. No cheap beer in this house.

Greg laughed. "Half the food budget went straight to your stomach. I remember once telling your mother I should just sign over one paycheck a month to Kroger."

Tony sipped his beer. "I don't remember that."

"Didn't last long," his mother said, setting the bowl down in front of Colton. "About the time you turned sixteen you just stopped eating. I was worried to death about you." She grinned at Lori. "Then I realized you had other things on your mind besides food."

"Yeah," Tony said. He glanced at Lori and caught her gaze. "Must've been it."

Lori pulled her phone out and slid out toward the formal dining room. "I'm just gonna call my mom," she said. "I'll be right back to help you clean up,

Kathy."

"Don't worry about it. I'll put on a pot of coffee and we can all go relax in the den."

Tony stretched, feeling the knotted muscles in his back tense and release. "I need to go stretch out," he said. "Tired from driving all day." He slid back from the table and headed up the darkened hallway to the den.

"I'll join you," his father said.

The Christmas tree glittered brightly in the dim room, and a small fire burned merrily in the fireplace. The room smelled of pine and bayberry.

Tony pulled off his boots and stretched out on the sofa. "You never used to burn a fire when I was a kid," he said.

Behind him, Greg grunted, and Tony could hear him pouring himself a drink. Probably bourbon. Probably expensive bourbon. "We had the fireplace converted to gas logs a few years back. Sure keeps the room nice and cozy." He eased into a leather recliner with a sigh. "Want to watch some TV? Might find a ball game on."

Tony shook his head. "Not really. I'd just like to rest for a while." He watched the lights on the tree, letting his gaze drift over the ornaments, most he remembered from childhood. A few new ones stood out, and he wondered if his parents had picked them up on their travels since Greg had retired. "So what are you doing with yourself now?" Tony asked.

"I do some pro bono work over in Springfield occasionally," Greg said. "Try to help out here in the community as much as I can. I'm on the city council now, did you know that?"

"No, I didn't."

"Damn thankless job," Greg said and took a sip of his bourbon. "No one wants to help do anything for the town, but they sure like to bitch when nothing gets accomplished. All part of public office, I guess."

"Yeah." Tony could feel himself drifting off, his arms and legs heavy as stones.

"Oh, here's something that will interest you," Greg said. "That old fishing hole you and your friends used to go to, the one on the north end of the lake? Some guy's wanting to purchase that land from the state and build a boat ramp there."

"Really?"

"Says he got a couple of investors already. They want to make it a little harbor. Boat dock, concrete ramp, general store, the works."

"What do you think about it?"

"I think the guy will lose his shirt. I mean, there's nothing up there on that end of the lake except forest and a few private hunting lodges. But maybe that's his point. Who knows." He took another sip of bourbon. "Oh, and get this. He says he also wants to buy that old quarry up on 232."

Tony came instantly awake. "What? Why?"

"Wants to put a bed and breakfast in there, or some fool thing. Maybe offer diving there during the summer."

Panic stabbed in Tony's belly. "You think that will happen?"

"It's possible. That's all state land, too. State's in such a budget crunch, they'd probably feel lucky to unload it."

Tony took a deep breath. This was something he hadn't counted on. Divers at the quarry? It would only be a matter of time before they discovered the truck.

And Melvin inside it. But surely by now there would be nothing left to point to them. Even Melvin's body would be nothing but scummy bones after thirty years. But maybe this was the break he'd been looking for. If private divers found the truck and traced it to Melvin, Melvin could have a proper burial, and Tony wouldn't have to be involved.

Except it might or might not happen, and even if it did, it was too far out in the future. This would have to be resolved in a matter of days, not months or years. And Tony knew he couldn't chance his family's safety on a vague whim by some nameless real estate developer.

No, the ritual was still his best bet if he intended to get this over with. And if he went through with the ritual. . .

He swung his head around, getting a side glace at Greg. "Hey whatever happened to Gabe Devons' mother?"

"Sheila?"

"Yeah. She's still here in town, right?"

"Still lives where she always did as far as I know, down there on Jones Street."

"She still work at The Sail?"

Greg shook his head. "Nope. Retired like most of us. I heard she's got cancer."

"Really?"

"Yeah. Pretty bad from what I understand. Lung cancer." He clucked his tongue and took a sip from his glass. "Sad. She's had such a sad life. Losing her husband and her son and her grandson. Got no other family that I know of. Never remarried. Kept to herself mostly after Gabe was killed. Your mother tried to reach out to her a couple of times, trying to get her involved in activities, church, things like that, but Sheila never wanted any part of it. Preferred to lock herself up in that tomb of a shack down there and wither away."

Tony sat up. "I need to go see her."

Kathy stepped into the room, drying her hands on dish towel. "You know, she would probably like that. She asks about you every time I see her."

"I'd like to talk to her," Tony said. "Ask her some things about Gabe."

"She's always willing to talk about Gabe," Greg said.

Kathy shook her head. "I don't think she ever got over the police not finding who killed him."

"Helluva thing," Greg said. "Nobody ever saw that truck or the out-of-towner Harold Felter claimed he'd seen up there. Poor old Harold was even a suspect for a while."

"Harold didn't do it," Tony muttered.

"No," Greg said. "Harold Felter never hurt anybody his whole life. Leastways a thirty-year-old boy who could have whipped his ass in nothing flat. The police always said it must have been a drifter, but they never located him."

"Just like they never found whoever pushed Craig Marston out his office window," Kathy said.

Greg looked up at her. "Craig killed himself, Kathy. Everyone knows that."

"I was never convinced." She twisted the towel around her hand and turned back to the kitchen. "Coffee's brewing."

* * *

Later, with Colton safely ensconced in the guest room, Tony and Lori unpacked their bags in Tony's old bedroom. His mother had never bothered changing the décor after he left, and posters of Van Halen, U2 and Michael Jackson papered the walls. Tony's old stereo still sat on the bookshelf beneath the window, and on a whim he pulled out the mixtape and popped it into the player. Lionel Richie's velvet voice growled out of the speakers.

"You could probably get a fortune for this stuff on eBay," Lori said.

Tony came up behind her and wrapped his arms around her waist, kissing the back of her neck. "I was hoping I'd get something else."

"Now?"

"Not at this exact moment." He kissed her again.

She turned and kissed his lips. "At least let me brush my teeth first."

And when the lights were low and they had finally nestled into Tony's old double bed and they were wrapped around each other, Tony said, "This is where we did it the first time. This same tape was playing."

"Your parents were out of town," Lori said. "We were supposed to go to the movies, but we ended up here instead."

"What were we going to see anyway?"

"Does it matter?"

He laughed. "Nope." He nuzzled her neck and she giggled. "We had a better show right here."

"Remember how scared we were?"

He drew back and looked at her. "*I* was scared?"

"Tony, you tried to put the condom on inside out."

"It was dark, I couldn't see what I was doing."

She snuggled closer to him. "I'm scared now, too."

He held her tighter and rubbed his hands across her bare back. "Me, too, babe."

And suddenly their lips were pressed together, their hands searching, stroking, feeling. Tony tasted her mouth, her lips, her tongue, the same as he had tasted her for thirty years. But there was an urgency in her response that she'd never had before, as if she were afraid to let go, as if he could slip suddenly from her like a petal in the wind and never be retrieved. He felt that urgency, too, and it drove him to her breasts, to the flat of her belly and below. And when she cried out, stifling her voice against the pillow, her fingers grasped his hair with involuntary spasms, pulling him deeper, so deep that all he was aware of was her pulsing against his tongue and the rush of juices on his lips. He pulled away and in the dim light saw that she was crying. He brushed the tears away from her cheek with his fingertips and leaned down to kiss her, letting her taste herself on his lips. And then he was moving inside her, slowly and deliberately, rocking with a steady rhythm that burned to a fever pitch – a white light that blazed with an intensity he'd not experienced since that first night long ago. A feeling that seemed to go on and on even as his muscles relaxed and he fell away from her.

He lay spent and gasping beside her, and she snuggled against him, stroking his chest. And only then did she notice the cross on the chain around his neck. "What's this?" she said. "Is that the old cross you used to wear before we got married?"

"Yes. I thought I might need it."

She dropped the cold metal against his skin and ran her fingers up and down his torso. Across the room, the tape ended and clicked off. "You know," she said, "I don't think we ever made it to side two."

* * *

He awoke to muted light streaming through the
windows, coming out of a dream where he was running
through a hedge maze – the one in *The Shining*. Someone was chasing him, but it wasn't Jack Nicholson. He
knew it was Melvin, and he knew Melvin was going to
do things worse to him than chop him up with an ax.
Music was playing, a roaring cacophonous dirge that
droned along like a chainsaw. He opened his eyes. The
music still played, and he realized it *was* a chainsaw.
Somewhere over on the next block. He stretched and
felt the ache in his back from sitting tensed over the
steering wheel. He reached out his hand toward Lori,
but his fingers brushed only the rumpled sheets.

Tony sat up and the covers fell to his waist. Across
the room he looked at his reflection in the dresser mirror. God, he looked like he'd been on a three-day
drunken bender. Dark circles loomed beneath his eyes
and his cheeks were dusted with two days' worth of
black and gray stubble. The cross dangled in the center
of his bare chest, glistening in the light, and he wondered again whether God would hear a prayer uttered
by a lamb who had strayed so far from the path.

He fingered the chain and thought of the Hendersons – both long dead. And he wondered about the
great-grandson that never got this cross that Christmas.
Who was he? Where was he now? And had old Mrs.
Henderson ever told him the things she'd told Tony?
About first loves and half-remembered nightmares
about moon shadows? Did he still think of his great-
grandmother? And had she ever placed a hand on his
arm the way she had with Tony and said, "I'll pray for
you"? Did the great-grandson know that sometimes

moon shadows became real?

He glanced at the clock and saw it was after ten. Jesus, he never slept this late. He pulled on a pair of jeans and a sweater and padded down the hallway to the guest room, knocking lightly on the door before easing it open. The bed was empty and unmade, the sheets barely disturbed. As if Colton had slept deeply and soundly and undisturbed by dreams.

From downstairs wafted the aroma of coffee and bacon, and his stomach rumbled at the thought of food. Everyone was gathered around the table in the kitchen, and by the looks of their empty plates, Tony had slept through breakfast. "We saved you some," his father said, looking up from his newspaper, "although we had to beat Colton back with a stick."

Colton glared at Greg over the top of his phone. "I was hungry."

Tony pulled a mug from the cabinet and filled it with coffee. "Why didn't you wake me up?"

"Thought you needed the extra sleep," Lori said. "Besides, it's Saturday and we're on vacation."

He leaned back against the counter and sipped at the coffee. "I want to go see Gabe's mother this morning."

"I'll go with you," Lori said.

He shook his head. "I'd rather go alone."

He glanced at Lori, expecting her to protest but she merely nodded in understanding. "Then you can drop Colton and me off at Mom's," she said. "I promised we'd swing by there today. She's found some old family pictures she wants to show me."

Colton rolled his eyes. "Oh, great."

Kathy placed a hand on Colton's shoulder. "You can always stay here and help me do my Christmas baking."

He looked at her. "No offense, but no thanks." His phone buzzed, and he looked at it and smiled. "Tim just texted that it's snowing back home."

Greg folded his paper and laid it on the table beside his plate. "Kids and their gadgets," he said. He glanced up at Tony. "I remember that Christmas you wanted a Sony Walkman. What were you, eleven or twelve?"

Tony smiled. "Something like that."

"Then later it was an Atari. And then a Nintendo. The older you got, the more expensive your toys became."

Tony took another sip of coffee. "Still that way. Nowadays it's phones and tablet computers and X-Boxes and a dozen other things you've got to take out a second mortgage to buy. Kids are expensive."

His father laughed. "Don't I know it. Just wait 'til Colton gets to college."

Tony slid into the chair next to Greg. "I just hope he goes to college."

"He'll go," Kathy said. She stroked Colton's hair and he gave her a crooked smile. "And he'll finish. If something's worth doing, it's worth finishing."

Tony laced his fingers around the warmth of his mug. "Well, apparently it wasn't worth doing for me."

"You've done all right for yourself," Greg said. "You've got a good job. A nice home. And don't forget the most important thing of all – you've got a good wife."

Lori blushed. "Thanks, Greg."

Greg winked at her and picked up his coffee cup. "Now that boy of yours is hardly worth shooting, though."

Colton looked up. "Hey!"

Greg grinned at him and took a sip from his cup, then turned back to Tony. "You're a decent man, son. It doesn't matter that you didn't finish college. You've made me very proud."

"Thanks, Dad," Tony said. But he couldn't meet his father's eyes.

* * *

Outside the morning was crisp but the air was thick, as if it could barely contain the moisture it held. Any snow today would be heavy and wet. Good packing snow like the kind Tony remembered from his childhood. He started the Outback, and while it warmed up he brushed the night's light accumulation off the windshield. He looked down the driveway and saw with irritation that the plows had piled a good solid foot of snow between the car and the street. He would need a shovel. He remembered now why he hated winter.

"You might want one of these," his father's voice called. Greg was trudging toward him wielding two aluminum snow shovels. "I'll help. We'll get it done in half the time."

For a while they said nothing, concentrating on whittling down the dense wall of ice and slush at the edge of the drive. Scoop and throw, scoop and throw. Tony's heart hammered in his chest, and sweat began trickling down his forehead, and finally he stopped and stabbed his shovel into the drift. "I've got to rest," he said, trying to force his breath to even out. He leaned over with his elbows on his knees.

Greg set down his shovel. He had hardly broken a sweat. "You all right?"

Tony managed a nod. "I'm okay. Just out of

shape."

"Don't overdo it." He walked closer, and Tony kept his gaze on the toes of his father's boots. "I don't want you keeling over from a heart attack."

Tony gulped in the cold air, felt it burn deep inside his lungs. "You probably think I'm pretty pathetic."

"Why would I think that?"

Tony closed his eyes. "I can't even finish shoveling the driveway." He took a deep breath. "I can't seem to finish much of anything."

"Hey," Greg said. "Look at me."

Tony turned his gaze up to his father.

"I meant what I said in there. You've got nothing to be ashamed of. So you didn't finish college. Big deal. If it bothers you that much, go back and get your degree. Hell, you're only forty-five, you've got plenty of good years left."

Tony straightened and looked down the curve of Lakeview Drive, at the houses lining the street under the thick blanket of snow. "It's not just that."

Greg's eyes narrowed. "What else is bothering you?" He leaned closer. "You and Lori having problems?"

"No."

"Are you guys all right financially? You know, I can loan you a few bucks – "

"It's nothing like that."

"Is everything okay with Colton?"

"Colton's fine, Dad." Tony blew out a breath. "Everything's fine. I just. . . " He glanced at Greg and then back down the street. "I just needed this trip to work out something personal. Something private."

Greg nodded. "All right." He put a hand on Tony's shoulder. "But I'm here if you need to talk."

Tony gave him a tight-lipped smile. "I appreciate that."

Lori and Colton emerged from the front door, and Lori flung her scarf around her throat. "I think it's colder than it was last night."

"It's not," Colton told her. "Granddad's thermometer said twenty-four when we got here last night, and right now it's almost thirty."

"Well, it feels like it, anyway." She looked at Tony and Greg. "How's it coming? We going to get out of here before spring?"

"I think we got it," Greg called to her. He looked at Tony and gave him a pat on the back. "You guys be careful."

* * *

The streets in town were surprisingly passable considering the amount of snow that had fallen. Traffic barely crawled along Lake Shore Drive, but many of the businesses along the strip seemed to be doing a booming business, especially the hardware store and the small grocery.

"Wonder how much snow we're getting back home?" Lori said.

Colton leaned forward. "Tim says it's already stopped. I told him how much they have here and he's big-time jealous."

"Well, he can have it," Tony said. "I've seen enough snow on this trip to last me a lifetime."

He maneuvered the Outback up Russell Street, slipping a bit as he made the turn off Lake Shore, and came to a crunching, sliding stop in front of the Wilsons' house. "I'll be back in a little while," he said.

"You know Mom and Dad will want to see you."

"Yeah, I know. Your dad will want to give me a hard time about the OSU basketball team."

Lori smiled and leaned over to kiss his cheek. "Good luck."

She and Colton climbed out of the car and Tony watched as they carefully made their way up the freshly-cleared sidewalk. The front door opened and he saw Lori's mother grab them both in a big hug. She waved to Tony, and he waved back, then eased the Outback down the street.

He had no idea what he was going to say to Gabe's mother. Part of him hoped that maybe Gabe had confided in her at some point before he died, that maybe he couldn't hold it inside any longer and told her everything. But he couldn't imagine Gabe doing that. Gabe was always loyal. He never would have broken a promise to Craig or Tony, no matter how much it ate away at him inside.

Tony coasted back to Lake Shore and hung a left toward Jones Street. Down here the houses were smaller, a little shabbier. Few of them were decorated for Christmas. Two small girls around six stood motionless in a front yard and watched him pass by. They had been playing in the snow, and Tony saw that neither was wearing gloves; their fingers were raw and chapped, and it made his joints ache to look at them.

Gabe's old house stood away from the others, its brown cedar siding faded and cracking. A white Buick LeSabre sat in the drive, its hood and roof mounded over with snow. It didn't appear anyone had gone in or out of the house since the storm. The side porch held two wooden rockers, their back slats broken and loose, their white paint faded and worn. He could see a lamp burning in the front window, and for a moment he thought about driving on past, about leaving the stone unturned and the dead buried. But it was too late for that. These days the dead weren't resting quietly, and if he had any chance of getting out of Harper's Lake alive, he was going to have to face this.

He pulled up behind the Buick and climbed out. The neighborhood was silent as a tomb, and closing the car door seemed obscenely loud. He ascended the creaky wooden steps to the porch watching the dilapidated chairs rock back and forth in the breeze as if two ghosts rested in them. Two ghosts. Gabe and Craig. He shivered.

He had just raised his hand to knock, when the door swung open and Sheila Devons appeared before him. She was gaunt and pale, and Tony thought he had never seen anyone alive look so dead. She was pulling a portable oxygen tank, and the hose snaked its way from the apparatus up to her face, then parted and disappeared into her nostrils. Her sunken eyes flared in recognition, and her mouth opened in what Tony at first thought was a grimace of pain, but he realized she was smiling at him.

"Tony!" she said, and her voice was like gravel. "I've been expecting you."

7

THE LIVING ROOM HADN'T CHANGED AT ALL in the twenty years since Tony had dropped by after Gabe's funeral. The same tired furniture, the same faded curtains. The same sun-bleached pictures on the paneled walls. Curtis' old green recliner still sat in its place, the vinyl cracked and stained now. It seemed as if the house was a time capsule of the night Gabe died, that no air, no light, no life had entered since.

Sheila motioned for him to sit in the recliner, and he did so, cringing as the jagged edges of the torn vinyl snagged his jeans. She wheeled the oxygen tank over beside the sofa and sank down into the cushions. The television was blaring some news program and she muted it with the remote. A cup of cold coffee sat on the table in front of her, the cream curdled on top like a bull's-eye. "I know why you're here," she said, not looking at him.

"You do?"

She nodded. "It's about Melvin. Isn't it?"

Tony turned away from her. "How did you know?" He chuckled humorlessly. "I guess Gabe finally told you, didn't he? Before he died?"

The respirator on the oxygen tank wheezed. "Gabe never told me anything about it," Sheila said.

He looked at her. "So how did you find out?"

She met his gaze evenly. "Melvin told me."

For a few seconds his mind reeled at the possibilities. Was Melvin alive? Had he survived that night and run away to Mexico like most of the town thought? But that was impossible. Tony could sooner believe in ghosts than he could accept the idea of Melvin being alive and well. He studied Sheila's lined face, her red-rimmed eyes and faded hair. Had she lost her mind? Had the loss of everyone she held dear finally driven her over the edge?

"Melvin comes to me in my dreams," she said. "He. . . *shows* me things." She looked at him then, and gave that grimacing smile once more. "I'm not crazy."

He nodded. "I know." After all he'd experienced over the past few days, nothing was impossible.

"He and I were close." She shifted her gaze to the silent television. "I'm sure you heard rumors all over town."

"Yes."

"That he and I were having an affair right under Curtis' nose?"

Tony nodded, staring at the floor.

"Well, it's not true," she said. Tony stole a glimpse at her and saw a tear crawling down her cheek. "I did love him. I loved him all my life. But I never would have been unfaithful to Curtis. Even when Curtis turned mean. Melvin would come see me every once in a while. Sometimes at the diner, sometimes here at the house when Curtis was out. I guess that's what got people talking."

Tony rubbed his hand across the stubble on his face. On the wall was Gabe's twelfth-grade portrait, the same one Tony had in his yearbook back in Tulsa. "Gabe always thought. . . "

"I know. So did the whole town." She leaned back on the sofa. "It was right before Gabe died that I first started dreaming about Melvin. He was far away at first. But over time he came closer. Close enough that I could see his burned face. I asked him what happened."

Tony took a deep breath. "What did he say?"

"He wouldn't tell me. Not for a long time. Not after Gabe died. Not even after Craig was killed."

"But you know now."

She nodded. He followed her gaze and saw that she, too, was looking at Gabe's picture on the wall. "Melvin was wrong to provoke Gabe like that. He knew what Gabe thought about him. He used to laugh about it. He enjoyed trying to get a rise out of him."

"Why? Couldn't he see how much it upset Gabe?"

Sheila shrugged. "That's just the way he was. I don't think he meant any harm."

Tony looked at her. "Gabe didn't mean for Melvin to fall into the fire that night."

"I know."

"Gabe was so. . . *angry.* I'd never seen him that angry before."

"Gabe was always an emotional boy," Sheila said. "Even when he grew up. That's why it was so hard on him when Mikey died and he and Julie split up. It damn near killed him."

"You have to understand," Tony said, "we were just

kids. We were scared shitless. I know we should have gone to the cops. I know that now. We just didn't want Gabe to get in trouble. Because Gabe took that piece of wood. . . "

Sheila nodded. "I know what Gabe did."

"He was terrified," Tony told her. "If you could have heard Melvin, if you could have heard him screaming."

Sheila closed her eyes. "I *have* heard him," she whispered. "I hear him every night when I dream." She looked at him and leaned forward. "I know what Melvin did to Gabe. I know what he did to Craig."

"He's after *me* now," Tony said, his voice cracking.

Sheila nodded. "You're in terrible danger, Tony. Melvin won't rest until all three of you are dead and in the ground."

Tony felt ice course through his veins. "I think there's a way to stop him."

"You can't stop him."

"I believe I can." He told her about his visit with Shinko, about the three options she gave him, including her description of the ritual he needed to perform. "Short of sending a team of divers down to the quarry to bring him up, it's the best alternative."

"It's a long shot," Sheila said. "I don't think it will be that easy."

"I've got to *try*," Tony told her. "I need to do this. And then if it doesn't work I'll go to the police."

"You don't have much time," Sheila said. "I think he's getting stronger. And rest assured, he knows what you're up to."

"Then we need to hurry," Tony said. "Tomorrow night will be thirty years since it happened. If I'm going to do this, it has to be before then."

She sat up straight. "What do you need me to do?"

"I need something of Gabe's," he said. "Something that was important to him. Something that will burn easily."

Sheila put her hands to her mouth, thinking. "I know just the thing." She struggled to her feet, and Tony rose to help her up. "I'm all right," she said. She grabbed the oxygen tank and pulled it toward the kitchen. "Come with me." He followed her through the house. It was dusty and dark and smelled of old grease. Piles of books and newspapers lined the hallway. "Watch your step," she said, wheezing slightly. "I can't clean anymore like I used to."

She pushed open a heavy door and stepped into a cold, pitch-black room. She flicked on the ceiling light and Tony realized they were in Gabe's old bedroom. Boxes overflowing with clothing and video tapes and papers filled the space, stacked precariously atop one another. At one side of the room was a twin bed, its green cotton spread covered in a thick blanket of gray dust. Sheila looked at Tony. "When Gabe died I boxed up everything in his place and just brought it all back here. I never had the strength to go through it." Tony wondered if she meant physically or emotionally, but looking at her he realized it was probably a little of both.

She pulled open the top drawer of a chest and brought out a plastic bag holding a wallet and a cheap plastic Casio watch, and he shuddered as he recognized the watch as the one Gabe wore in high school. And then he knew: this bag was from the police. It was all the personal effects Gabe had on him when he died. Sheila pulled the wallet out of the bag. It was light brown, and Tony's stomach lurched as he saw the dark stain of blood on the leather. "I haven't done anything with this since I brought it home," she said.   She opened it and gave a sad smile. "It still has money in it." She fingered the bills. "Seven dollars." Tears were welling up in her eyes and her breathing had become labored.

Tony stepped toward her. "Mrs. Devons – "

"You call me 'Sheila,'" she told him.   "You've known me way too long to call me 'Mrs. Devons.'"

"Sheila, if you don't feel like doing this. . . "

She looked at him squarely. "We have to. Gabe is dead. Craig is dead. And you're next if we don't do this." She thumbed through the wallet's contents. "Here it is." She pulled out a small photograph and handed it to him.

It was a snapshot of a little boy with blond curly hair. His eyes were full of mischief but his smile was innocent and sweet. The photograph was worn around the edges; Gabe had evidently carried this picture in his wallet for a long time. Tony looked at Sheila. "Mikey?"

She nodded. The tears were spilling freely down her cheeks now. "He loved that boy more than anything. Gabe was never the same after Mikey died. Mikey was his whole reason for living. He told me once, 'Mom, I just don't want to go on anymore.' And I said, 'Gabe, you've got to. Mikey would want his daddy to be strong.' But after I lost Gabe, I finally understood what he meant. I've got no one. No reason to stay alive."

"Sheila. . . "

"Look at me," she said. "I'm dying, Tony. I've got maybe three months left, if that long. It's been twenty years since Gabe died. Longer than that since I lost

Curtis and Mikey. I'm ready to go, Tony. I'm ready. Sometimes I think about taking Curtis' old pistol and just. . . " She sank back against the chest of drawers. "Weak all of a sudden. I. . . I think I need to sit down."

Tony helped her back to the living room and eased her back down on the couch. "Can I get you something?" he said. "Can I do something for you while I'm here?"

She waved him away. "Nah. I'm all right. I've got a girl that comes by every afternoon. She helps me wash up, cooks dinner for me, that kind of thing." She smiled at him. "Don't worry, I'm fine."

"If you're sure. . . "

She reached out and patted his hand. "Sweet of you to worry, but you run on. You've got more important things to do."

He nodded. "Thanks for the picture." He started toward the door, then turned back to her. "Mrs. Devons – Sheila. . . would you like to go out there with us tonight?"

"I don't know. . . "

"I can understand if you don't want to. I just thought it might. . . help bring some closure. You know?"

She nodded. "Gabe never really told me what you boys did out there."

"Talked about things mostly," Tony said. "Drank a few beers."

She smiled. "I figured that. I'm not stupid."

"Well, you're more than welcome to join us." He reached out and touched her shoulder. The sharpness of her bones through the thin sweatshirt was enough to give him a start. "It would mean a lot if you can make it. I don't know what's going to happen. I might need your help."

"I'll think about it," she said. She motioned toward the oxygen tank. "I'm not exactly built for travel anymore."

"I understand."

She ran a hand across her face and her eyes squeezed shut. "I'm just so tired. So tired." She looked up at him. "Tony, what are you going to do about the third object? Something from Craig?"

He took a deep breath and slid the photo into his jacket pocket. "I've got an idea. It may be crazy, but it's all I got."

* * *

Back in town, he stopped at the hardware store and threaded his way through the cluster of men in Carhartt bibs and camouflage jackets standing around outside the front door. They were shooting the shit, talking about the snow and taking their ATVs out into the fields and woods around the lake. He recognized a few of them, some he had gone to high school with, but no one seemed to know him, and he didn't stop to make small talk. He made his way through the store and found the few items he needed, then carried them to the front register. He was relieved to see the place took Visa, and even more relieved when his card didn't get declined for being over the limit.

He loaded everything into the Outback and headed up Lake Shore toward the outskirts of town. The plows had cleared most of the snow off the pavement, even outside the city limits, and he had no trouble reaching his destination. After he had seen what the plows had left in their wake across his parents' driveway, he was a little concerned with what he would find when he got here. But he was lucky; something, a big state highway department truck maybe, had turned around here and left two slushy ruts that gave him easy access.

He pulled off the highway and sat looking at the yellow crossbars barricading the grown-up path into the woods, the path that led to the old fishing hole. As he had glimpsed last night, the forest had encroached upon the turnout, and anyone who wasn't aware of the path would never see it.

Tony climbed out of the car and opened the hatch-back. The wood-handled pick he'd bought at Kesterson's Hardware lay on the mat. He grabbed it and felt its heft in his hand.

He ducked under the barricade and headed down the remnants of the path. Briars snagged the sleeves of his coat, and his boots caught on vines and brambles beneath the snow. The silence was overwhelming. Not even a bird to disturb the quiet. The massive pines rose from the dark, dead woods, stark and heavy against the gray sky. From somewhere drifted the odor of woodsmoke. Fitting, he thought.

He emerged from the forest onto a flat sandy shoreline ringed with shrubs and saplings. No evidence of a fire still existed, having been long washed away by time and flood. How strange to be standing here again. And though he had often thought of coming back to this spot, he'd always imagined it would be warmer. Summer maybe. And there would be boats on the water, and the sound of kids squealing on the beach across the lake. Not like this. Not with everything entombed in ice and snow.

He pulled his gloves from his pockets and slipped them on, bracing the pick between his knees. He wondered if anyone in the houses across the lake could see him, if anyone would be watching while he did this. And he decided it didn't matter. Let them watch. Maybe they would call the state police. And then maybe he would confess to all of it and the decision would be made for him. But he thought of Lori and Colton and knew he couldn't let that happen. Not yet. Not while there was still a chance he could do this on his own.

Up from the old fishing hole the snow-covered riprap covered the banks. He climbed upward, heading for the vaguely remembered spot where they had buried Craig's jacket that long-ago December night. He had no idea whether it was still there. Or whether he would even be able to find it if it were. But he knew he had to try.

If something's worth doing, it's worth finishing.

And he knew he had to finish this, even if it killed him in the process.

He swung the pick into the snow-covered rock and tugged, dislodging some of the riprap. It was going to be a long, back-breaking process. He wasn't even sure he was digging in the right place, but he had to start somewhere. "Fishin' in the dark," he said aloud. Below the top deposit of rock was another, dark and muddy, and he wondered how many times the riprap had been layered over in thirty years, whether they ever cleaned the old rock out before they lined the bank anew. It didn't matter. He was going to do this. He had to.

Strike. Tug. Strike. Tug.

He felt like a tired cliché, an extra in one of those old prison movies where the inmates hacked away mindlessly at a rock pile.

Strike. Tug.

After fifteen minutes his shoulders were screaming with pain and sweat was pouring down his body. He stripped off his coat and tossed it aside. The cross rubbed against his chest, and he fingered it with his gloved hands through his drenched sweater.

More time passed, and he had cleared a section about ten feet long and ten feet wide. He arched his back, and his aching spine popped like gunfire. He would definitely feel this tomorrow.

He forced himself to get back to work. He had only delivered three more blows when the handle of the pick snapped in two. He sank to his knees and looked at it stupidly. He would have to continue by hand.

He had just bent over the rock when a shrill noise roused him out of his thoughts. His cell phone. Ringing in his coat pocket. He pulled off his gloves and reached for it. Lori. "Hello?"

"Where are you?" she said, clearly irritated. "You've been gone for three hours."

Jesus Christ. "Sorry, I got busy."

"What are you doing? You were supposed to come by here and pick us up at Mom's."

He looked out across the colorless expanse of water. "I'm out at the lake. At the old fishing hole."

"What are you doing out there?"

"Looking for Craig's jacket."

For a moment she was quiet, then she sighed heavily. "Are you insane?"

"I've got to find it, Lori. I've got to have something of Craig's." He listened to her breathing, panicked by her silence. "Lori?"

"I'm here."

"I've got to do this. As 'insane' as it may be."

"I know."

"Just sit tight. I promise I won't be much longer. It may not even be here anymore. If I don't find it in the next little bit, I'm giving up."

"What are you saying?"

He sighed. Across the lake three ducks skimmed the surface of the water and rose back toward the sky. "I'm saying if I can't find this jacket, there's no point in doing the ritual. And if I can't perform the ritual, I've got no choice but to go to the police and tell them everything. Let them dive the quarry and bring Melvin up."

"Maybe we can come help you," Lori said. "Maybe with all three of us looking we can find it."

"No," he said. "I'm too tired to do much more. We don't even know if it will work. It was all a crazy idea anyway."

"But you can't give up," she said. "Come get us. We can help."

He took a deep breath. He had never felt so weary, so defeated. He grabbed the broken handle of the pick and flung it toward the water. It hit with a dull splash. This had all been for nothing. He looked back at the area he had excavated. Nothing but mud and gravel and rot.

And something else. Something that just barely glinted in the dull light.

"Tony?"

"Hang on," he said. "I see something."

Keeping his gaze on the spot, he crawled toward it. There was definitely something there. He reached his fingers toward it, brushed away the black sandy grit. It was a metal snap. He dug deeper and felt the softness of old wool. And another snap.

Tears filled his eyes. "I found it," he whispered into the phone. "I fucking *found it*."

He crumbled to his hands and knees, sobbing with exhaustion and relief.

8

LORI CLIMBED INTO THE OUTBACK, catching her breath as she looked at him. "You look like shit," she said.

He glanced down at himself. He was smudged from head to toe with dirt and sand, and his damp sweater clung to him like a second skin. "Probably smell like it, too," he said.

Colton slipped into the back and buckled his seatbelt. "So you found it, huh?"

Tony eased the car down the street. "Yep. It was still there. After all this time."

Lori leaned back against the headrest. "So tonight we perform the ritual. And that should be the end of it?"

Tony glanced at her. "I sure hope so."

"This is so crazy," Colton said. "I can't believe you're actually going to perform black magic."

Tony caught Colton's gaze in the rearview mirror. "This isn't some kind of game, you know."

"I know."

"It's dangerous. We're dealing with something we don't understand."

Colton glared at him. "Dad. I get it."

"And you know what you'll have to do."

"I know."

They arrived back at his parents' house, and Lori managed to keep Greg and Kathy occupied while Tony snuck upstairs to take a shower and change his clothes. He didn't need any questions from them right now, especially questions he couldn't answer. He was already worried about the logistics of sneaking his family out of the house just before midnight without waking anyone, but they would just have to deal with that when the time came.

The afternoon ticked by slowly. His mother and Lori baked cookies while Tony sat with his father and Colton in the den. He pretended to watch a college football game with them on the television, but he found himself staring out the window at the sky as it turned orange, then purple, and finally faded to black. His stomach roiled, and more than once he found himself fingering the cross around his neck. If only this were one of those old Universal horror flicks and he could simply repel Melvin with a wave of a crucifix. But this wasn't a movie and Melvin wasn't Dracula. He was much worse. And Tony wondered again whether this silly ritual of Shinko's was going to be enough to drive him away.

If he had been more religious, perhaps he could have chosen a man of God to help him. Someone with a direct line to the Almighty. Someone who might have said a special prayer to drive away demons and rescue Tony's soul from the lips of hell. Like he had many times over the past few days, he thought back to sitting on the pews at the First Methodist Church as a gangly teen before the incident with Melvin and tried to remember what it felt like to be innocent and carefree and in God's good graces. But that part of him seemed dead. As dry as dust. Tomorrow his parents would probably insist on dragging them to worship services – it was Christmas time, after all – and maybe Tony could rekindle some of that belief that was now nothing but cold ashes. But tomorrow was too far away. And if tonight didn't go well for him, tomorrow might not come at all.

Dinner was baked chicken and mashed potatoes and green beans, and all the good things Tony remembered from living at home. After the meal was over, they lingered around the table, talking and laughing and swapping stories, and Tony looked at his parents, at Lori and Colton, and he knew he would always remember this moment. His father, smiling in that way he had of making his eyes mere slits, his white mustache barely tickling his upper lip. His mother, always with her hands folded and her cheeks, still unlined at her age, rosy with joy at having them all here. Colton, his perpetual Raiders cap turned backward on his head, his dark hair peeking from beneath it and that crooked grin that was already driving the girls crazy. And Lori, her eyes meeting his across the table and giving him a glance that conveyed not only affection but also an understanding of the weight of what tonight meant for all of them. He stared at her as the others talked on, knowing he had never – and could never again – love anyone more deeply.

Kathy pushed back from the table. "Well, these dishes won't wash themselves."

"I'll help," Tony said, rising to his feet and stacking

plates. He carried them to the sink and started the water.

Behind him, Kathy carried over two serving bowls. "Lori's taught you well over the years," she said.

Tony let the water play over his fingers as it heated up. "She didn't teach me anything you hadn't already drummed into me."

Kathy pulled out a container and spooned the remaining green beans into it. "Well, I tried."

Tony smiled at her. "You saying you did the best with what you had to work with?"

She laughed. "I didn't have to do much. You were always a good boy."

Tony felt a stab and looked away, squirting soap into the rising water. "Not always," he said.

Beside him, Kathy leaned against the counter. "You were good enough that I wish we'd had about three more just like you." She looked at the others filtering out toward the den. "I'm so glad you guys came in. Your dad's really happy, too." She glanced at him. "You know, what he said this morning was the truth. We couldn't ask for anything more. Any parents would be proud to have you as their son."

He smiled at her, then leaned over and gave her a quick kiss on her cheek.

* * *

When the late news was over and Greg and Kathy had gone up to bed, Tony sat with Lori and Colton in the darkened den, pretending to watch *Saturday Night Live* but paying no attention to it. After fifteen minutes Lori switched it off and they sat in silence as the minutes ticked by, not looking at one another, no one daring to speak about what was to come.

Finally, at eleven-thirty, Tony took a deep breath. "I guess we should go on." His heart hammered in his chest and his hands were shaking. He thought he had become accustomed to the sick feeling in the pit of his stomach throughout the day, but now it gnawed like sharp teeth.

"You have everything we need?" Lori asked.

"In the car."

As quietly as possible, they slipped into their coats and eased out the front door. The clouds had thinned since sunset, and now dim stars flickered in the moonless sky. Somewhere a dog barked, probably at a cat or a rabbit, then quieted.

Tony started the Outback as Lori and Colton climbed in, then hastily scraped the thin frost off the windshield. Something had nagged at the back of his mind all day, and now he suddenly realized what it was. He'd had no dealings with Melvin, visually or otherwise, since they'd arrived in Harper's Lake. And that worried him. He wondered if Melvin had been storing energy, waiting for tonight, waiting to unleash on them.

The streets were deserted, and though downtown was still brightly lit, Tony couldn't help but feel they were driving through a ghost town. They passed the theater just as the marquee winked out for the evening, and he glanced over at Lori and smiled. "Don't forget, you promised me a movie when all this is over." She reached over and squeezed his hand and her watery eyes gleamed in the dim light from the dash.

They climbed the grade outside of town, winding through the pine forest that lined the road, and Colton said, "What if it doesn't work?"

Tony kept his eyes on the road. "It'll work."

"But what if it doesn't?"

"It *has* to," Tony said. He wouldn't let himself think of what might happen if they failed tonight. There might be more to worry over than just going to the police. All they might manage to do was seriously piss off an already vindictive spirit. And that wouldn't be good for anyone.

They reached the turnout, and Tony pulled the car off the road, stopping just shy of the crossbars. He turned off the engine and they sat in silence for a moment, watching the woods disappear into the darkness as the headlights faded out. "Well, here goes nothing," he said.

Outside, he lifted the hatchback and grabbed the garbage bag containing the remnants of Craig's jacket, Gabe's photograph, and his own mixtape. A sack from the hardware store held a package of Duraflame fire-starter logs, a container of charcoal lighter fluid and matches, as well as a box of Morton's salt he'd swiped from his mother's pantry. He handed the sack to Colton. "Hang onto this." Lori was pawing through the back seat for the first aid kit; Tony hoped it was well-stocked because they were going to need it. He flicked on his flashlight and led the way, ducking under the crossbars.

"What time is it?" Colton asked.

"Ten minutes to midnight," Lori said. "How far is it through here?"

Tony played the light over his footprints in the snow from earlier. "Not far." A small limb caught him just above the eyebrow with a stinging stab. "Watch out," he told them. "It's kind of close through here. There's briars and tree branches."

"I can't see where I'm going," Lori said. "Slow

down."

"We're almost there," Tony told her. "It's just past these shrubs up here."

"I can't see any shrubs."

Tony emerged onto the shore, and Colton and Lori followed.

Before he had left this afternoon, he had gathered firewood from the woods and piled it in a heap on a flat area just above the waterline. He led them toward it now. Across the black water he could see the lights of the houses on Lake Shore, and he noted how much the area had built up over the last thirty years. There were never that many streetlights when they came out here as kids. "We'll do it here," he said, dropping the garbage bag at his feet. He handed the flashlight to Lori. "Hold this for me."

He took the hardware store sack from Colton and pulled out two of the Duraflame logs, then stuffed them in the center of the firewood. He opened the charcoal lighter fluid and doused the wood. The fumes were suffocating. The container of salt was almost full, and he would have to remember to pick up another one for his mother. He flipped open the metal spout, wrenching it out of the cardboard in the process, and stepped around the pile of wood, pouring the contents carefully to make an enclosed circle.

From the garbage bag he pulled out the ragged jacket. The wool was still damp, and he prayed it would burn and not merely smolder. He placed it on top of the Duraflame logs, then added the photograph and his cassette. He stared at the objects in the yellow beam of the flashlight. "What time is it now?"

"About three minutes 'til," Lori said.

Tony took a deep breath. He fished his pocket knife

from his jeans pocket and opened it. He had sharpened it earlier on his father's whetstone out in the garage and now it could slice through newsprint. "Colton, are you ready?"

"I'm ready."

Tony took another breath. He could feel his pulse throbbing in his neck. His stomach was clenched tight as a rock. He pressed the knife into Colton's hand. "You know what you have to do."

Colton nodded. He squatted next to the circle and held out one hand. With the other, he drew the blade along the tip of his index finger, gasping at the sudden pain.

Tony placed his hand on Colton's shoulder. "You're doing fine."

He watched his son dangle his bleeding finger over the objects in the circle. Red droplets spattered on the soiled letters on the back of the jacket and across the peeling paper label of the cassette, fell on the face of Mikey Devons in the faded photograph and left a crimson trail across his chest.

Colton stood and Tony hugged him close. "Perfect. Let Mom get you bandaged up."

Lori was already digging into the first aid kit. "One minute left."

For a moment everything was still. Tony had just enough time to notice the sound of the waves lapping at the shoreline, the reflection of the lights across the water, the sharpness of the December air against his face.

Then Lori said, "It's time. It's midnight."

9

TONY STRUCK A MATCH and dropped it into the circle. The lighter fluid caught with a solid *whunk* and orange flames shot toward the sky. Mikey's picture was the first to go, his face fading into gray. The paper browned and curled, then shriveled into nothingness. As the lighter fluid burned off, the flames off the firestarter logs grew, and in moments the fire was blazing and crackling.

The cassette was next. It blossomed outward like a strange flower, and the ribbon of tape inside unspooled into the flames like a burning snake. Then the exterior shell melted into a black pool with an eruption of dark smoke.

The jacket smoldered, the moisture within it hissing and sputtering like a cat, but it stubbornly refused to ignite.

Tony grabbed a thick branch and poked at the bundle of tattered wool, sending a shower of sparks into the black sky. "More lighter fluid!" he called.

Lori grabbed the can and squirted it toward the

flames. The fire instantly flared, then died down.

"Dad!"

Tony whirled around. "What's wrong?"

Colton was pointed toward the edge of the woods with his freshly bandaged hand. "Something's over there."

Just at the edge of the firelight, Tony could see the shape lumbering through the trees toward them. Tall and spindly, moving with graceless fluidity as it parted the brambles and saplings. And even as the form came closer and Tony realized what he was seeing, even as he remembered the black shadow he had faced in the hallway back home, he refused to believe this was possible.

"It's not real," Tony heard himself whisper. "It's a moon shadow."

A low rumbling laugh emanated from the shape, watery and thick. "Oh, I'm real," it said. "I'm *fucking real*, Tony."

And suddenly the light hit it, and Tony saw the moldy misshapen skull, the tattered strips of cloth that still clung to its lichen-covered bones, the hideous unending grin of blackened teeth and the rotting leather boot wrapped around one decimated foot. And for a moment, all he could do was stare at the thing as it drew closer to them.

It laughed again, and its voice seemed to come from within Tony's head – from nowhere and everywhere at once. "Did you actually think you could get rid of me with a cheap trick?"

Tony moved in front of Lori and Colton. "Get out of here, Melvin," he said, his voice quivering. "I won't let you hurt my family."

The walking corpse moved closer. "I don't want

your family," it said. It pointed a bony finger at him. "I just want you."

"I'm not afraid of you," Tony said.

It laughed again. "Oh, yes, you are. You're about to piss your pants."

Tony realized he was still holding the branch. He held it up like a club. "Go on, Melvin," he said. "Leave us alone."

The thing stopped and locked its black eye sockets on him. "Or what? You gonna hit me with your little stick?" It took a step closer. "Gabe already did that, remember?"

From somewhere inside him, Tony felt the rage welling up, overpowering the fear, pushing it aside like a feather. This had made him miserable for thirty years, had haunted him all his life. Had caused him to doubt not only his own self-worth, but his sanity. Had fucked up his whole goddamned life. He glanced behind him at Lori and Colton, at their pale, terrified faces, then turned back toward the thing before them. He ran toward it.

"No!" Lori screamed.

He hit the corpse with everything he had, felt a sharp pain and tasted the bitter tang of blood as his teeth clamped down on his tongue. The bones were slick with slime and stank of fish and decay. He fell into them, bringing them down with him into the snow. But the thing was surprisingly strong, and even as his hands searched for something substantial to grab onto, he felt the ice-cold fingers close around his throat. The skull was inches from his face now, and in the glow of the fire Tony could see the jagged shards of bone where the driftwood had dealt the lethal blow all those years ago. The fingers gripped tighter, and Tony flailed helplessly at the grinning corpse, his chest heaving for air, his vision growing dim around the edges.

And suddenly Gabe appeared out of nowhere, the driftwood in his hand. And Tony thought, *Gabe came back, too. Gabe came back to save me.* But then Tony's vision cleared and he saw that it wasn't Gabe, but Colton, and he was wielding a hunk of wood. He swung at the skull, but the thing was too quick for him. It grabbed Colton's arm before the wood could connect and flung him aside like a doll.

Tony tried to cry out but he had no strength, no breath. He was vaguely aware of Lori screaming, of Colton whimpering where he lay crumpled in the snow. The fire was dying out and the darkness growing thicker. He had failed. It was all for nothing. He'd never see Colton graduate high school. Finish college. Start a family. He'd never grow old with Lori. Play with his grandchildren. The snow beneath him was no longer cold. In fact, he couldn't feel it at all. He couldn't feel anything. Everything was fading, turning to gray. His pulse thudded heavily in his ears, a slowing, dying rhythm. *He* was dying. He knew that now, knew he should be afraid, but he wasn't. Not anymore. He was falling backward. Falling and falling and –

The thing's icy grip let go, and Tony tumbled to the ground, gagging and heaving as glorious air filled his lungs. Lori was beside him at once, saying something, but her words were far away and unintelligible.

A solitary figure had stumbled from the path into the clearing. "Melvin." The voice was raspy, breathless.

Tony sat up and saw Sheila Devons' face in the glimmering light of the dying fire. Her chest rose and fell beneath her thin coat as she labored for breath, and

Tony realized she was without her oxygen tank. "Sheila!" he managed to gasp. "What are you doing here?"

The corpse rose to its full height, its eyeless face turned toward the approaching figure.

Sheila looked at the hulking thing above Tony. "You leave him be, Melvin. You leave him be." Every word seemed to be a great effort.

The thing took a step toward her. "Sheila."

"Take *me*," she said. "You take me instead. But you leave this boy and his family alone."

The living corpse turned from Sheila to Tony and back again.

"What's the matter?" Sheila whispered. "It's what you always wanted, ain't it? Me and you together forever?"

"Sheila, don't," Tony said. He scrambled to his feet and took her hands, trying to lead her away.

Sheila pulled away from him and kept her gaze steady on the decimated skull. "Tony," she said, barely audible, "get your wife and son and get out of here."

Lori was pulling Tony back toward the path. "Tony, let's go."

Colton caught up with them and took Tony's arm. "Dad?"

Sheila and the thing faced each other. Sheila's skin was gray, almost translucent. "Tony," she sputtered, "go on!"

The entity that had once been Melvin Hart, that now was more than a mere projection of what his rotted body had become, reached out a skeletal hand to Sheila's face. And in that instant, flesh weaved to cover bone, and body became whole again, burning with an ethereal light. And Melvin was no longer a putrefying corpse, but a young man, tall and handsome, the Melvin

Hart that Sheila Devons had fallen in love with all those years ago. The way he must have been before cheap whiskey and bad decisions turned him into a frail shell. "I love you, Sheila," he said, and his voice was boyish and strong. "I always loved you."

Sheila was looking into his eyes. Her lined cheeks glistened with tears.

"You can come with me," he told her. "You can be young again. *We* can be young again."

"Melvin," Sheila whispered. She closed her eyes. "You killed my boy. You killed Gabe. He was all I had left, and you took him away from me." It was only then that Tony saw the knife in her hand, saw the blade glint in the fading firelight. She thrust the knife upward. "Go to hell."

For one moment, Melvin stood rigid, looking down at the handle protruding from his chest. In the next, the ghostly light was gone and he was changing, turning back into the slimy, skeletal, dead thing from the quarry. Blackened, bony hands grasped Sheila's throat.

"Sheila!" Tony cried. He made a move toward them, but Lori caught his arm.

Sheila's eyes rolled back in her head. Her tongue lolled from between her lips.

The thing opened its putrid mouth and a roar emanated from it, deep and guttural, a sound of fury and rage and pain. It dropped Sheila's limp body to the ground and turned toward Tony.

"You heard the lady," Tony said, surprised at the steadiness in his voice, "go back to hell where you belong."

It roared again, even as its skull continued to blacken and fragment. Bone fell upon bone, landing in a heap of muck and rot and gore. And as they watched, the mold-covered bones melted like wax, pooling into a slime that hissed as it mixed with the snow. The puddle belched one last gasp of foul-smelling steam and was still.

Tony rushed forward and took hold of Sheila's lifeless hand. "Call 911," he told Lori.

Lori knelt down and took Sheila's wrist, feeling for a pulse.

"Is she alive?"

Lori shook her head. "No."

"Is it over?" Colton asked.

Tony reached over and closed the half-open eyes with his fingertips. "I think so. He got what he really wanted." He looked into Sheila's face, marveling at the expression of peace. "I guess in some way, she did, too."

Lori pulled her phone from her coat pocket. "The police will have questions."

"I know," Tony said.

"What will we tell them?"

Tony looked at her. "I don't know."

She kept her finger poised over the keypad. "So. . . what do you want me to do?"

Tony blew out a breath. "I'm thinking."

EPILOGUE
DECEMBER 2015

TONY CLINKED HIS GLASS against Greg's. "Merry Christmas, old man."

Greg gave him a crooked smile. "You watch yourself. You're getting on up in years yourself."

Tony took a sip of the bourbon and felt the warmth spread through him. Woodford Reserve. The best of the best. "Good stuff, Dad."

Greg studied the amber liquid through the glass. "You know, I almost balked when I saw the price, but then I thought, what the hell, it's Christmas." He set the glass down and stared into the fire. "Really glad you guys decided to come in again this year."

"Yeah, me, too. It's been a good day."

There had been no snow for the holiday in Harper's Lake this year, but after the previous Christmas and the harsh winter that had followed it, no one was complaining. The air had warmed to the balmy fifties, and Tony had even seen a boat out on the lake yesterday. He thought of this time last year and felt a shiver.

Outside the window, bare tree limbs rose against the purple sky, and from the kitchen came the sounds of Kathy and Lori clearing the table – the clink of dishes and conversation – and the aroma of a fresh pot of coffee. Tony settled into the corner of the sofa, his glass of bourbon resting on his belly, and sighed with pleasure. He was home in Harper's Lake, his belly was full of Christmas dinner, and he was surrounded by his family. It just didn't get much better than that.

Colton appeared in the doorway, his face flushed and eager. He had muscled up over the past six months, ever since he'd turned sixteen, but Tony was sure playing football had something to do with that. His Raiders cap and ragged jeans had disappeared around the same time, and now his hair was always combed and his clothes spotless, but Tony figured they had Chelsea to thank for that.

Chelsea stood behind Colton wearing the diamond pendant he'd given her, the one he'd worked weekends at the Lazy W Steakhouse washing dishes to pay for. They'd started dating in June. Colton had insisted on bringing her with them to Harper's Lake for Christmas, and Tony and Lori had insisted there be some fairly rigid ground rules. They liked Chelsea, and she had been good for Colton, but Tony and Lori had been sixteen once, and there was no sense in letting a wildfire go untamed.

"We're going down to the movies," Colton said.

"Come straight here after," Tony told him.

"We will."

Tony listened as they said goodbye to Kathy and Lori and headed outside and to start up the car. He took another sip of his bourbon. "It's great the old theater's still going. I figured it would have closed already."

Greg nodded. "Seems to do pretty well. Especially in the summer."

Tony sat up. "Hey, whatever happened with that guy that was going to build the bed and breakfast out at the old quarry?"

"I think all that fell through," Greg said. "Couldn't get the financing I heard."

Tony nodded. "Probably just as well. Who'd want to stay out there at an old quarry when there's three nice hotels on the lake?"

Greg took a sip of bourbon. "Yeah, especially after poor old Sheila Devons killed herself out there."

Tony shook his head. "So sad."

Greg clucked his tongue. "Helluva thing, driving her car over the cliff like that."

"Well, she was terminal."

"Yeah, I guess the poor old thing just couldn't take being sick any longer." He downed the rest of his bourbon. "I'm just sorry you all had to see it happen. If you hadn't seen her drive through town that night, if you hadn't followed her, they might never have known what happened to her."

Tony nodded. "I was so worried after talking to her that day. I just knew something was wrong when I saw her car heading out of town."

"Imagine the odds. You all going down to the convenience store at that moment because Colton had a craving for Combos." He chuckled. "I'd have made his ass wait 'til morning."

"He was pretty insistent," Tony said.

"Oh, that truck they found out there with Sheila's car – police traced it back to Melvin Hart. He went missing back in the 'eighties. You probably don't remember it."

Tony shook his head. "No."

"Ah, well, he was a drunk. Everybody thought he'd run off to Mexico or some fool thing, but now they think he was three sheets to the wind and just drove off into the quarry. What're the odds – them finding him after all this time."

Kathy stepped into the room carrying a mug. "Coffee's ready if you two want any."

Lori followed, balancing her mug with both hands. "I think they've already had something else," she said.

"Dad got the expensive stuff," Tony said.

Kathy shuddered. "That's so nasty. I don't know how you can drink it. And straight, too."

"It's an acquired taste," Greg said.

Kathy sank down into her chair. "This is so nice, having everybody here again. That Chelsea's a charmer, isn't she?"

"We like her," Lori said.

"Lovely girl," Greg agreed.

"Wonder if they'll still be together next year?" Kathy said. She blew on her steaming coffee.

Greg shrugged. "They're young. Who knows?" He looked at Tony. "Your mother's already marrying them off."

Kathy sighed. "Oh, Greg, I just was going to say if they are, she's welcome to come back. That's all." She set her cup down on the side table and looked around at them. "I just love Christmas."

"Yeah, me, too," Tony said, catching Lori's gaze across the room. "Christmas is a real blast."

About the Author

Author and sometime banker Will Overby lives with his wife, a dog, and a menagerie of cats in the rural lakes area of western Kentucky. Between dodging mergers and drafting policies he writes novels. Connect with him on his website, *www.willoverby.com*, on Facebook, or follow him on Twitter (@Will_Overby).